'Fair Ophelia':

A Life of Harriet Smithson Berlioz

Théâtre Anglais à Paris.

*I cannot chuse but weep, to think,
they chould lay him in the cold ground.*

Melle SMITHSON, Rôle d'Offélia dans Hamlet.

Harriet Smithson as Ophelia in *Hamlet*. Lithograph by A. de Valmont, 1827.

'Fair Ophelia':

A Life of Harriet Smithson Berlioz

PETER RABY

CAMBRIDGE UNIVERSITY PRESS

Cambridge

London   New York   New Rochelle

Melbourne   Sydney

Published by the Press Syndicate of the University of Cambridge
The Pitt Building, Trumpington Street, Cambridge CB2 1RP
32 East 57th Street, New York, NY 10022, USA
296 Beaconsfield Parade, Middle Park, Melbourne 3206, Australia

First published 1982

Printed in Great Britain at the University Press, Cambridge

Library of Congress catalogue card number: 81-21601

British Library cataloguing in publication data
Raby, Peter
'Fair Ophelia': a life of Harriet
Smithson Berlioz.
1. Berlioz, Harriet Smithson   2. Actresses
– Ireland – Biography
I. Title
792'.028'0924   PN2601
ISBN 0 521 24421 8

To Liz

Contents

Illustrations

Preface

~~~~~~

Harriet Smithson is not perhaps the most obvious personality to arouse obsessional interest, a judgment which may help to explain Berlioz's own lasting absorption in her. In fact, it was through the eyes of a less subtle Romantic, Dumas, that I first came to form an image of her: he wrote that she made a divine Ophelia, and it was then that for the first time in a theatre he saw real passions felt by men and women of real flesh and blood. The 1969 centenary exhibition at the Victoria and Albert Museum, 'Berlioz and the Romantic imagination', provided further stimulus, and by its focus on performance encouraged speculation about the nature of the experiences which Berlioz and his contemporaries enjoyed at the Odéon and the Théâtre des Italiens. I found myself wishing to know more about the woman who could arouse such heights of enthusiasm, even ecstasy, and yet be so lightly sketched a figure both as an individual and within the history of the theatre.

Harriet herself remains, I think, a little indistinct. She was by nature modest and retiring. There are few personal documents to provide an alternative picture to the detailed and yet biased portraits provided by Berlioz himself; and most other descriptions inevitably place Harriet in a perspective dominated by Berlioz. Harriet's letters, few in number and widely scattered, are largely concerned with arrangements for her professional life until the time of her marriage; afterwards, the fact of living in a country whose language she spoke with difficulty and wrote hesitantly restricted her correspondence. Undoubtedly, there is more to be retrieved about the details of her early life, especially in Ireland, and during her long years of apprenticeship at Drury Lane.

I hope, however, that the kind of actress Harriet Smithson became emerges from the welter of detail about plays and dates and places I discuss here. Some may feel there is too much included, though there could have been far more. But it was from the stage that she made her impact, and I believe that her dedication to her career at a troubled period for the theatre deserves attention and respect. Whatever the judgment about her qualities as an actress, there is no doubt that she embodied a powerful and yet refined series of images whose influence reached further than the most widely known and personal instance of Berlioz, and that alone might be thought a sufficient claim on our interest.

I acknowledge gratefully those who have given me permission to quote or make use of copyright or unpublished material, notably David Cairns, Victor Gollancz Ltd and W. W. Norton and Company for the extracts from *The Memoirs of Hector Berlioz translated and edited by David Cairns*, Weber Commemoration and Oswald Wolff Ltd; Dr Paul Joannides; the British Library; the Chatsworth Settlement Trustees; the Garrick Club; Mr Richard Macnutt; the National Library of Ireland.

The following have kindly answered enquiries or made illustrative material available: Professor Hugh Macdonald; Mr Richard Macnutt; the Theatre Collection, the Victoria and Albert Museum; the Department of Prints and Drawings, the British Museum; Mme Geneviève Viollet-le-Duc; Harvard Theatre Collection; the National Gallery of Canada, Ottawa; the Art Gallery of Ontario, Toronto; La Bibliothèque de l'Arsenal; La Bibliothèque Nationale; La Bibliothèque de l'Opéra.

The almost unfailing helpfulness to be found in every library, sometimes in inverse ratio to its size, has been a constant encouragement. I should like to thank especially the librarians and staffs of the University Library, Cambridge; the British Library and the Newspaper Library, Colindale; the Victoria and Albert Museum; the Garrick Club; Birmingham, Carlisle, Margate, Nottingham and Plymouth Public Libraries; the Folger Shakespeare Library; the Harvard Theatre Collection; Yale University Library; the National Library of Ireland; the Royal Irish Academy; Ennis Public Library; Le Musée Berlioz, La Côte Saint-André; La Bibliothèque de l'Arsenal; La Bibliothèque de la Conservatoire; La Bibliothèque Nationale; Universiteits – Bibliotheek, Amsterdam.

During the preparation of this book I was fortunate to be granted a period of study leave, for which I am grateful to the Principal and Trustees of Homerton College. I have received encouragement, information and help from many sources, and should like to record my warm appreciation in particular to Philip Barnard, Jock Burnet, David Butler, David Cairns, Paul Joannides, Barry Jones, Chris Kelly, David

Male, John Moore, Steve Otto, John Parmenter, Juliette Ryan, Georges and Nicole Simon, and Frank Whitford; also to Andrew Brown and Maureen Leach of the University Press. I am deeply indebted to Professor Julian Rushton and Mr Richard Macnutt, each of whom undertook the thankless business of reading an early draft and generously gave me the benefit of their wide knowledge: they saved me from error and made numerous suggestions for improvement. Lastly, I thank my wife and children, who were forced to live with my obsession for several years, have patiently suffered detours to fusty libraries, decrepit theatres and even cemeteries, and encouraged me to reach the end.

The author and publisher would like to thank the following for their permission to reproduce illustrations: the Theatre Museum, Victoria and Albert Museum (frontispiece and illustrations 2, 3, 6, 7, 8, 15, 20, 21, and 28); Department of Prints and Drawings, British Museum (illustrations 4, 5, 10, 12, 16, 17, 25, 37, 42 and 43); Bibliothèque Nationale (illustrations 9, 11, 13, 14, 18, 22, 23, 24, 26, 27, 32, 34, 38, and 39); Harvard Theatre Collection (illustrations 1 and 19); Musée Victor Hugo (illustration 31); Académie de France, Rome (illustration 33); National Gallery of Canada, Ottawa (illustration 41); Reboul-Berlioz Collection, Paris (illustration 36) and Richard Macnutt (illustrations 29, 30, 35 and 40).

1 Childhood in Ireland

Harriet Smithson is known today because in 1827 she chanced to play Ophelia and Juliet in a season of English theatre in Paris; Hector Berlioz was present, fell in love with the Shakespearean image, and pursued it in his life and in his music. Harriet comes to the world first through the medium of his music, his letters and his memoirs, and secondly as an aside on record sleeves and programme notes or as a diversion in books whose emphases properly lie elsewhere. The tone of many of the comments (other than those by Berlioz) is faintly dismissive and disparaging, suggesting that the *coup de foudre* which the actress so unconsciously delivered was slightly absurd, a romantic aberration, almost a figment of Berlioz's own imagination; the image of Harriet–Ophelia–Juliet is regarded as a self-engendered, self-delighting ideal which bears only a tenuous relation to the shadowy reality that was Harriet. There is enough truth in the general attitude to make it simple to accept. Berlioz's personal absorption was echoed, though to a lesser degree of intensity, by a generation of French writers and artists, Hugo, Dumas, Vigny, Delacroix, but in their case the interest can be accounted for as a temporary fashion, a tactical episode within a long and complex reaction against the classical tradition. What Harriet did, and how she acted, becomes submerged. Even the form of the name by which she is known – Harriet, Henrietta, Henriette – is variable and elusive.

The faintness of Harriet's image is to some extent inevitable, given the ephemeral nature of theatrical performance. Berlioz, quite apart from his greatness as a composer, is a supremely evocative writer, and his letters and memoirs are the most important evidence about Harriet and the events of her later life, and more vivid than any other description could hope to be. Harriet herself left comparatively little in writing from which to construct a portrait, most of her few surviving letters

I

being concerned with business arrangements and stage performances. Yet there is sufficient in the way of external comment to encourage an attempt, and it is right that the focus should be on Harriet's professional career, for it is her acting which brought her, however fortuitously, to the notice of Paris and Berlioz, and on which her wider claims to attention, together with the response she aroused, must rest.

Harriet Smithson's whole life was controlled by the theatre. She was born Harriet Constance on Tuesday, 18 March 1800 in the west of Ireland, at Ennis, County Clare, where her father had settled his family for a few months while he organised one of several short seasons in the playhouse.[1] In view of Harriet's later career, it seems suitable to anticipate the actual date of birth and associate her first public appearance with a performance given the previous week on 10 March for her mother's benefit. Smithson had himself enjoyed a remarkably successful benefit at the end of February, with more people turned away at the doors than had gained admission, which moved him to insert a fulsome acknowledgment in the *Ennis Chronicle*. Mrs Smithson, an occasional actress over the years, was not a regular member of the company and can scarcely have taken a part on this particular evening; probably Smithson calculated that her advanced state of pregnancy might draw sympathetic interest from the Ennis public. The entertainment was a contrasting programme consisting of a new musical play, *The Irishman in Naples* (including a 'distinct view of Mount Vesuvius on Fire'), and *Romeo and Juliet* accompanied by 'a solemn Dirge and Funeral Procession'[2] (these obsequies for Juliet Capulet were part of Garrick's interpolations): hardly the most auspicious greeting for the expected arrival, but an entirely apposite association for Harriet.

Harriet's father, William Joseph Smithson, was 'descended from a family of that name in Gloucestershire'.[3] Harriet was anxious later in life to stress the English connection and the polite circles of society in which she moved. But whatever her father's ancestry, for years he had been earning a slightly precarious living in the country towns of Ireland. Towards the end of the eighteenth century provincial theatrical activity expanded there as rapidly as in England, and Ireland as a whole provided an attractive alternative for the growing ranks of professional players; besides the people's enthusiasm for drama, there was a generally more open and welcoming attitude towards the actors themselves, in contrast to the social condescension which still prevailed in England. Smithson earned himself a modest place in Ireland's theatrical history. In 1784 he was acting for Robert Owenson in the theatre at Fishamble

Street, Dublin. Three years later, he was engaged to appear in Chalmers's company at Kilkenny but left in mid-season because, according to his explanation in the *Leinster Journal*, he was not allowed to perform the roles which had been agreed. Showing the independence and enterprise which his daughter inherited, he took up the hazardous business of strolling manager, and for the next twenty years moved principally between Wexford, Kilkenny, Galway, Waterford and Ennis.[4]

Ennis, however, was the place with which the Smithson family formed the strongest ties. Sited on the banks of the River Fergus, the town was an important market as well as the county capital, with assizes and race-meetings to draw people to it in addition to the ten thousand or so inhabitants. Smithson's energy and ambition had been apparent there from the start. Towards the close of 1789 he had busied himself in fitting up a building in Cooke's Lane, formerly Bridewell Lane,[5] as a playhouse to accommodate two hundred or so spectators, which would be 'as neat and comfortable, for the size, as any in the Kingdom, an Agreeable surprise to those who were accustomed to the temporary theatres hitherto made use of in this town'.[6] With entrance fees of two shillings for the pit and one shilling for the gallery, Smithson's budget was tight, and it may well be that he carried out much of the reconstruction with his own hands. Later plans for a purpose-built theatre were never fulfilled. The repertory he provided, though trimmed to the shifting capacities of his company and relying heavily on comedies and light musical plays, suggests a man of wider taste or higher ambition than the common run of strolling manager. Otway's *Venice Preserved*, later a favourite context for Harriet, was given in the first season. For his own benefit in 1791 Smithson presented *The Sheep Shearing*, an adaptation of *The Winter's Tale*, with himself as Autolycus, while contemporary events were reflected in the concluding item, a 'Grand Transparency of that terrifick Mansion, the Bastille, on Fire'.[7]

Smithson was a Mason, and used this connection to swell the attendance whenever he could. On special occasions – such as his benefit – the Ennis Lodge Number Sixty would parade in full regalia through the streets, and were then disposed upon a specially constructed amphitheatre at the back of the stage, where the members formed a colourful backdrop. Those brothers who might be reluctant to appear in so public a position were cordially assured that they were welcome to purchase tickets in the regular manner. In ways like this Smithson prudently cultivated his audience, and the *Ennis Chronicle*, which consistently supported his efforts, seems to indicate a genuine warmth (and perhaps a fellow Mason in the proprietor Foster Parsons) when writing of him that 'as an Actor he has been much caressed, as a Brother much beloved, and as a Fair Dealer, much admired'. Not all his actors shared this view.

No manager, however popular, could afford to stay in such a comparatively small centre as Ennis for long. The 1800 season was extended for a number of additional performances, and concluded on 3 April with yet one more Benefit for Brother Smithson: the play chosen, wishfully, was Dibdin's *Five Thousand a Year*. Mr and Mrs Smithson departed with the proceeds and their baby daughter in the direction of Waterford.

The common experience of strolling actors' children was to pass their infant years trailing tediously from one playhouse and town to another, and then to find themselves at an early age eking out the company's resources on stage. Harriet was spared this phase. The Smithsons returned to Ennis in October 1801 to mount another short season.[8] Either then or shortly after, it was agreed to leave Harriet in the care of the Reverend James Barrett, who became her guardian and brought her up as though she were his own daughter.[9] The Smithsons came to see her from time to time, certainly in 1803 and 1805, but Ennis was Harriet's childhood home. According to Oxberry's *Dramatic Biography*, whose writer seems to have relied upon Harriet's own account, Harriet was 'the pet of the inhabitants'.

Dr Barrett was in his eightieth year, and for forty years had been Pastor of the Church of Ireland parish of Drumcliffe, and latterly Dean of Killaloe. He was greatly loved in the district, by Protestants and Catholics alike, and Harriet was fortunate to be in his care, and to grow up in the calm of his house in Chapel Lane. Dr Barrett instructed Harriet 'in the precepts of religion', states Oxberry, adding that 'everything connected with the stage was carefully kept from her view'. This comment is difficult to reconcile wholly with an announcement for 15 February 1808 for 'Theatre Ennis', headed 'By desire, and under the patronage of the Rev. Dean Barrett, For the Benefit of Miss A. Smithson'[10] – a remarkably tolerant gesture on the Dean's part for that age. The initial of the Miss Smithson who was to dance and sing remains a puzzle; conceivably it is a misprint, which would advance Harriet's début by some six years.

However, that well-intentioned involvement with the theatre was Dr Barrett's last public action. Early the next morning he died, 'a character as near perfection as the lot of humanity admits of'.[11] The Ennis shops closed down, and a general gloom settled on the community; at his funeral, Protestant and Roman Catholic clergy alternated in the procession while tears ran down the faces of all the spectators;[12] and in the Pro-Cathedral some years later a monument was placed by members of 'All Religious Persuasions' to 'Perpetuate the Memory of so good a Man'.

Harriet had not lost a parent; but she had lost the person who for the greater part of her eight years had provided her with affection, a home and education. Once again, the Smithsons had to decide whether to take their daughter with them on their travels, or to provide some alternative. They chose stability in the form of a school at Waterford kept by a 'Mrs Tounier'[13] – an 1824 directory lists a ladies' boarding-and-day academy in William Street, headed by Mrs Mary Tourner. Oxberry comments, relying 'on the information of a friend', that Harriet then showed herself 'actually averse even to witnessing dramatic exhibitions'. This attitude suggests an attempt on Harriet's part to distance herself from the humdrum family theatrical background. Certainly, her early isolation from the world of theatre did nothing to prepare her for the unglamorous realities to come.

Whatever Harriet's own hopes and inclinations may have been, the joint pressure of family tradition and pinched finances swiftly prevailed. Her father's health began to fail; and there were others in the family, a brother Joseph and an invalid younger sister to provide for. The explanation of failing health given by Oxberry may conceal a straightforward commercial disaster. Some manuscript verses by an anonymous actor accuse Smithson of every conceivable misdeed of a provincial theatrical manager. Entitled 'The Smithsoniad, or Chapter of Managers',[14] and set to the tune of 'Scots wha hae', it contains 'an Actor's advice to such of his brethren of the Sock and Buskin, as may have been trepann'd into the company of a certain Manager, in the South of Ireland'. Harriet might well wish to dissociate herself from the dismal life outlined in these verses:

> Wha wad be a Strolling Gag?
> Wha wad be a Barn vag?
> Wha for Benefits wad beg, –
>   and in a Garret lie?
> Wha wad e'er be Smithson's slave?
> Wha wad e'er support a knave?
> Or for him chaunt a single stave, –
>   an' by starvation die?

The verses are provided with copious notes and glosses: 'Strolling Gag' – 'An Itinerant humbugging performer'; 'Smithson' – 'William Joseph Smithson, Manager of the South, universally and execrated by the Whole Profession – "Ecce Homo!"'

> By your wives' an' children's moans!
> By the Gall'ries Shouts an' groans!
> Yea! By Frederick Edward Jones –
>   The Royal Patentee!
> I conjure you fly wi' haste: –
> Your precious time na longer waste;
> For if ye stay ye'll be *uncased* –
>   Ay, surely *dudded* be!

'Dudded' – Performers who have continued any length of time in Smithson's Co know too well the meaning of this phrase to need any explanation; however for the information of others I must remark that the word undudded would be more applicable, as it signifies being *dispossessed of a wardrobe*, an accident to which Smithson's Co is often subject!

Smithson is not the only manager to be lambasted in this diatribe, but the others serve largely as a standard of comparison for his supposed villainy:

> Yield not to Joseph's knavish tricks,
> Iwit his paltry rags and sticks,
> Leave him to his Hods and Bricks,
>   For if ye stay ye'll die!

The writer notes that Smithson 'was a Bricklayer before he embark'd Theatrical Manager'. Various other shortcomings are ascribed to him – 'rude austerity', 'ferocity', 'cursed malignity'; 'There's no one can dissemble more, Iago none resemble more' – before the actor concludes with a pious hope:

> May I my once bless'd country see
> From Managerial Tyranny,
> From *Swadlers* and from Smithson free,
>   and then I'll die content.

It is clearly impossible to assess the justice of these complaints, though the general background seems authentic. Managerial failures were becoming a common occurrence now that the tide of public enthusiasm for theatre was perceptibly receding, as Harriet would have frequent cause to know. Mr and Mrs Smithson were in Plymouth in 1813, which may have marked a tactical withdrawal. The following year they returned to Ireland and decided to launch Harriet upon the world. Among those who had taken a kindly interest in Harriet as a child was Lady Castle Coote. Lady Castle Coote spoke to Lord Castle Coote, and Lord Castle Coote spoke to Frederick Jones, patentee of the Theatre Royal, Dublin. On Friday 27 May 1814, as Albina Mandeville in Reynolds's sentimental comedy *The Will*, Harriet made her début.[15]

The Theatre Royal, Dublin, was a favourable setting for the start of an acting career. The resident company was of good quality and Jones, a 'gentleman by birth and education', had the reputation of a thoughtful manager with firm views about the conduct of his actors – to encourage them to behave like gentry he paid at rates appreciably higher than the normal provincial scale. He had less control over his audiences. The Crow Street building was to suffer badly in December 1814 when the public rioted because the advertised afterpiece was withdrawn. This was to have been *The Forest of Bondy*, an adaptation from Pixérécourt, starring a trained Newfoundland dog; when the animal's owner demanded what Jones considered to be exorbitant terms in the form of a perpetual free pass, the manager countered with an unannounced substitution: the outraged audience broke up the seats and benches, wrecked the chandelier, and was narrowly prevented from setting fire to the place.[16] Dublin audiences, apart from being volatile, were perceptive and outspoken. They were used to seeing the best-known performers from Drury Lane and Covent Garden: a visit to Dublin became established as part of the regular summer pattern for actors like the Kembles, Liston, Kean and Macready. The audience acquired the habit of forming, and voicing, independent judgments: Elliston found his Hamlet compared unkindly to that of the regular interpreter, Holman, and Charles Kemble was left in no doubt that he could not match Talbot in the latter's best comic roles.

There was no shortage of girls eager to try to make a name for themselves on stage. The theatre was one of the very few occupations open to women of wit and ambition but with limited means and influence, and even there influence of some kind was almost essential initially. As late as 1840 Tomlins, in his *Brief View of the English Drama*, described the profession of actor as the worst an 'intellectual man' could at that time select. 'Its requisites are more various, its difficulties greater, its remuneration (except to an exorbitantly paid few) worse, and more uncertain, and its duties more harassing, than those of any other.'[17] Macready, for one, would have agreed with that assessment. But for a woman, intellectual or not, the question of selection of career barely arose. The actor Walter Donaldson, who abandoned piano making for the Dublin stage and was later a member of the English theatre in Paris with Harriet Smithson, considered that no occupation, such as governess or lady's maid, could equal the stage when a female 'was thrown on the world to gain a living'. It was 'the only position where woman is perfectly independent of man, and where, by her talent and conduct, she obtains the favour of the public. She then enters the theatre emancipated and disenthralled from the fears and heartburning too often felt by those forced into a life of tuition and servitude.'[18] A succession of talented actresses had launched their careers in Dublin. Three years or so before, in the same theatre, Miss Eliza O'Neill had made her first appearance; in October 1814 at Covent Garden, she would create an outstanding impression as Juliet, and overnight become the undisputed successor to Mrs Siddons in tragedy. She was still a member of the Crow Street company, and acted in another part of the bill on the evening of Harriet's début.

Harriet's part as Albina Mandeville was described as 'her first appearance here' rather than 'her first appearance on any stage'. It may well be that she had in fact acted for her father elsewhere in Ireland, but chose later to suppress so humdrum an initiation. Certainly the tone of the *Freeman's Journal* the next day implies no particular surprise at her accomplishment, and, strangely, makes no reference to her extreme youth:

Miss Smithson met a most warm reception last night, and it is only justice to say that she did not receive one plaudit which she did not eminently deserve. She certainly is a most interesting and promising young actress, and there is no doubt she will prove a great acquisition to Crow-street, in the line of performance which her taste, as well as her talents, incline her to pursue. In the last scene she was particularly successful in hitting off all the peculiarities of the gay, the volatile, and amiable *Albina Mandeville*. During the entire performance she was cheered with the most flattering testimonies of approbation, and at the fall of the curtain she received the compliment of three distinct peals of applause.[19]

She was granted a benefit, and chose to play Lady Teazle on 1 July.

Her father and mother now joined Talbot's company in Belfast. For their début there Smithson played Flutter and Mrs Smithson Letitia Hardy in Mrs Cowley's *The Belle's Stratagem*; the gentleman's flippancy and 'light neat figure' called to mind Richard Jones of the Theatre Royal, Covent Garden; the lady, commented the *Belfast Newsletter*, 'is a fine woman, both in face and figure, but as she does not possess that airyness of proportion which implies if it does not denote extreme youth, we think her choice of character was rather injudicious'. This

8

1. Montague Talbot as M. Morbleau in *Monsieur Tonson*. Etching, *c.* 1821.

tendency to stoutness, along with the role of Letitia Hardy, was passed down to Harriet. At the close of 1815 Mr and Mrs Smithson returned to Dublin while Harriet took their place in Montague Talbot's company.[20]

Talbot, a graduate of Trinity College, Dublin and excessively proud of his aristocratic ancestry, had abandoned the law for the stage and had taken charge of the Belfast theatre in 1809 after making a reputation in

9

Dublin as an actor of refined comedy. Mrs Jordan thought him the best Mirabel of his time; and in the *Familiar Epistles* Croker evaluates his qualities:

> A baby face, that sometimes shows
> Alike in transports as in woes,
> Will ne'er permit him to resemble
> Or soar the tragic heights of Kemble;
> Yet in some scenes, together placed,
> With *greater* feeling – *equal* taste
> From a judicious audience draws
> As *much* and as deserved applause.[21]

Talbot was a robust and eccentric figure who seems to have provoked mildly uncomplimentary anecdotes – he was reported to have played the Ghost in *Hamlet* with a pair of tin eyes fastened over his own. However, he was a polished actor to have as a model, and as a manager he gave Harriet ample opportunity to extend her range of roles. The season opened on Monday, 1 January 1816, and Harriet was given parts in a succession of comedies: Mrs Mortimer in another Reynolds piece, *Laugh When You Can*; Amelia in Mrs Inchbald's *Lovers' Vows;* Floranthe in Colman's *Mountaineers*. The *Belfast Newsletter* enthused about her appearance in a melodrama, *The Magpie*: 'There is in this young lady's beauty so much of innocent softness, mingled with playful, even childish archness, a sort of rustic shyness of countenance which seems to stamp her the very *Annette* who the author drew.'[22] She was more child than woman. For her benefit on 1 April she filled, far more appropriately than her mother, the role of Letitia Hardy opposite Talbot in one of the most effective characters, Doricourt.

After the Belfast season there was a spell at Newry, and then Harriet accompanied Talbot to Cork and Limerick before returning to Dublin. Among the parts she added to her repertoire was that of Mrs Haller in a version of Kotzebue's *The Stranger*. This, for a sixteen-year-old, was a more demanding and slightly incongruous role. Created originally in England by Mrs Siddons, Mrs Haller is a disguised countess who has fallen in love with another man and run away from the count and her children when the affair comes to an end; remarkably for the age, the countess's adultery does not sentence her to a dramatic death, and she is eventually reconciled with her forgiving husband. It was a role which Miss O'Neill had inherited, and marks Harriet's first attempt at a character of greater weight and seriousness.

Harriet was now thought to have enjoyed sufficient success and experience to be submitted to a more demanding test. Once again the offices of the Castle Cootes were invoked, and Harriet left her parents in Dublin and crossed the Irish Sea to go to Birmingham, where Robert Elliston had been persuaded to offer her a place in his company.

In joining Elliston, who was to have a powerful influence on her development as an actress, Harriet came into contact with one of the most talented theatrical men of the time, and certainly the most flamboyant.[23] Elliston was a compelling actor, specialising in high comedy and yet sufficiently versatile for Leigh Hunt to call him, in 1807, 'the greatest actor of the present day'.[24] Elliston never stopped acting. 'Wherever Elliston walked, sate, or stood still,' recalled Lamb, 'there was the theatre. He carried about with him his pit, boxes, and galleries, and set up his portable play-house at corners of streets, and in the market-places.'[25] There were moments when it seemed as if he was intent on taking over every theatre in England. Apart from the Olympic in London and the Theatre Royal, Birmingham, he currently owned or leased playhouses in Croydon, Worcester and Shrewsbury, and would shortly add King's Lynn, Leicester, Northampton and Leamington to his sphere of control. Actor, manager, impresario, Elliston had unbounded faith in the power of the theatre to attract interest; his own involvement in an enterprise was a guarantee of vigour and ingenuity, if not invariably good taste and decorum.

Birmingham, for all its size and wealth, was a difficult place to please. The prevailing philosophy was too conservative to ensure ready support for the drama. Even so astute a manager as Macready had failed to make the theatre pay in recent years, and the committee of proprietors told Elliston that the town could not sustain performances more frequent than three a week. This was the kind of challenge Elliston liked. By 1817 he had won increasing audiences by gathering a more distinguished company and by providing a far greater variety of entertainment. The critic from the London *Theatrical Inquisitor* even descended on Birmingham that July, a rare accolade for a provincial theatre. Elliston, free for a while from his commitments to Drury Lane, acted regularly, and a procession of visiting stars fulfilled engagements, Grimaldi, Junius Brutus Booth, Liston, and Charles Mathews among them.

Harriet's first appearance at Birmingham was on 30 June 1817 in one of the roles she had played in Ireland, Lady Contest in Mrs Inchbald's *The Wedding Day*.[26] She remained until October in her lodgings in Lichfield Street, where she must have spent much of the time available after her calls at the theatre in learning her lines. In a little over three months she appeared in more than forty different roles, and all but two of these were new to her – because of the company's strength and the presence of Miss Somerville and Miss Brunton, she was generally restricted to a line of parts inferior to those she had grown accustomed to in Ireland. It is true that some of these roles were extremely slight, and that many were constructed to a clearly defined and familiar formula. Yet the season still provided a formidable apprenticeship, and is evidence both of Harriet's eagerness to learn and the good impression she made on Elliston. She acted in farce and comedy, in Shakespearean history and tragedy, appearing as Lady Amaranth in O'Keefe's *Wild Oats*, Margaret in Massinger's *A New Way to Pay Old Debts*, Celia in *As you Like It*, Blanche in *King John*, Virgilia in *Coriolanus* and Lady Anne in *Richard III* – such a range being partial fulfilment of Elliston's stated aim to present 'the very best example of the British Drama'. She played with three of the greatest comic actors of the day: Mathews, Liston and Elliston. To ensure the widest possible appeal, the repertory also included of necessity a substantial amount of melodrama, pantomime and romance, and T. P. Cooke, a specialist in spectacle, had been hired to supervise that area: Harriet featured in such unclassical roles as Madame Perouse in *The Desolate Island*, Ardenelle ('the Fairy of the Lake and Protectress of Ali Baba's Family') in *Forty Thieves*, and Agnes in *The Bleeding Nun*. It was a broad and thorough theatrical education.

The chief financial reward for all these endeavours was the granting of a benefit, and *Aris' Gazette* pleaded on Harriet's behalf for 'that kind interference and patronage which the ladies of Birmingham have on many occasions exerted for the countenance of unassuming worth'.[27] More important was the fact that Henry Johnston, the 'Scottish Roscius', had approved of her ability, and agreed to recommend Harriet personally to the committee at Drury Lane. Having survived the preparatory phases, Harriet was judged ready to face the far more daunting conditions of a London patent theatre, and the astringent critics of the London newspapers and journals.

2 Years of apprenticeship

Harriet made her London début on 20 January 1818 at the Theatre Royal, Drury Lane.[1] The role was one she had already performed in Ireland, Letitia Hardy in *The Belle's Stratagem*, a comedy frequently chosen to present a relatively inexperienced actress to a fresh audience. Letitia Hardy is a rich heiress about to be married to a childhood friend, Doricourt, who has returned to England from the continent disillusioned with the insipidity of English beauties after meeting the 'resistless charmers' of Italy and France. Miss Hardy longs for her husband-to-be to fall romantically in love with her, and resolves to make him first dislike her, 'Because 'tis much easier to convert a sentiment into its opposite, than to transform indifference into tender passion'; she therefore intentionally repels Doricourt by acting the part of a gauche, forward, ill-educated girl before contriving to meet him in disguise at a masquerade, where he duly falls in love with the mysterious woman who seems to him to possess all the spirit and fire he could wish for. The play has a deftness and vitality which raise it above the common level of sentimental comedy, and while celebrating the 'innate modesty' of English women implicitly criticizes that very quality as itself a form of affectation. The part of Letitia Hardy is in the nature of a compliment to the actress who plays it, inviting her to unfurl her accomplishments, for in addition to the demanding range of masks required, it calls for her to sing and to dance: an ideal, if ambitious, audition piece.

The playbill description, 'Miss Smithson from Dublin', was as traditional as the choice of play. Miss O'Neill and Miss Fanny Kelly were only the latest of a long line of predecessors on the London stage who were of Irish descent or connection. The timing of her début alone worked to Harriet's disadvantage. Both the great patent houses, who held the official monopoly in London of legitimate drama, had entered upon a period of marked decline. This tendency was affecting theatre

13

throughout the country, but it was accentuated at Drury Lane and Covent Garden by a transfer of allegiance on the part of the fashionable audience in favour of Italian opera. At Drury Lane the general difficulties had been compounded by administrative folly. The management had been placed in the hands of a committee, including for a time Byron; its members proved even more incompetent than the individual managers whom they succeeded. The box-office receipts for the 1817–18 season were half those for five years before. The quality of acting, with certain exceptions, was notoriously poor. The standard of production suffered from lack of clear policy and consistent direction. So strained were the theatre's finances that no free orders for admission could be issued. When Mrs Smithson arrived from Dublin to see her daughter act, she had to pay her money at the door like everyone else.

It would have required exceptional talent to overcome these rather depressing circumstances. Harriet's freshness and striking features were enough to make her appear promising in Dublin or Birmingham. To force her way into the front rank in London required more polish and technique than she yet possessed. The supporting company offered limited help, for while Dowton as Letitia's father and Mrs Glover as Lady Racket gave good performances, Stanley as Doricourt 'wanted discrimination' while the rest of the play was indifferently cast. One scathing notice catalogued Harriet's defects and dismissed her in terms which have a certain prophetic irony, considering her as 'likely very soon to occupy a place among the forgotten persons whose memories are lying in cold abstraction in the tomb of all the Capulets'. *The Times* was cool, praising her face and features but questioning her talent, adding the patronising suggestion that she might appear to more advantage in the line of country rustic.[2] Other reviews were much more encouraging: 'She is naturally graceful in her action, but perfectly capable of assuming the awkwardness which some of the situations required.' If the broad comic part seemed a little overacted, it was

conceived and executed with spirit. The speaking voice is rather distinct than powerful, and she gave the song of 'Where are you going, my pretty maid' in a style more remarkable for humour than sweetness. The Minuet de la Cour was substituted for the song at the masquerade, and in it her fine figure and graceful movements were displayed to advantage.[3]

All in all, she was reckoned to be a useful acquisition to the company.

However nervous her initiation, Harriet was given a further opportunity as Letitia Hardy, and the critic of *Bell's Weekly Messenger* paid her the compliment of a second notice, commenting on the more favourable impression she made the second time:

> She poured out a great portion of comic spirit. She adapted herself to the various parts of the character with propriety as well as with facility; and though she did not execute all that might have been done with the materials which had been placed in her hands, yet she managed them with such a gay and artless air, as veiled her deficiencies. She has a great deal in her favour, her youth, her figure, her countenance, her incessant animation; and these in a comic actress, are no mean or common qualifications.[4]

Harriet was soon attracting further positive commendations. In February, she took the 'arduous' part of Ellen in George Soane's melodrama *The Falls of Clyde*, and, wrote the *Theatrical Inquisitor*, 'played it in very good style. We are ardent and professed admirers of Miss Kelly's acting in this afterpiece, and we therefore consider that we are bestowing no trifling praise in saying, that we believe Miss Smithson to be second only to that lady in this difficult line of her profession.'[5] This was a less backhanded compliment than it might appear: Fanny Kelly, ten years senior to Harriet, was vastly more experienced and extremely accomplished in a particular type of role. She had obtained leave from Drury Lane to go to Dublin, and Harriet's success as Ellen encouraged the committee to entrust her with the part of Mary in *The Innkeeper's Daughter*.[6]

This was a melodrama, again by George Soane, and loosely based on Southey's ballad, *Mary the Maid of the Inn*. Fanny Kelly played the original Mary at Drury Lane in 1817 to the mingled sobs and cheers of the audience, and Soane, who dedicated the published version of his adaptation to her, was under no illusion as to the extent of her contribution. It was one of the earliest melodramas to have a specifically British setting (the ballad, it was claimed, was based on an 'actual' series of events in Wales) and contrived to unite a central relationship of true but humble love, an improbable and rapid tale of smugglers, coastguards, shootings, stabbings, shipwrecks and drownings, and several Gothic set-pieces in the shape of tangled wood, moonlit churchyard, ruined belfry and storm-lashed rocks. It may be taken as broadly representative of its genre, and an example of the indirect contribution of the English Romantic writers to their contemporary theatre.

There are eight scenes, and eight settings, in this relatively brief two-act afterpiece, and the stage directions for act one, scene four suggest how important a part of the total effect was conveyed by the visual, rather than the verbal, element:

2. The villain Harrop in action in *The Innkeeper's Daughter*. Engraving, c. 1817.

The village church-yard. – The moon shines brightly at first, but at intervals is completely overcast by large black masses of cloud that roll rapidly along. – On the left hand is the Church. – At the back is a small river, skirting the church-yard, and dividing it from a thick wood. – In front are several tombstones, on one of which is the following inscription so large as to be distinctly visible to the audience – 'In memory of Ellen, wife of John Frankland, who died October 7th 1698, aged 44 years.' Near it grows a large yew-tree. – A little farther on are several simple hillocks bound with willow.

The features described are integral to the action. Into this churchyard stumbles Mary Frankland the innkeeper's daughter (as well as almost every other member of the dramatis personae) on her way to win a wager and a purse of five guineas by bravely cutting a slip of yew from the tree. Bells toll, the wind howls, shots and screams echo, a woman is fatally wounded by her husband the villain, a freshly murdered corpse is tossed into the river, and corresponding music accompanies all. As the scene closes, the luckless Mary wrongly identifies her betrothed Richard as the murderer and secures his eventual arrest.

In the second act the pace quickens. In the hope of making himself secure, the villain Harrop has helped Richard escape from the belfry and persuaded him to take to the sea, although no boat can be expected to survive the howling storm. To make doubly sure of Richard's death, Harrop climbs the lighthouse to remove the lamp which might conceivably guide Richard to safety; just as Richard gains the rocks on the long sands, the lighthouse railings collapse and the villain plunges to his death. But the rocks are swept by the floodtide and Richard, now known to be innocent, is certain to perish. Enter the Romantic heroine:

(*Mary rushes in pale and breathless, and her hair streaming wildly to the wind. During the whole of this scene the water rapidly gains on the rock of the sand, and with so strong a rise as to be distinctly visible to the audience.*)
MARY: Is he gone? – Is it too late?

Fifty guineas is the reward offered to anyone who will try to save Richard; William, the old seaman, would not be that man for five hundred – it would be merely throwing away life. Mary, anticipating Grace Darling, leaps into the storm-boat.

MARY: Death was a promise, and I go to keep it – let it be written on my grave – 'A woman braved the storm which a seaman shrank from'.

Spurred by the taunt, old William follows Mary into the boat, and with a cry of 'Life or death with Richard!' the boat darts away before the wind. The stage directions crescendo:

(*Music. – A furious burst of the Storm – The thunder peals along in violent claps, that, for a few seconds, follow each other without intermission. – A broad flash of lightning blazes around the boat, which is seen at the very top of a mountainous wave, and in the next moment is lost to the sight.*)

But the boat survives and a rope is cast towards Richard, who leaps from his rock as the waves burst over it and can be glimpsed by the lightning flashes swimming towards safety and Mary. As the curtain slowly drops to music, the onlookers cheer and cheer and the boat is seen steadily making for the shore.

For all the banality of the dialogue and the predictability of the scenario, audiences were powerfully engaged by this and similar theatrical experiences, and it was a kind of drama which formed an important part of the repertory even at the major theatres. The emotive music contributed greatly to the impact – the music in *The Innkeeper's Daughter* was not continuous, but the piece could not be given without the proper accompaniment: when the parts were mislaid one night at Drury Lane, the management was forced to substitute a farce, to the disgust of the half-price customers. But these plays were equally popular with the more fashionable and educated sections of the audience, who responded with tearful enthusiasm to the stage pictures. The purely visual element assumed increasing significance, and made huge demands on the ingenuity and resources of the scene-painters and stage directors. With the advent of gas lighting and the introduction of more advanced machinery, visual effects were susceptible to far finer control and became more ambitious in their approximation to the real. For the actor or actress, the emphasis was on situation. With sparse and unsubtle dialogue, the weight of interpretation had to be expressed through posture and mime. Appearance was paramount. Harriet as Mary had to look beautiful, distressed, frailly courageous, and to project the successive phases of her extremes of emotion. As simple image, a silent actress, she was highly effective.

Appearance was now the dominant factor at Drury Lane whatever the type of drama. 'Henceforward theatres for spectators rather than playhouses for hearers', had been Richard Cumberland's reaction to Holland's Drury Lane.[7] Even after Wyatt's remodelling of 1812 the auditorium still held over three thousand, and only the broader effects could be appreciated from many parts of the house. (Illustration 3 gives a sense of the problem; with the addition of the stage doors, replaced in 1814, this represents Drury Lane as Harriet initially knew it.) The installation of gas lighting in 1817 was an important advance; Leigh Hunt called it 'a very great improvement' which, 'if it is managed as well as we saw it on Friday, will enable the spectator to see every part of the stage with equal clearness'.[8] But many of the spectators could see little in the way of detail, and heard even less. The *Examiner* commented on Kean in 1819 that 'a great part of the house can neither see nor hear him to any purpose, especially when his voice is exhausted, *another* consequence, by the way, of the space which he has to fill with it'.[9] This was a description of Kean at the height of his powers. Actresses were frequently criticised for inaudibility, and the task of making

3. Theatre Royal, Drury Lane. Engraving by W. Hopwood after N. Heideloff, 1813.

themselves heard in such a vast building, often against a background hubbub from a boisterous and easily distracted audience, contributed in many cases to an artificial and monotonous style of delivery. The alternative, as explained to the Parisian visitor Pichot, was to address any speech chiefly to the pit, for the actors 'well know that the frequenters of the dress boxes are, for the most part, indifferent to the performance, and that the company in the gallery only come to see the last act of the tragedy, which usually terminates with a battle, or the afterpiece, which is a mere display of splendid dresses and scenery'.[10] The proportions of the theatre, as much as the taste of the times, pushed the repertory towards spectacle, farce and melodrama, and away from the great strengths of English drama, Shakespearean tragedy and the comedy of manners. Developments in scene arrangement and lighting tended to draw the actor upstage, within the scene, separating him from the audience, and supporting the shift to a representational from a presentational style. For Harriet, the professional environment was far from ideal, but it may be said to have contributed to the development of one especially strong element in her technique, her command of mime.

In terms of making a living, these six months in London brought one distinct advantage. When the season closed at the end of June and Harriet, like most of the company, left London to take up engagements in the provinces, or to embark on tours to Scotland or Ireland, she would be entitled to have placed after her name on the playbills the words 'Of the Theatre Royal, Drury Lane' – a somewhat tarnished decoration, and often appropriated on the flimsiest of excuses, but still the guarantee of a certain respect in Buxton or Wisbech.

Drury Lane reopened in September, and Harriet returned from Ireland to take up a place in the company at a salary of £5 a week.[11] This moderate figure was reasonably encouraging considering her limited experience, and one she would not attain again for another five years. The members of the subcommittee, conscious of their collective failure, had appointed Stephen Kemble to be in day-to-day control of the season. Kemble, a brother to John and Charles and manager of the Newcastle circuit, was known less for his ability than his girth – he could play Falstaff without stuffing – and the theatre's fortunes sunk even lower. The only thing which could be laid to the management's credit was that Drury Lane had not yet been 'degraded, as Covent Garden had been, by the performances of horses and rope dancers'.[12] The theatre closed on 5 June 1819 with stated debts of over £90,000.

The outlook for Harriet as an actress at this moment was uncertain. Her family background, however, prepared her for the persistent effort required to secure work. That summer, it was arranged that she should go to Margate, to the Theatre Royal in Addington Street. Margate's era as a fashionable watering-place was passing in favour of Brighton, but the town was only a few hours by packet from London and it remained an attractive engagement, partly because of its convenience and partly because of a number of wealthy and influential people among the regular audiences.

Among these were the banker Thomas Coutts and his expansive second wife Harriot, formerly the actress Miss Mellon and later to astonish society still further by marrying the youthful Duke of St Albans. Coutts, reputedly the richest man in England, had always been a lover of theatre and a consistent patron of the arts; Harriot Coutts, unlike many from her profession who made advantageous marriages, never forgot either her humble origins or her own stage career, which

4. Harriet Smithson. Engraving by J. Hopwood after a painting by Rose Emma Drummond, 1819.

ended at Drury Lane but which began in a barn – in fact, she was almost too insistent on alluding to the past. She and her husband noticed Harriet at Margate in such roles as Kate Hardcastle in Goldsmith's *She Stoops to Conquer*[13] (in which Mrs Smithson made a rare appearance in the part of Mrs Hardcastle), were generous supporters of her benefit, and continued to show her kindness in London. When Thomas Coutts died in 1822, Harriet was so overcome with grief that she was unable to play that night at Drury Lane.

Such unexpected and warm-hearted support, though useful and encouraging, brought only temporary security. At Drury Lane a minor revolution was in progress. Various bids to take over control of the theatre were being considered, and on 14 August Harriet was in London knocking on the door of the man most likely to succeed:

Miss Smithson presents her respects to Mr Elliston, would feel most happy if honoured with any communication from him relative to her engagement at Drury Lane next season; Miss Smithson call'd at the theatre with the hope of seeing Mr Elliston for which purpose she solely came up to town from Margate but not being so fortunate begs leave to address him and requests he will favour her with an early answer.[14]

There is a note of pathos in this brief letter which will be heard again. On 8 September Elliston was confirmed as lessee on a fourteen-year term. One of his first actions was to prune the existing company by over forty, and though he offered terms to several of his Birmingham company, there was no place for Harriet.

While waiting for an answer, Harriet had been appearing for the first time at the Theatre Royal, Bristol, managed at this period by Macready, father of William. Announced on the playbills originally as engaged for six nights, she was retained for a further week. Most of the roles she had acted before, in Ireland or Drury Lane, though the tragic heroine Imogine, in Maturin's Gothic drama *Bertram*, was a new departure. If she had so far escaped the rope dancers at Drury Lane, she had ample opportunity now to study them at close quarters. She had already come into contact with Il Diavolo Antonio at Margate; preceding her to Bristol, Antonio was shot in the eye by Junius Brutus Booth in a duel in Queen's Square, after Booth had pressed his attentions too forcibly on Antonio's wife. Harriet found herself performing in Bristol in repertory with more enthralling feats: 'at the end of Act the First Madame Saqui will Dance her much-admired Pas-Seul, on the Single Rope, And will, both with and without the Balance Pole, make her Grand Ascent from the Back of the Stage to the Gallery!!!'[15] This was bagatelle for Madame Saqui, who crossed the Hippodrome of the Porte Dauphine forty feet above the ground at the age of seventy-five; but in Paris her acrobatic feats were usually confined to her own theatre on the boulevards, and not played side by side with legitimate drama. The varied entertainment at Bristol was at least a suitable introduction to Harriet's next job. Since she was not required at Drury Lane, she took lodgings in Lambeth and accepted an offer from Glossop to join the permanent company at the Royal Coburg for the 1818–19 season.

The Royal Coburg theatre – now the Old Vic and still, like the Margate and Bristol Theatres Royal, surviving as a Georgian construction – had only been opened the previous year. Lambeth had become easier of access since the building of Waterloo Bridge, though the marshy and less civilised surroundings obliged the management to provide special lighting and patrols for the comfort and safety of the audience. Licensed for that loosely defined and contentious category 'burletta', the theatre was constructed to house melodrama and panto-mime, and had an interior almost as elaborate as the shows which were staged there. Something of the atmosphere may be sensed from J. R. Planché's description of the unveiling of a much-heralded 'looking-glass' curtain:

After an overture, to which no attention of course was paid by the excited and impatient audience, the promised novelty was duly displayed; not one entire plate of glass – that could not have been expected – but composed of a considerable number of moderately-sized plates – I have seen larger in some shop-windows – within an elaborately gilt frame. The effect was anything but agreeable. The glass was all over finger or other marks, and dimly reflected the two tiers of boxes and their occupants . . . There was . . . considerable applause at its appearance. The moment it ceased, some one in the gallery, possessing a stentorian voice, called out, 'That's all werry well! Now show us summut else!'[16]

Hazlitt, most sympathetic and sensitive of critics, went to the Coburg 'all attention, simplicity and enthusiasm', and had his expectations turned topsy-turvy.

It was the heartless indifference and hearty contempt shown by the performers for their parts, and by the audience for the players and the play, that disgusted us with all of them . . . The genius of St George's Fields prevailed, and you felt yourself in a bridewell, or a brothel, amidst Jew-boys, pickpockets, prostitutes, and mountebanks, instead of being on the precincts of Mount Parnassus, or in the company of the Muses. The object was not to admire or to excel, but to vilify and degrade everything. The audience did not hiss the actors (that would have implied a serious feeling of disapprobation, and something like a disappointed wish to be pleased) but they laughed, hooted at, nick-named, pelted them with oranges and witticisms, to show their unruly contempt for them and their art.[17]

Interestingly, Hazlitt ascribed this 'indecency' of attitude in part to the comparatively small size of the theatre, which destroyed the dramatic illusion and brought the audience into too great an intimacy with the actors.

Although a substantial part of the audience came from the south bank, there was plenty of fashionable patronage for the kind of enter-tainment in which the Royal Coburg specialised. Music, dance, and spectacular scenery were the major constituents of presentation, and the repertory emphasised every popular element in the English drama-tic tradition: villains and heroines, ballads and hornpipes, acrobats, clowns, combats, performing dogs and racing cats, trained birds, even on one occasion an elephant. The intellectual demands made on the human performers were small; in terms of energy, timing, physical control and versatility, they were formidable.

Hazlitt was shocked by the prevailing tone among the audience, in contrast to that of the patent houses (itself remarkably unrefined). In terms of repertory, the gulf between the major and minor theatres was not nearly so wide as either might claim. One of Harriet's roles was the heroine in *Mary, the Maid of the Inn*, which was merely an alternative version of *The Innkeeper's Daughter*. The hero was played by Harry Kemble, who inherited a powerful pair of lungs but little else of the family technique or sensitivity: his name looked well on the playbills. Junius Brutus Booth also featured during the season in *King Richard III, or The Battle of Bosworth Field*, nothing, so the advertisements claimed, to do with the well-known play of that name, but a melodrama in three acts, founded on Cibber's compiled tragedy from Shakespeare, with music by Mr T. Hughes. For this and other pieces of poaching on the patent theatres' preserve, Glossop was taken to court. Harriet, who had played with Booth in Birmingham, appeared again with him in a 'New Grand Classical Melodrama' with one of the less alluring titles in English theatrical history, *Horatii and Curiatii*, which provided a cast-iron excuse for a Grand Combat for six.

The role of Harriet's that was most representative of this Coburg season was that of Zelima, surnamed Beauty, in *Beauty and the Beast*.[18] In terms of spectacle the minor theatres yielded nothing to their competitors. The marine painter J. T. Serres was Glossop's first scenic director, and the young Clarkson Stanfield was on the staff. *Beauty and the Beast* was produced 'with every possible degree of Splendor', and included choruses of 'Slaves, Genii, Pandeans, Satyrs, Officers, Guards, Dancers, Peasants, and Banner Bearers'. Scene three, which presented a 'Pavilion of Pleasures in the Palace of Scanderberg', had a typical scenario: 'Grand Bridal Procession of the Cloud King over the Mountains, with Nuptial Presents, Military Band etc., to claim the hand of Zelima.' The piece concluded with the defeat of the Cloud King (Harry Kemble) and the Union of Beauty and the Beast, alias Prince Azor (T. P. Cooke). After her winter in Lambeth, Harriet can have sustained few illusions about the nature of her profession.

Harriet spent the summer in Dublin. Henry Harris of Covent Garden had become patentee of the Theatre Royal there, and while searching for a suitable site he fitted up the round room of the Rotunda as a playhouse. Harriet enjoyed a far more satisfactory selection of parts, although she had to give precedence to Miss Booth, playing Celia to her Rosalind. However, when Macready joined the company she acted Lady Anne opposite his Richard III, and Virginia in Knowles's *Virginius*, with Macready in the title-part.[19]

In the autumn of 1820 she was relieved to continue within the so-called legitimate theatre when she rejoined the Drury Lane company, albeit on a reduced salary. James Winston, Elliston's acting manager, was notoriously mean when it came to striking terms with the less important members of the company. Joseph Cowell attributed Winston's attitude to disappointment in his hopes of becoming an actor himself:

With the same acrimony of feeling an elderly virgin hates a blooming bride, he detested the professors of an art he hadn't warmth of soul enough to advance in. It was his province to measure out the canvas and colour for the painters, count the nails for the carpenters, pick up the tin-tacks and bits of candle, calculate on the least possible quantity of soap required for each dressing-room, and invent and report delinquencies that could in any way be construed into the liability of a forfeit.[20]

The complex system of fines for backstage indiscipline set up by Elliston could make large inroads into an actor's weekly salary. The penalties ranged from a half-a-crown forfeit for 'any one standing upon the stage at Rehearsal, when not concerned in the scene' to a massive £30 and nine nights' salary for a refusal to 'study, rehearse and perform any Character, or Part, or Prologue or Epilogue'.[21] This season Harriet received only £3 a week, which relegated her to the second green-room. The contrast with Fanny Kelly's £20 and Madame Vestris's £12 underlines Harriet's status as the walking lady, restricted to a minor line of parts unless illness or some other cause for absence gave rise to greater opportunity.

The virtual ownership of roles by permanent and influential members of the company made it extraordinarily difficult for a newcomer, however talented, to advance. The status of a particular part was judged to a nicety; if Lydia Languish or Lady Teazle lay within an established actress's accustomed purview, it was not lightly relinquished. There was one occasion this season when a kind of inverse pecking order worked to Harriet's advantage. On 20 February 1821 Winston recorded that 'Miss Kelly, finding Thérèse was to be performed tomorrow night, Vestris being ill, said she would not play tragedy No 2, and therefore Miss Smithson's name was put in the bills.'[22] This particular production illustrates both the English theatre's growing dependence

25

on French boulevard drama, and Elliston's urgent search for novelty. *Thérèse* was a version of a Pixérécourt melodrama, whose text was despatched from Paris and delivered to John Howard Payne who was in prison at the time; Payne contrived to translate and reshape it in four days, and Elliston hustled it on to the stage within a week to forestall possible opposition – which did not prevent Glossop from mounting a rival version at the Coburg, in spite of a court injunction.

That evening's unexpected promotion did not lead to any permanent improvement in the parts offered to Harriet, but she was beginning to impress herself more vividly on the London public's imagination, even though it was her face and figure which attracted notice as much as her acting. She was clearly developing into a beauty of an uncommon kind. The *New Monthly Magazine* might have been defining one prototype of the Romantic ideal when writing of Harriet in *Geraldi Duval* that 'she looked beautiful enough to justify any frenzy but one which would destroy her. She lies fainting in the arms of her enemy, pale and lovely, with reclined head, like a lily snapped by an ungentle hand.'[23] The qualities of delicacy and refinement which she projected were frequently noted. As Adolphine, in Moncrieff's farce *Monsieur Tonson*, 'Miss Smithson, the heroine, acts like a lady, and looks like an angel',[24] an opinion placed in perspective by the more reserved *Examiner*, which commented that Miss Smithson 'made a very pretty French Girl, and it was not her fault if she had nothing to say'.[25]

Probably the most balanced criticism of this period comes from the *Theatrical Observer*, whose caustic analyses of the deficiencies at Drury Lane led eventually to Elliston withdrawing the magazine's free pass. Of Harriet's performance as Louisa Courtney in Reynolds's *The Dramatist* the critic wrote: 'We feel great pleasure in being able to commend this amiable young lady. She improves on us: but she must give a little more distinctness and natural tone to her delivery.'[26] The *Theatrical Observer* had been castigating the management's general policy, deploring the conversion of this *'great national theatre'* into a *'School* for *Scene-painters, Tailors,* and the *training* of *Theatrical Horsemen'*;[27] it welcomed the return of Edmund Kean in November 1821, and evenings therefore chiefly devoted to the legitimate drama. On 12 November Kean acted Richard III, with Harriet as Lady Anne; two days later, she was given her first major Shakespearean role in London when she played Desdemona to Kean's Othello. The *Theatrical Observer* reviewed Kean with enthusiasm, and called Harriet's Desdemona highly interesting, adding a few days later that it was 'very satisfactory to observe the rising merit of the amiable Miss Smithson, who as Desdemona gave a faithful, pleasing, and impressive portraiture of the hapless lady'.[28]

In later years, when Harriet's extravagant reception in Paris was set against the long period of comparative neglect, even obscurity, at Drury Lane, a number of reasons were put forward to explain her lack of advancement in London, among them her 'strong' Irish accent. There is little contemporary evidence to support this explanation. Fanny Kemble, in a retrospective and waspish appraisal of the Paris season which she had not witnessed, wrote that Miss Smithson's 'super-fluous native accent was no drawback to her merits in the esteem of her French audience';[29] nor was it a drawback to her twice being offered terms by Charles Kemble to act for him at Covent Garden. The French critics often proposed the theory that Harriet had been overlooked because of her Irish pronunciation. During Harriet's years at Drury Lane, however, comments about her voice centre rather on her over-precise, stilted enunciation, as in the following advice: 'there is rather too much obvious endeavour to be correct. She should study a more *natural* delivery.'[30] This over-precision might conceivably be an attempt to conceal the 'superfluous' accent behind an assumed refinement, but it is just as likely to have arisen from the strain of making herself heard in the cavernous recesses of Drury Lane. In November 1821 there was a comment in *Bell's Weekly Messenger* which is relevant: 'Miss Smithson improves nightly, and is rapidly losing that drawl, which we presume she brought from the blarney districts of her native country.'[31] Even here the writer is clearly referring to a pattern of intonation rather than pronunciation, for he continues: 'It has frequently fallen to our lot to see many handsome Irish women, some as handsome as Miss Smithson, but we have never seen one of them without feeling a wish to infuse a little more quickness and spirit in their mode of speaking.' If there had been substantial evidence behind Fanny Kemble's charge, the critics would certainly have returned to it again and again, for the age was quite as given to the harsh dismissal as to the anodyne compliment. It would, too, be surprising if years of living and acting, largely in England, had not enabled Harriet to modify any problems of accent.

The critiques on Harriet were by no means universally favourable, but the general picture which emerges at this time, in the face of limited opportunities and the daunting conditions at Drury Lane, is that of an actress of recognised potential, increasing range, and slowly maturing powers of interpretation.

There are several indications that Harriet was either unluckily or unjustly overlooked during this period after achieving a notable measure of success, for to play opposite Kean at Drury Lane at the age of twenty-one was an accomplishment even in the conditions of the 1820s. One hint is supplied by the strength of Harriet's personal following. At the close of the 1820–21 season, Harriet shared a benefit with Edward Knight – this was 'Little' Knight, who had moved to a career as actor after a spell as a painter, first of miniatures and then for the stage. The theatre's standing costs were £221, and on many normal evenings these were barely covered by the box-office receipts. Knight and Miss Smithson drew in the astonishing total for 'small people' of £627, of which £428 were the proceeds of tickets sold on Harriet's behalf.[32] However assiduously she may have worked at persuading friends and acquaintances to support her benefit, such a response, which would have pleased Kean or Kemble, testifies to the strength of Harriet's popularity as an actress, at least among the wealthier sections of the audience.

It is clear, too, that Harriet was an entirely respectable member of the acting profession, a quality which commended her to society but which did little to advance her cause at Drury Lane. No breath of scandal touched her reputation in England at a time when the moral atmosphere in the theatres, both in the auditorium and behind the scenes, was flagrantly lax. Of audiences, wrote Scott, 'one half come to prosecute their debaucheries, so openly that it would disgrace a bagnio'.[33] Backstage there was little improvement, certainly at Drury Lane – the atmosphere of Covent Garden was infinitely more respectable. James Winston may have taken pleasure in disapproval, but he had no reason to exaggerate the drunkenness and sexual licence of Elliston, Kean and various other members of the company which he records in his diary. Oxberry ends his article on Harriet in the *Dramatic Biography* with a pointed implication that other actresses had not hesitated to use traditional methods of securing attention which she had shunned: 'Beautiful beyond the common run of beauty, yet as virtuous as beautiful; affable to all the members of the theatre, servile to none; *she* has never *coquetted* a manager into favour, nor marted her feelings for the sake of her interest.' Oxberry's complaints that Desdemona had been entrusted to others after Harriet had filled the character successfully, and that other suitable roles such as Juliet, Imogen and Cordelia had been unreasonably withheld from her, seem sufficiently justified, especially when coupled with similar pleas on behalf of other actresses.

The most obvious reason for Harriet's lack of further opportunities lies in Elliston's commercial judgment, not so much about her personal ability and drawing power, but about the general strategy which might wring support from a grudging audience. During his tenure at Drury Lane Elliston pursued many, often conflicting, ways to restore the Theatre Royal to popularity and prosperity. However, after a brief, fruitless attempt to draw new work from the 'best writers' in England, most of his decisions moved the theatre further in the direction of novelty and spectacle, and towards a reliance on star names and lavish production. During the 1820–21 season evenings of opera and melodrama outnumbered programmes of legitimate drama by two to one, while a spectacle such as the facsimile of George IV's coronation ceremony, with Elliston as an uncannily accurate double of the King, played night after night.

Harriet could not expect to figure prominently in such a repertory. For one thing, although she worked in the chorus and from time to time took minor singing roles, she was not an accomplished singer like Fanny Kelly, Madame Vestris or Catherine Stephens. Nor could it be argued that she had star quality: her innate modesty, and her sweet but at this point somewhat passive stage personality, restricted her appeal. Elliston must have had a certain respect for her ability, since he renewed her engagement throughout his tenure, but he obviously regarded her primarily as a decorative utility player. Soon after Harriet's apparent breakthrough as Desdemona, Elliston offered improved terms to Mrs West, who first played Juliet (much to the *Theatrical Observer*'s disgust) and later supplanted Harriet as Desdemona. Next, Miss Edmiston, a protégée of Kean, was introduced in Rowe's *Jane Shore* as the heiress apparent to the vacant throne of tragic heroine. Harriet retained Lady Anne, and a few other classical parts such as Margaret in Massinger's *A New Way to Pay Old Debts*, but she was as a general rule restricted to juvenile roles in afterpieces and to such routine tasks as a 'singing witch' in *Macbeth*.

Harriet's personal life was centred on her family. 'We question if a more beauteous or happy domestic circle can be found, than that of which Miss Smithson forms a prominent feature', was Oxberry's rather fulsome description. 'Wherever she steps, the praises of approving friends attend her; and, wherever she is once introduced as an acquaintance, she is sure to be cherished as a friend.' Harriet, for all the apparent independence which a professional career in the theatre afforded, was closely protected within her immediate family, and the affection did nothing to ease the pressure laid upon her, for after her

29

5. Harriet Smithson as Miss Dorrillon in *Wives as they were and Maids as they are*. Engraving by R. Cooper after a painting by George Clint, 1822.

father's death she became the principal support, financial and otherwise, for her mother and crippled sister. They were joined in London from time to time by Harriet's brother Joseph. He appeared at Covent Garden in April 1822 in a scenic fairy-tale, *Cherry and Fair Star*, which played regularly to the close of the season and was revived the following autumn; but Joseph was something of an adventurer, and his speculations in management tended to take him abroad.

In the business of earning a living and gaining experience, the summer months away from London became more lucrative and enjoyable for Harriet. In her first provincial engagement after her début at Drury Lane, a correspondent complained that she had 'kept her voice at its town pitch';[34] now, absolved from the critical responsibility to make herself heard, she learned to relax, and the impact she made in the more intimate theatres was infinitely more confident and sensitive. In July 1822 for instance, she opened at the Theatre Royal, Liverpool, and spent a successful four weeks there. She played eighteen different parts, largely from comedy – established favourites such as Letitia Hardy, Lydia Languish, Kate Hardcastle, and the heroines of the comedies of Mrs Centlivre, Colman, Morton and Murphy. She also appeared as Lavinia in Moncrieff's *The Spectre Bridegroom* – 'as originally acted by her in London' – and as the victim of seduction in Payne's *Adeline*, while for her benefit she chose Mariette in *Therèse*. According to Broadbent's *Annals of the Liverpool Stage*, 'her talents procured her many friends, notably Mr Arthur Heywood, the banker'.[35] The friends swelled the proceeds of her benefit, but only a favourable marriage could release her from the constant need to make a living, and the tedious coach journey to the next town and engagement. By September Harriet was at Gloucester, where the theatre was under the management of Farley and someone she would later be closely associated with, William Abbott. At the least, these summer tours gave Harriet the chance to act more varied and demanding roles, to see her name at the head of the bills and to feel herself the focus of an audience's attention. Then it was once again time to return to lodgings in London, and to await the delayed start of a new season at the Theatre Royal.

3 The walking lady

Even by Drury Lane's existing low standard, the 1821–22 season was reckoned a conspicuous failure. Elliston had been furiously active during the summer, spending £20,000 on re-structuring the theatre's interior. Criticisms about the quality of the accommodation were met by increasing the number and size of the boxes, and decreasing the capacity of the pit. The stage apron was cut back by six feet, the stage doors replaced by boxes, and backstage arrangements redesigned to facilitate the production of spectacle.[1] Over the next few months the team of scene-painters and designers was strengthened; Marinari was already on the staff and he was joined by Clarkson Stanfield at Christmas and, early the next year, by David Roberts, while William Barrymore, the master of pantomime, was inveigled from Covent Garden. To inject vitality and drawing-power into his acting company Elliston lured several leading Covent Garden performers, who had been refused an increase in salary by Kemble, with the promise of exceptionally high fees, although these were negotiated on a nightly rather than a weekly basis. This meant that as a supplement to Kean, Elliston could announce future appearances by Young, Catherine Stephens, Madame Vestris, and the comedians Liston and Munden. While Charles Kemble at Covent Garden was doing his utmost to restore the theatre's prosperity through stringent economies, Elliston strove to out-manoeuvre him by boldly expansionist policies.

For Harriet, there was little to be gained. Her salary, still a mere £4 a week, marked how little she had risen in Elliston's estimation: Mrs West and Miss Edmiston at £10, Miss Copeland at £9, of the regular company, blocked Harriet's path to roles which might give her more chance to excel.[2] She continued to be thought agreeable, amiable, engaging; her benefits were far better attended than her status in the company would suggest, and she was supported in them by Kean and

Young; but her more habitual employment was to be cast in such spectacles as the pantomime *The Chinese Sorcerer*, where she took the part of O-Me, niece of the emperor and princess of China. Crabb Robinson's comment is enough to define the involvement: 'the scenery is so beautiful that I actually cared nothing for the execrable stuff of words by which it was accompanied. As a ballet of action how delightful it might have been made!'[3]

Frustrated by Harriet's lack of progress, the Smithson family decided to explore the possibility of independent management. Joseph Smithson had experience of continental theatre: he organised a season in Amsterdam in 1821 which included productions of *Hamlet* and *Othello*. He thought that Paris might provide a suitable opening for himself and Harriet. On 9 October 1823 he wrote to the British Ambassador, Sir Charles Stuart, using as his address the Theatre Royal, Drury Lane:

I take the liberty humbly to entreat your Excellency's interference with His Most Christian Majesty's Minister to grant me a licence for the performance of a select Company of English Comedians in France under my management, and I pledge myself that the Talent and Respectability of the Performers shall not be unworthy of your Excellency's Patronage.[4]

In view of the hostile reception given to Penley's company at the Porte-Saint-Martin the year before, Smithson's plan was either ignorantly rash or amazingly far-sighted. The request was turned down, although not absolutely: it was suggested that an application should be made to the director of an already licensed theatre for a limited season by means of subscription. This approach seemed too complicated, and Joseph decided to make his base at Boulogne and Calais where there was a substantial nucleus of English residents, even if many of them were living there reputedly to escape from their creditors. Smithson conducted the 1824 season in Boulogne with great spirit but only fair success, and Harriet travelled over in September to support her brother. It was her first visit to France and she played a few nights in Boulogne as well as in Calais, appearing with Wallack and also with Penley, who was slowly withdrawing with remnants of his company after his failure in Paris. The arrangements for Harriet's benefit have a pleasant blend of informality and grandeur: 'Tickets and Places to be had of M. Hoad, Pastry-Cook, No 10, Grande Rue; and of Miss Smithson, at the Hotel de l'Europe.'[5]

Back at Drury Lane for the 1824–25 season, there were few changes in Harriet's fortunes beyond an advance in salary to £5 a week which also brought with it the coveted right to use the first green-room. She added a few relatively minor Shakespeare parts to her range – Lady Percy, Anne Bullen in a production of *Henry VIII* in which Macready played Wolsey, as well as Celia, Virgilia and her regular appearances as Lady Anne. But these next three years served as little more than mechanical consolidation so far as Harriet's career was concerned. Even the *Theatrical Observer*, which usually referred to Harriet as 'our favourite', reported that she had 'stalked' through her role in Colman's *The Heir at Law* with 'determined indifference'. The short step from her rooms in Great Russell Street to the theatre and the undemanding repetition of a minor role grew tedious. In retrospect Harriet's time at Drury Lane might be judged useful preparation. Towards its close it must have seemed monotonous and dispiriting, with only the annual flurry of excitement over her benefit and the summer visits to Cheltenham or Liverpool to vary the pattern.

Even Shakespeare was beginning to assume a supporting role at Drury Lane. The great event of the 1823–24 season had been *The Cataract of the Ganges*. This 'Romantic Drama' written to order by Moncrieff capitalised on the skills of Roberts and Stanfield and moved to a much-heralded finale in which James Wallack as the hero made his escape on horseback up the cataract, with fire threatening him on every side. For all the *London Magazine*'s sneer that the effect was 'something like the pouring of a good tea-pot, only flatter', every performance had a distinctly uplifting effect on the receipts. For the following season Elliston declared his artistic intentions even more openly and brought in Ducrow and his entire troop of horses for *The Enchanted Courser*, while Kean himself was persuaded to appear mounted in *Masaniello* – an unrepeated experiment. Productions with more substance were Soane's adaptations of *Der Freischütz* and *Faust*; but it was the spectacular staging and the brilliantly conceived visual effects which drew the audience's attention, not the interpretative powers of the singers and actors.

Although for a while Elliston seemed to be bringing about at least an economic recovery at Drury Lane, his personal behaviour was growing alarmingly erratic. The bouts of drinking and debauchery increased, and his temper became so volatile that he resorted to kicking almost anyone with whom he was in dispute, some of whom retaliated by taking him to court. Kean's dissipated life and unconventional morality had similarly become public knowledge. In January 1825 Alderman Cox sued Kean in the Court of King's Bench for 'criminal conversation' with his wife Charlotte. This was a strange action to bring since Cox would seem to have known about the affair for some time: certainly, everyone else did. Mrs Cox had first come to Kean's attention in 1816 when she fainted in her box at the power of his Othello, whereupon Kean halted the performance and had her carried over the stage to his dressing-room; he and 'Little Breeches' had been lovers since 1820. The trial was itself a highly theatrical business, with Newman, Kean's dresser, and Drury Lane box-attendants and doormen as witnesses. The jury found for the plaintiff and awarded Cox £800 damages; the newspapers, led by *The Times*, printed full details and denounced Kean, who promptly took even Elliston by surprise by announcing his immediate return to the stage.

The Times thundered with moral indignation:

We ask Elliston – and here we do not speak of respectable females who are to attend plays as spectators and auditors, but we speak of the female performers of plays – what women, who are they, and from whence do they come – what women, we again say, are THEY, whom Elliston will bring forward on the stage, to be fawned on and caressed by this obscene mimic? One, perhaps, as his daughter, another as his sister, another as his wife, and even, in *Douglas*, one as his mother? Is it not shocking that women should be forced to undergo this process with such a creature, for the sake of bread, before an assembled people?[6]

Apart from the social attitude towards the acting profession which this diatribe reveals, it is also interesting to note how realistic an idea of the process of imitation is implied. Kean played Richard, with Harriet as Lady Anne and Mrs West as Queen Elizabeth, on 24 January 1825, though most of the drama was taking place in the auditorium. When Richard offered his sword to Lady Anne, someone in the gallery yelled out to Harriet, 'Stick him, little breeches, stick him!' and the reaction to lines like 'Now all's cock-sure!' made certain that most others were inaudible. On 28 January Mrs West was fawned on and caressed as Desdemona; again, scarcely a word of the play could be heard. Three days later Harriet had to undergo the process of playing Margaret to Kean's Sir Giles Overreach. The ranks of Kean's opponents and supporters had grown, and were evenly matched.

When Mr Kean appeared with Miss Smithson . . . several pieces of orange peel, and an orange nearly whole, were thrown at him, from a box on the right hand of the stage. This excited a terrible commotion; and the look and gesture of Mr Kean, who pointed to the lady and seemed to ask – 'Is this fit treatment for a woman?' drew down very general applause.

Elliston, who seldom missed a chance to make a speech, came forward but failed to obtain a hearing. A young man scrambled on to the stage and threatened the orange-thrower with a stick. Elliston picked up the orange and pointed 'significantly' to Miss Smithson.

This piece of pantomime was received with great approbation. The manager then retired, Mr Kean put on a forced smile, and proceeded with his part; but it was still all dumb show. The only words we heard Mr Kean utter during these three acts, were those with which the third act concludes, viz. – 'What men report I care not', which he gave in a very triumphant tone, and which were received with a tumult of applause and disapprobation.[7]

This ragged episode is uncomfortably indicative of the tenor of the contemporary English stage: Elliston as lessee seizing the opportunity to mouth and posture; the audience, one half officiously belligerent, the other suffering from one of those periodic English attacks of prim outrage, rioting not over any matter of artistic or political consequence but about an unrelated question of morality; the plays of Shakespeare passing unregarded and unheard; the greatest English actor of his generation, diseased and dishevelled, shouting his part defiantly against the uproar; while Harriet, a beautiful piece of stage-dressing, stands forlornly in a litter of orange peel. Faced with this and similar if milder events, it seems appropriate to ask where the strength and quality of the English theatre lay, if any claim for its influence on French Romanticism is to be made, to say nothing of Harriet's personal impact.

The answer lies partly in the repertory, especially the Shakespearean element in it, and partly in the genius and technique of individual actors. A nucleus of major Shakespeare tragedies and histories was still to be seen at Covent Garden and Drury Lane. *Othello, Macbeth, Hamlet, Richard III, Romeo and Juliet, Coriolanus, Julius Caesar* were regularly given and, after George III's death, *King Lear* was reintroduced. *Henry VIII* offered the part of Wolsey for Kean or Macready, *King John* was the subject of a famous production by Charles Kemble with costumes supervised by J. R. Planché which had claims to historical accuracy; *Henry IV Part 1* provided the role of Falstaff, and both *Richard II* and *Henry V* were performed from time to time. The taste for Shakespeare's comedies had not yet been fully reawakened. Macready appeared in *Measure for Measure* in 1825, but *The Times*'s reaction was that 'all must turn with disgust from the circumstances out of which the action arises'. (Disgust was in part responsible for keeping *Antony and Cleopatra*, surely a play which would have appealed to the French Romantics, in obscurity.) *The Winter's Tale* was also revived for

Macready, and *As You Like It* was frequently played, but in general Shakespearean comedy was looked on as suitable material for musical elaboration unless it happened to offer a star role like Shylock, so closely identified with Kean: star roles for actresses scarcely came into the reckoning. Alongside the gradual broadening of the standard Shakespearean repertory came a tentative process of textual restoration. It would be years before an unexpurgated and unadulterated Shakespeare text was common practice, but at least the issues of textual completeness were being discussed, as a natural accompaniment of the movement towards greater historical, even archaeological, accuracy in costume and setting.

With few additions, the Shakespeare canon provided suitable contexts for all the major British tragic actors who, since the retirement of John Philip Kemble in 1819, were Edmund Kean, Macready, Young, and Charles Kemble in a limited number of parts (a judgment with which Macready would fiercely disagree). Amédée Pichot, in the *Historical and Literary Tour* which he made through England and Scotland, described in detail his impressions of the state of the English theatre. Although he made a significant contribution to the influence of English Romanticism in France through his translations of Byron and Scott, Pichot was far from being an unblinkered Anglophile, and his commentary and criticisms are well-balanced. On the merits of the tragic actors, he is unequivocal:

There are better tragic actors in London than in Paris, where, for my part, I generally feel very much inclined to fall asleep during the performance of tragedy. In Paris, tragedy is a literary entertainment, and in London a dramatic treat. This is as much owing to the difference of acting, as to the difference of style in tragic composition.

Pichot was able to compare Kean's Othello, at Drury Lane, with that at Covent Garden, where both Macready as the Moor and Young as Iago were 'worthy of Shakespeare'. At Covent Garden, much greater attention was paid to balanced casting, and it was possible to see *Julius Caesar* interpreted by Macready as Cassius, Young as Brutus and Charles Kemble as Mark Antony; or *King John* with Young as the King, Kemble as the Bastard and Macready as Hubert. At Drury Lane acting was a more competitive business and Kean, who had acted Booth's Iago off the stage in 1817, was to vie similarly with Macready as late as 1832. In *Othello*, Pichot was especially struck by the actors' interpretation of the sequence after Desdemona's death, when Othello becomes conscious of the full extent of his loss.

37

6. Edmund Kean as Othello. Published by M. and M. Skelt.

At this point, Kean and Macready produce a surprising effect, by one of those natural and sudden bursts of feeling, which I cannot bring myself to look upon as trivial. When Othello is made acquainted of Iago's villainy, he gives vent to his anger and despair, by the exclamation of 'fool! fool!' a phrase which has been generally esteemed vulgar, and to which the English actors used to endeavour to give a degree of importance by the vehemence of their action. Kean was the first to give it due effect, by a rapid, and almost inarticulate mode of utterance, accompanied by a sort of half smile, at his fatal incredulity.[8]

Kean's Othello was called by Hazlitt the 'finest piece of acting in the world'[9] and by Leigh Hunt 'the masterpiece of the living stage';[10] it was the detailed naturalism of his acting which, as noted by Pichot, revealed the nice fluctuations in the state of a character's mind and was the chief strength of English dramatic presentation. 'The energy of passion, as it expresses itself in action, is not the most terrific part' (Hazlitt again on Kean), 'it is the agony of his soul, showing itself in looks and tones of voice.' It was effects such as these, the product of careful technique for all Kean's spontaneous flashes of genius, which made English tragedy so emphatically dramatic rather than literary.

Delacroix's early admiration for Shakespeare was reinforced on his visit to London in 1825 by his evenings at the theatre, where he saw Kean as Shylock, Othello and Richard – one scene in *Richard III* he thought 'terrifyingly played'.[11] Again, it is the impact of the physical experience of being at the play which is remarked on. Delacroix, who was impressed by the staging of *Der Freischütz* and *Faust*, thought that 'the English understand theatrical effect better than we do, and their stage sets, although they are not so carefully carried out as ours, provide a far more effective background to the actors'.[12]

The intensity of the dramatic and visual image is stressed by Pichot in his description of Kean as Richard.

It must be confessed that Kean displays, throughout its performance, extraordinary energy and truth in the management of his countenance, voice and action. His bitter words and terrific glances go like a poignard to the heart. His attitudes are always such as a painter would employ in representing a similar subject, and yet they seem not so much the effect of study, as the natural expression of passion.

The actresses of the time received comparatively little attention from French commentators. Their silence was caused partly by a temporary shift in English taste. It would be another twenty years before Shakespeare's plays were reassessed for their insight into women's lives and characters, and the change supported by a spate of illustrations picturing Juliet on the balcony, or Desdemona listening to the story of Othello's life. Since the retirement of Miss O'Neill, no actress had been judged first-rate in tragedy and neither the choice of plays, the textual versions used nor staging traditions favoured the women's roles, with the exception of Juliet. Pichot thought Mrs West, though certainly beautiful, 'too much of the woman' to be able to personify Lady Macbeth, while Miss Foote relied 'wholly on her natural charms' in the character of Desdemona. For Delacroix, the English actresses were 'divinely beautiful' and often 'more worth seeing than the play itself'[13] – he is referring to the poverty-stricken non-Shakespearean repertory.

39

MISS SMITHSON.

AS

MARIA.

7. Harriet Smithson as Maria, probably in Jameson's *A Wild Goose Chase*. Engraving by J. Rogers after a painting by Rose Emma Drummond, 1825

Actresses such as Harriet were little more than supporting players for the great tragedians during most of the decade.

Oxberry's plea, in 1825, that Harriet was well suited to play Cordelia, Juliet and Imogen as well as Desdemona went unheeded. The flattering portrait he gave of her and the complimentary verses at the close of his memoir must have given pleasure; it was her nature, as well as her beauty, which was praised in these and other tributes:

> Let Envy's rancour, Sorrow's darts,
> Pass by that lovely breast alone;
> Let her, who lightens other hearts,
> Feel not a pang within her own:
> But let her happy moments rise,
> Pure as her soul, bright as her eyes.

So much public praise, and Harriet's wide circle of acquaintance, might be expected to lead to an offer of marriage. At twenty-five, she was in her bloom, and even her severest critics acknowledged her loveliness. But she remained firmly enclosed within her family circle, continuing to provide for her mother and sister even in the pinched circumstances to which she was reduced.

From 1825, and for several years more, the English theatrical world became even more fragmented and insecure in spite of its isolated glories, especially at Drury Lane where Harriet's salary was cut back to £3 10s. 0d. Kean sailed to America, claiming that he had been driven from England by the 'machinations of scoundrels'. Elliston suffered a stroke but promoted his son to be his deputy and struggled on for one more season until he was forced to relinquish the lease and eventually declared bankrupt. During 1826 Weber made his tragic visit to London; Charles Kemble had persuaded him to come and conduct the *Oberon* he had commissioned from him, to a libretto by J. R. Planché. Typically, Elliston hustled a makeshift *Oberon* on to the stage in a futile bid to forestall Covent Garden, with scenery by Stanfield and Roberts, and Harriet in the decorative but sketchy role of Amanda. Weber, whom Berlioz to his deep regret had missed seeing in Paris, went to view this rival affair in some trepidation: to his obvious relief he found it idiotic.

A few pretty decorations and hired sparkling costumes. The changes of scene without any interest as if cobbled together, and frightfully badly presented, the music especially miserable. The overture was from Lodoïska, by Cherubini, some choruses and ballet music from the Opferfest by P. von Winter. Particularly awful was the mess when the whole stage was supposed to be a stormy sea, in the middle of which a ship was wrecked, from which the Turks finally hurled Huon and Amanda into the water. Then some fantastic spirit-costumes, decked out with all sorts of filmy stuff, and in Titania's fairy garden large movable birds, peacocks, colibris, in most garish colours, really magical.[14]

Weber was hardly an objective observer, but his judgment that the whole thing was without effect and could do the Covent Garden production no harm proved correct. No one thought much of it, though a dog was singled out for the melodramatic effect it made in the part of the tiger. Harriet had a ghastly song:

> Oh haste thee, gallant Christian knight,
> To sad Amanda's bower,
> Where love's own rose is blooming bright
> And Fate would mar the flower.

But only the stage-picture appealed, and on this occasion the Romantic moment passed Harriet by.

The following season, 1826–27, she remained in the company, an ensemble with less and less to commend it. Macready was on tour in America. Kean returned, but his powers were beginning to fail and he only spasmodically revealed his former brilliance. Towards the end of the season he gave several performances of Richard, and after the last, on 28 June, in one of his sudden and characteristic acts of generosity, he presented Harriet with £50 to thank her for her Lady Anne.[15] It was more than five years since she had first acted the part with him, and she had had the chance to play opposite him more often than any other of the great actors; although no two personalities could be less alike, his influence on her technique and on her approach to interpreting a character may have been more far-reaching than anyone supposed. By this time plans for a season of English theatre in Paris were well advanced, and it was understood that Harriet was to form part of the company. Kean predicted greater success for her in Paris than she had ever known in London.[16]

4 Shakespeare in France

In France close interest was being taken in the projected Paris season to which Shakespeare was central. The work of Shakespeare, so powerful an influence and rich a source for French Romanticism, was even as late as 1827 imperfectly known. The earliest printed translations were those of La Place, in his *Le Théâtre anglois;* these were in fact not so much translations as scenarios, rendered in a mixture of prose and verse with summaries, omissions and alterations. Theatrically they were of some historical importance since Ducis, who knew no English, used them as the basis for his adaptations. The first of these, and the first French adaptation of a Shakespeare play for the stage, was *Hamlet* in 1769.

Ducis, whose devotion to Shakespeare was so intense that he observed the fête de Saint Guillaume by decorating the bust he kept in his study with a wreath, offered the French public a Racinian *Hamlet* in alexandrines which bore only slight affinities to the original. Hamlet, Claudius, Gertrude remained, with Ophelia now Claudius's daughter. Polonius became a confidant, together with Norceste (ex-Horatio) and, inevitably, an Elvire. The 'terrible ghost' was reluctantly omitted as a character, existing simply in Hamlet's mind and so anticipating Allerton at the Princess Theatre by a century and Jonathan Pryce at the Royal Court by two. Laertes, Rosencrantz and Guildenstern, Fortinbras, strolling players and gravediggers were all jettisoned. The plot, drastically altered and condensed, caused Gertrude to die by her own hand, Claudius by Hamlet's, and left the melancholy but never mad Hamlet to rule in a future which might or might not include marriage to Ophelia.[1]

However changed, Ducis's *Hamlet* was received with some admiration in the theatre, and survived in a revised form in the repertory of the Théâtre-Français until 1852. Diderot, on the other hand, condemned it roundly, concluding that he could 'more readily put up with Shakespeare's monster than with M. Ducis' scarecrow'.[2]

Ducis followed his adaptation of *Hamlet* with versions of *Romeo and Juliet*, *King Lear*, *Macbeth* and *Othello*; each would form part of the English 1827–28 season. So far as translation was concerned, there was gradual but distinct progress over the years towards a more accurate and fuller rendering. From 1776 to 1783, the twenty volumes of Le Tourneur's prose version appeared. Their publication received a testy acknowledgement from Voltaire:

Now, gentlemen, we are being told about a translation of Shakespeare's works and instructed that he was the *Creator* of the sublime art of theatre, and that *the theatre* received its existence and perfection from him. The translator adds that *Shakespeare* is in fact unknown in France, or rather that he has been distorted here. Things have changed considerably in France since that moment fifty years ago when a man of letters, who has the honour of being one of your colleagues, was the first among you to learn the English language, the first to make Shakespeare known by translating some passages by him freely into verse – as poets must be translated.[3]

One of the changes which had occurred was Voltaire's own attitude to Shakespeare. He, the translator of 'To be, or not to be', seemed to regret the effect he might have caused by his extraction of a little gold from the 'slime' where Shakespeare's genius had been plunged by his century. Fifty years before Voltaire had written of Shakespeare's 'strong and fertile genius, innate and sublime', for all the lack of good taste and awareness of the rules; he had recognised the many beautiful scenes and the many 'great and awesome' fragments to be found in the plays, while designating them not as tragedies but as 'monstrous farces'. Now he subjected Shakespeare's lack of decorum to renewed criticism, addressing the Académie-Française on the example of the guard's reply in *Hamlet*, 'Not a mouse stirring':

Very well, gentlemen; a soldier may give such an answer in the guard room; but not on the stage, before the most distinguished people in the nation who express themselves with nobility and who have every right to expect that others will do likewise in their presence.[4]

Nothing could illustrate more clearly the contrast between the Classical and the Romantic approach; for the Romantic spectator, the stage ceased to be a stage and became a guardroom, palace or mountain top in quick succession. For Voltaire, the approach of Shakespeare signified a descent toward a barbarous chaos. 'Mon cher ange,' he wrote to the Comte d'Argental,

the abomination of desolations has entered the house of the Lord. Lekain . . . tells me that almost all the youth of Paris supports Letourneur; that English scaffolds and brothels are winning out against the theatre of Racine and the noble scenes of Corneille;

that there is no longer anything majestic or decent in Paris except this Gilles of London, and, finally, that a prose tragedy is going to be staged in which there will be a gathering of butchers, which should create a splendid effect. I have seen the end of the reign of reason and good taste. I am going to die, and leave a barbarous France behind me; but fortunately you are living still, and I flatter myself that the queen will not abandon her new country . . . to be the prey of savages and monsters.[5]

Voltaire foresaw the aesthetic controversies of the 1820s and 1830s with dreadful clarity. No doubt they would have occurred earlier had not revolution and war interposed. One obvious result of these events was to create an additional cultural barrier between France and England, and the unresolved argument about Shakespeare was placed to one side. During the years of Napoleon there was, however, at least one important contribution to the French perception of Shakespeare when Talma took the part of Hamlet in 1804 and persuaded Ducis to revise his adaptation for him. There were no drastic alterations, but the fifth act was reshaped, and 'To be, or not to be' retrieved from dialogue and cast again as a soliloquy. Talma's influence on French theatre was as substantial as Garrick's in England. As an actor, he was supreme, and even his consistently hostile critic Geoffroy admitted that he possessed 'every gift of nature'; he exemplified a less mannered, more natural style of acting. Napoleon was rumoured to have given him advice on the subject of simplicity in the portrayal of great men: 'You do not find we continually strain our voices and make violent gestures'; the royalists claimed that Talma coached Napoleon how to mount a throne and make an effective speech. Talma had lived in London, seen John Philip Kemble and Sarah Siddons act, spoke the language fluently and was able to analyse Shakespeare in English. He was superbly fitted to the role of Hamlet both by technique and temperament, and within the classical constraints of Ducis's text he contrived to convey the intense melancholy and passionate agony of Hamlet in a performance that was Romantic in spirit. Stendhal, while despising Ducis, thought Talma sublime.

Stendhal had a very personal interest, or absorption, in Shakespeare. Wishing to read him in the original, he began to learn English and as early as November 1802 he produced a rough draft for his own adaptation of *Hamlet*, quite as free in its treatment of the plot as that of Ducis. In 1821, having seen Kean as Richard in London, Stendhal adopted a distinctly more purist attitude, complaining in a letter to the London *Examiner* about the adulterated text he had been forced to listen to: 'When a modern pretender resolves to give us his own paltry sentiments instead of the great thoughts of Shakespeare, I detect the last stage of the ridiculous.'[6] French commentators were generally far more concerned than their English counterparts about the integrity of the Shakespeare texts used in the theatre. The following year Stendhal was present at the first attempt to perform Shakespeare's plays, in English, before a Parisian audience.

Penley, a relatively undistinguished actor–manager with two pretty daughters, had made something of a speciality of mounting continental tours. Junius Brutus Booth, not himself noted for delicate sensibility, had tramped round Belgium and Holland with him between 1813 and 1815 and referred to his productions of Shakespeare as 'Penley's butcheries' – though the performances of *Hamlet* in Brussels in 1814 with Charles Kemble in the title role have some interest as the first professional production of the century in English on the continent. Penley later established himself temporarily at Calais and Boulogne, and then approached Merle, the director of the Porte-Saint-Martin theatre, to allow him to put on a short season in Paris. After the formidable array of necessary permissions had been sought and granted, the first night was announced for 31 July 1822 in the following terms: 'By His Britannic Majesty's most humble servants will be performed the tragedy of *Othello* in five acts by the most celebrated Shakespeare.'[7] The flourish about 'His Majesty's servants' was based on Penley having acted at Windsor; it was a highly injudicious reference. If there was already a mixture of interest and suspicion about the venture, this notice ensured outright hostility, since it succeeded in offending both republicans and classicists by its unfortunate association of monarchy with the implied superiority of Shakespeare. The theatre was crowded and so boisterous that one of the company, Pierson, had to come forward and ask if the audience wished to hear the play. The actors staggered through the first half among a shower of eggs, vegetables, coins and several pairs of sabots, before making the mistake of trying to cut their losses by jumping to act five. *Othello* was the example in chief of Shakespeare's barbarity. The spectacle of Desdemona being smothered by the Moor appalled the audience who reacted so violently that the curtain was prematurely dropped to cries of 'à bas Shakespeare! C'est un lieutenant de Wellington!' The afterpiece fared no better. Miss Gaskill received a direct hit from a coin and retired hurt.

Two days later, the indefatigable English returned to the fray with Sheridan's *The School for Scandal*. Merle doubled the entry prices to secure a more restrained audience, but this strategy benefited only his receipts. English drama had been irrevocably identified with military invasion and the slogan was now 'Out with the English, no foreigners in France'. Armed police had to be called in to clear the building, and the crowd which lingered outside was finally dispersed by a cavalry charge.

The English took refuge in a small hall in the rue Chantereine more normally used for concerts. There, from 20 August until 25 October, they gave a series of performances to a subscribing audience, not all that numerous but highly attentive. Among the plays they performed were four Shakespeare tragedies, *Othello*, *Hamlet*, *Romeo and Juliet* and *Richard III*; and among the spectators were the *comédiens* of the Théâtre-Français, including Talma and the doyenne of classical comedy, Mlle Mars. The significance of the season lay not so much in its artistic effect, for the stage was cramped and the company second-rate, as in its usefulness as a necessary preliminary and preparation. Stendhal confidently predicted that Shakespeare's influence in France was bound to increase: the bell was tolling for the end of Classicism.

Stendhal's major contribution to what was more and more clearly a debate about the nature of art as well as of drama was *Racine et Shakespeare*, published in 1823. Some of the arguments had been already rehearsed by Guizot in *Shakespeare et son temps*, a preface to a revised and fuller translation of Shakespeare based on Le Tourneur. Guizot expressed the acute insight that Shakespeare did not in any way ignore the requirement for coherence in his plays, but achieved it by other means than the three unities. 'Unity of impression, the principal secret of dramatic art, was the very essence of Shakespeare's great conceptions and the instinctive end of his punctilious work just as it is the purpose of every rule formulated by every system.'[8] Guizot also suggested that the plays of Shakespeare would serve, not as models, but as a structural system, the use of which would enable contemporary writers to raise up monuments for the new age:

What form will it take? I do not know; but the ground in which the foundations can be set is already revealed. This ground is not that of Corneille and Racine; it is not that of Shakespeare; it is our own; but the Shakespearean system can provide, it seems to me, blueprints as a basis on which our own genius must set to work.[9]

The distinction between the two worlds and ages is made even more sharply by Stendhal in his often-quoted definition:

Romanticism is the art of presenting to people the literary works which, in the current state of their customs and beliefs, can afford them the greatest pleasure. Classicism, by contrast, presents them with the literature which gave the greatest possible pleasure to their great-grandparents.[10]

In the revised edition of *Shakespeare et Racine* of 1825, Stendhal creates a more radical definition of the new tragedy which implicitly increases the significance of Shakespeare: 'Romanticism as applied to the genre of tragedy, is a tragedy in prose which has a time span of several months and takes place in different settings.' While Shakespeare's plays are not of course predominantly in prose, Stendhal had argued elsewhere that mature Shakespearean verse possessed a freedom from the constrictions of rigid form and an expressiveness which enabled it to convey 'intimate knowledge' of a character quite precluded by the verse of, for example, Corneille's *Cinna*. Shakespearean construction offered a system which could be used to convey both the actuality and the sweep of historical events; Shakespearean language suggested a means of depicting detailed truth about the inner workings of the individual heart and mind. In the tragedies of Shakespeare could be found the passion, energy and immediacy which were apparently lacking in the French drama of the 1820s.

There seem at first sight several resemblances between the state of theatre in Paris and London during this decade. The Théâtre-Français was suffering from a stale repertory, a restrictive and hierarchical organisation within the company, and a consequent decline in support from the public. Unlike the practice, if not the charter, of the London patent houses, the Théâtre-Français could not seek to win new audiences by presenting spectacle and melodrama, which was the province of the more vigorous and innovative boulevard theatres like the Porte-Saint-Martin; it was specifically licensed and subsidised to perform a protected, traditional repertory, and any new works had to conform to strict definitions and be approved by a reading committee in which the leading actors' views predominated. Dumas and Vigny have left vivid, if partial, accounts of the indignities each suffered at the committee's hands, and these took place when circumstances had altered markedly in their favour.

In 1825, an important first step in the revival of the Théâtre-Français was taken with the appointment of Baron Taylor as Commissaire Royal. Taylor admired Shakespeare, was friendly with many of the young Romantic writers, and had himself worked in the boulevard theatres – he had been responsible, with Charles Nodier, for an adaptation of Maturin's *Bertram*. One of Taylor's first decisions was to invite Ciceri to design Pichat's *Léonidas* for the Comédie-Française; Ciceri extended into the sphere of stage settings the reforms which Talma himself had introduced so far as historical accuracy of costume was concerned. The partnership of Taylor and Talma promised much, but in October 1826 Talma died. The loss seemed irreparable, yet in some respects it may have accelerated the acceptance of new ideas in both the approach to acting and in the subjects, style and structure of dramatic composition. Talma's unique style of acting, 'a combination of Racine and Shakespeare', made the outmoded acceptable, as Delécluze noted: 'it is true to say that tragedy has only been tolerated in France because of him'.[11] The death of Talma left a void which demanded to be filled.

The writers who would thrust Romanticism on to the Paris stage had, in 1827, scarcely begun to demonstrate the new drama. Of those who gathered regularly at Charles Nodier's salon at the Arsenal, Hugo had already written *Amy Robsart* (not produced until 1828) and was working on *Cromwell*, which he had discussed with and originally intended for Talma. Dumas had two one-act pieces to his credit, but no full-length play. Vigny had as yet written nothing for the theatre. In other circles the debate remained largely theoretical, but none the less intense. After an evening at Viollet-le-Duc's, the more classically inclined Delécluze wrote: 'I have an idea that Stendhal is beginning to find us stupid, and this delights me. Yesterday he left very early. He had been bored all evening by a Classicist whom I was very careful not to interrupt.'[12] Arguably the most original dramatic writing of the time was Mérimée's *Théâtre de Clara Gazul*, plays which were published in 1825 as though they were the work of a Spanish actress. Although these pieces were never intended for the stage, they were read aloud in Delécluze's apartment and bear a clear relationship to the Romantics' programme of creating a new kind of historical theatre.

The boulevard theatres had already responded to the public's wish for dramatic experience infused with greater colour and excitement; the response commonly took the form of melodrama. J. T. Merle, the director of the Porte-Saint-Martin and Marie Dorval's second husband, had been keenly aware of what the English theatre was able to offer since his visit to London in 1819. Five years later he imported an English machinist, Tompkins, to supervise the stage machinery for his adaptation of *Frankenstein, Le Monstre et le Magicien* – 'mélodrame féerie en trois actes à grand spectacle'. He also brought over T. P. Cooke who had played the original Frankenstein at the Lyceum. Merle made his version of the monster a 'personnage muet', and Cooke's full-blooded mime was so popular that the production ran for eighty performances through the summer, and was revived with a French actor in the part after Cooke's return to London.

Following Cooke's triumph, and with the first symptoms of a wide-spread outbreak of Anglomania in the capital (volumes of Scott and Byron on every salon table, lavender water, Windsor soap and Whit-bread's Entire in the shops), Merle decided that the moment had arrived to risk a second English season. He promptly lost the direction of his theatre, which was not surprising since he was quite capable of cancelling a performance to continue an interesting conversation over dinner with his leading actor. The proposal was taken over by M. Emile Laurent, who was equally enthusiastic and impressively persistent.[13] The difficulties of securing official permission for the enterprise, the use of a suitable theatre, and an English company of sufficient quality, and of obtaining all three at the same time, were daunting. Laurent's first choice of English entrepreneur was Frederick Yates, manager of the Adelphi. Yates knew something of France and spoke the language well; as a junior officer he had acted before Wellington at Cambrai, and later made a short tour with Mathews. Yates travelled to Paris in February 1827 to make arrangements for the season, and gave two performances in M. Comte's concert-hall in passing. Application to share the Salle Favart with the Théâtre-Italien failed, however, and after appealing in vain to the Dauphine to use her influence Yates withdrew from the negotiations.

Laurent, who until this point had had little direct experience of theatrical management, revealed himself as a man of determination and ingenuity. Since he could not secure an existing theatre, he drew up a scheme under which state funds would pay for a new concert hall in a fashionable location to hold seven or eight hundred, where English plays could be presented three times a week. This plan was rejected as being prejudicial to the interests of the national theatres. Laurent then revised the idea and suggested raising the necessary capital from the subscriptions of expatriate English, but this variation met with no more approval than its predecessor. The Vicomte de la Rochefoucauld, Directeur du département des beaux-arts, advised Laurent to abandon the project.

Laurent, undeterred, now took up his original application again and succeeded in securing what he had first asked for, permission to play on alternate nights to the Théâtre-Italien. This concession seems to have been made as a diplomatic quid pro quo, for a French company starring the Junoesque tragic actress Mlle George had just been warmly received in London; it was also a shrewd financial move, as Laurent was to be charged sixty thousand francs for six months for the privilege. However, Rochefoucauld was overruled in a note of 27 August which stated that the members of the Royal Theatres Commission had not been able to approve the arrangement, and that the King shared their opinion. Rochefoucauld found himself snubbed, and Laurent in severe financial embarrassment. He had already spent considerable sums, and had signed contracts which came into effect on 1 September with twenty-five English actors and actresses who were beginning to arrive in Paris. In desperation, he finally managed to come to terms with the directors of the Odéon, at one time the second national theatre after the Théâtre-Français, for fourteen hundred francs a night – higher than the current average receipts, for the Odéon was suffering from a rapid turnover of directors and was neither financially nor artistically stable.

The company which Laurent engaged was collectively more capable and versatile than that of Penley; it was also more numerous.[14] It could not be described as especially distinguished. The nucleus was drawn from Covent Garden, with smaller contingents from Drury Lane and the Haymarket (which only had a company for the summer season), and a few from Bath and Dublin. William Abbott, the company's manager, was a sound enough actor who had been at Covent Garden for some years, and who had also had experience of management as lessee of the Theatre Royal, Dublin as well as with provincial English theatres during the summer. Abbott was not a first-rate actor. When Fanny Kemble made her début as Juliet, her father decided it would be inappropriate to play opposite her himself and asked Abbott to take his place. 'Must we speak of Abbott's Romeo?' enquired Leigh Hunt. 'We hear he is a pleasant person everywhere but on the stage and such a man may be reasonably at a disadvantage with his neighbours somewhere.' In supporting roles, however, Abbott, 'the prince of walking gentle-men', was more than adequate, and his tact and good humour fitted him admirably for his duties as spokesman and stage manager. Egerton was used at Covent Garden for the 'heavy business', a handsome but some-what corpulent figure with a reputation as a womaniser. The remaining actors at the start of the season – there was a certain amount of turnover in the months to come – were distinctly run-of-the-mill: Bennett, Brindal, Burke, Burnet, Chippendale, Dale, Grey, Latham, Mason, Power, Reynolds and Spencer. There was also a prompter, Broad, who had fulfilled the same job at the Hawkins Street Theatre in Dublin. According to Donaldson, who joined the company later, Broad was 'treasurer, stage-director, and everything where real judgment was necessary'.[15] The women, apart from Harriet and Mrs Vaughan, from

Dublin, were equally nondescript: Mrs Bathurst, Mrs Brindal, Mrs Gashall, Mrs Russell and for a brief period Mrs Smithson, who was awarded a courtesy title 'of the Theatre Royal, Drury Lane'.

Laurent's policy was to bring over to France a succession of famous actors for a limited number of appearances to lead the regular company. Journals in both countries were full of speculation about the English Theatre, not all of it enthusiastic. The year 1827 was, among other distractions, the year of the giraffe, which arrived in Paris as a gift from the Pasha of Egypt, and had a street named after it; some French commentators found the prospect of an English company at the Odéon equally monstrous. The *Theatrical Observer*, which had announced the engagement of Egerton and Miss Smithson on 10 August, was a week later reporting that Abbott had returned to London to escort some of the 'stars' back to Paris for the opening. Kemble, who should have performed on the opening night, was prevented by a previous arrangement at Norwich, so it was proposed to open with Kean in *Richard III*, and there were plans for Miss Foote, Madame Vestris, Young, Macready, Liston and Terry to follow. At the end of the month there were some hasty alterations and the idea was now to begin with Abbott and Miss Smithson in *Romeo and Juliet* – 'an arrangement of very questionable policy'[16] – for Kean was demanding £6 a night, and Liston was 'gandering' about the boulevards with little relish for facing a French audience. The French journals were equally confused about the swiftly changing plans, but it was clear that informed opinion wished to see the best English actors in Shakespearean tragedy, and that it would be unwise to make the attempt before Kemble's arrival. So Liston's misgivings were overcome and on 6 September 1827 the English theatre opened with Sheridan's *The Rivals* and, as an afterpiece, Allingham's *Fortune's Frolic*.

The first night of this long-heralded event was fully supported by both the French, many of whom came furnished with copies of the text or translations, and by the strong English colony. The British Ambassador, Lord Granville, was present with his wife, who wrote to her sister Lady Carlisle that 'Pozzo, Madame de Girardin and many others have taken boxes, and it makes a great sensation.'[17] The evening's preliminaries were a model of diplomatic tact: at seven thirty, the orchestra struck up *Vive Henri Quatre*, followed by *God Save the King*. Then Abbott appeared on the forestage and made a short speech in French, evidently intended to disarm any criticism which could possibly be made on aesthetic or chauvinistic grounds:

8. Théâtre de l'Odéon. Engraving, early nineteenth century.

53

Messieurs,

Called upon to present the masterpieces of our dramatic literature before an enlightened people whose own theatre possesses so large a number of excellent works, we cannot prevent ourselves from suffering a certain anxiety. The English poets have in no sense obeyed those established laws recognized by authors which France considers to be arbiters of taste. To instruct, to move, to please, such is the common objective; to attain it, the writers of the two nations follow different routes. But should a difference of system and theory raise real fears in our hearts? No, Messieurs; to reassure ourselves, we have only to say that we are in France. Every day, by the reciprocal influence of the fine arts, we see the signs of national prejudices being removed. Soon a long existing rivalry will have left in the highest minds only the wish to imitate. When French actors receive in London the welcome which is their undoubted desert, we may be allowed to hope that you will receive with indulgence English artists whose every endeavour and skill aspires to please you.[18]

Abbott's speech was very warmly received, and several times interrupted by applause. He then delivered a Prologue in English:

> From fertile England to your smiling shore
> We came as strangers – strangers now no more,
> Since you have deigned, with welcome warm and bland
> To make us free of France's fairy land. . . .[19]

And so on. The audience must have wondered if there was ever to be a play. But at last, at eight o'clock (only the Théâtre-Italien in Paris started so late) the initial ceremonies were complete and *The Rivals* began, with Abbott as Captain Absolute, Chippendale as Anthony Absolute, Liston as Bob Acres, Mrs Smithson as Mrs Malaprop and Harriet as Lydia Languish.

The performance was given a generous response although the nuances of dialogue were inevitably lost on many members of the audience, and in any case there was a consensus that in both the writing and acting of comedy the English had little to offer that could not already be seen to advantage in Paris. Liston's broad style of caricature made little impression, and there were several ironic comments about the overall quality of the ensemble. Mrs Smithson, who had acted most infrequently in recent years, was the target for several barbs – her voice was so feeble that all the comedy in her role was lost, even for the English: 'I have no idea what relation she [Harriet] may be to Miss [*sic*] Malaprop; but there seems to me to be no resemblance in talent between the two homonyms.'[20] Harriet was approved, at least for her grace and beauty; and it was an unexpected compliment for her when the *Journal des Débats* called for the swift production of one of

54

Shakespeare's great tragedies and associated her name with those of Kean, Macready and Charles Kemble as its preferred interpreters.

Financially, Laurent had every reason to be satisfied. The receipts were five thousand francs, and though they fell to three thousand on 8 September there was still a gratifyingly large and fashionable attendance for the second performance. This was for *She Stoops to Conquer*; Goldsmith's *Love, Law and Physic* was announced to accompany it, but the script had not been submitted in time to the censor, and the Allingham afterpiece was again played. Once more, Harriet found herself more highly praised than she had become accustomed to in England, or at least in London, not just for her appearance which 'won every Frenchman's heart', but for the 'art with which she combines the most extravagant gaiety with the most decorous modesty'.[21]

The true test of the English season was now to come, with the addition of Charles Kemble to the company. From the house in Westminster which her family had rented for reasons of economy, Fanny Kemble – who had been educated in France and was fully aware of the surrounding difficulties – confided her apprehension to her close friend Harriet St Leger:

My father is in Paris, where he was to arrive yesterday, and where tomorrow he will act in the first regularly and decently organised English theatre that the French ever saw. He is very nervous and we, as you may easily conceive, very anxious about it.[22]

Charles Kemble's nervousness contributed to the decision as to which Shakespeare tragedy should be selected for his début. A retrospective article in the *Gazette Musicale*, either written or dictated by Berlioz, suggests that Kemble originally intended to make his first appearance in Paris as Romeo. Such a plan, however, was impossible, since in his opinion there was no suitable Juliet within the company. Maria Foote, who had played Juliet opposite him at Covent Garden, was expected by 18 September, and it may be that Kemble wished to wait for her before committing himself to his most famous role at the age of fifty-two. In the event, he decided to begin with *Hamlet*. The part of Ophelia was nothing, and could be given to Miss Smithson.

According to the *Gazette Musicale*, the normally co-operative Harriet was for once reluctant to accept the allocation. First, she had not played Ophelia for twelve years, during her first stage experiences in Ireland. Secondly, she had a comparatively modest singing voice, and current English theatre practice emphasised the performance of the songs in Ophelia's mad scenes. At Covent Garden on 20 November 1821 Miss

Tree was praised not so much for her acting but because she 'sang the airs in [the part of] Ophelia with great feeling and sweetness'; and even though later in that season the *Theatrical Observer* reflected the movement towards realism by commenting that Miss Tree 'did not give the songs with the requisite *simplicity* of style. *Ornament* in the singing of a maniac is entirely out of character',[23] the role continued for some time to be regarded more for its musical decoration than its dramatic significance. When Miss Cubitt was unable because of illness to act Ophelia at Drury Lane in 1823, Miss Tree was borrowed for the evening from Covent Garden.

Harriet attempted to persuade several other actresses to take the part, offering a week's salary as inducement: piqued at being passed over in the first place, each refused. Harriet spent most of the two days available to her in preparation. She attended rehearsals with the rest of the company, where she carried out what was required of her in the accepted and traditional manner. No one else is likely to have shared her misgivings. The success of *Hamlet* was firmly centred on the actor who played the Prince, and Ophelia's role was made markedly subsidiary by a text cut even more heavily than usual. But Harriet was shrewd enough to realise that the Odéon provided a very different context to Drury Lane, and that the critical attention she had already attracted presented her with a more favourable opportunity than she had enjoyed for years. After the rehearsals she retired behind locked doors, and explored her own more personal interpretation of the role in private.[24]

5 'Fair Ophelia'

Hamlet was announced on Tuesday, 11 September, and even before the performance it was certain that the evening would be subjected to intense critical scrutiny. Already the more extreme views on either side had been declared. Charles Maurice in the *Courrier des Théâtres*, implacably hostile to Shakespeare and the English alike, had repeatedly advised the troupe to recross the Channel and so spare further disagreement. (The advertisement in the *Courrier* for the 11th read, 'At eight o'clock this evening, "Parnassus drowned in the Thames", tragedy by John Bull, and "Molière mocked or the Parisians and the English", farce by Milord London'.) The *Globe*, which had published an influential series of *Etudes sur Shakespeare* by Ernest Desclozeaux between November 1824 and October 1826 in which *Hamlet* had been singled out as a typical Romantic drama, commended the opportunity presented both to the French actors and to the coming generation of writers: 'particularly so that they can understand, in encountering these vivid and lively historical dramas of Shakespeare, that the history of France can also offer them noble and stirring subjects, so long as they do not sacrifice historical truth as a gesture of respect to the unities'.[1] After decades of theoretical debate, the great question as to the validity of Shakespearean drama within a French context could receive a public and practical examination. It was by no means a dispute confined to the drama. The conventions were fully as rigid and restrictive in music, poetry and the visual arts, and the fluidity of expression and form sensed within Shakespeare's work might be widely applicable. Both the upholders of tradition and the seekers after new truths intended to be present.

The Odéon provided, almost by accident, a neutral location. Isolated on the left bank, it lacked the basis of a fashionable audience; even when it held the status of second national theatre, it was usually in the shadow of the Comédie-Française in the rue de Richelieu, and its most recent seasons were notoriously unsuccessful. The Odéon is the focal point of a small, beautifully proportioned *place* close to the Faubourg-Saint-Germain. The theatre itself, rebuilt after a fire in 1818, is a handsome neo-classical building with a portico of eight Doric columns, and two elegant stone staircases leading up from the foyer. The auditorium, recently altered and redecorated and with a ceiling representing the signs of the zodiac by Daguerre, held about seventeen hundred. This was significantly more compact than Drury Lane or Covent Garden, though the Odéon's acoustics were reputed to be uneven, which encouraged the actors to shout.

The younger generation of artists flocked to the performances. The critic Ferrard de Pontmartin recalls, as a student, going to the Place de l'Odéon and sitting, ironically, in the café Voltaire where the legendary Madame Irma presided. There from his modest position in the background he observed the gathering of 'le bataillon sacré des claqueurs de Shakespeare, much the same company who three years later would cheer *Hernani* into acceptance: Victor Hugo, Alfred de Vigny, Alphonse Karr, Delacroix, Alfred de Musset, the brothers Devéria, the two Johannot, Emile Deschamps, Sainte-Beuve, Chenavard, Barye, Préault, Paul Huet, Louis Boulanger, Théophile Gautier, Philarète Chasles'.[2] Even if Ferrard de Pontmartin is exercising a raconteur's licencè – Musset, for one, cannot have been there on that occasion, since he was staying near Le Mans at the time and complaining about missing the chance to see Shakespeare – it is an impressive roll-call of the emerging leaders of the Romantic movement, who found it essential to expose themselves to the flame of Shakespeare's genius; it is also of interest that the list includes as many artists as poets and critics. For enthusiasm, no one could match the 25-year-old Alexandre Dumas. At this moment he was still a junior assistant in the secretariat of the Duc d'Orléans. He set aside fifty francs from his meagre budget to allow himself to gain knowledge of English dramatic practice and, above all, Shakespeare. He left his office at four and hurried to secure a place in the queue.[3] His precaution proved wise. The *place* and sidestreets grew choked with carriages, the theatre was completely filled, and the box-office takings an almost unprecedented seven-and-a-half thousand francs. As the *Journal des Débats* reported, 'A crowd inside, a mob outside, and everywhere stifling heat'.[4]

Everyone who visited the Paris theatres commented on the startling contrast between the demeanour of the French audiences and those of

London. In 1816 Lady Morgan attended a performance of *Britannicus* at the Théâtre-Français. Not without emotion, and in a *loge* procured for her by Talma, she observed the scene:

> However great my expectation . . . I soon perceived I was cold, languid, and inanimate to the genuine French audience that surrounded me. The house was an overflow at an early hour; the orchestra, cleared of all its instruments, was filled to suffocation; and the *parterre*, as usual, crowded with men (chiefly from the public schools and *lycées*, whose criticisms not unfrequently decide the fate of new pieces, and give weight to the reputation of old ones), exhibited hundreds of anxious faces, marked countenances, and figures and costumes which might answer alike for the bands of *brigandage*, or the classes of philosophy. Some were reading over the tragedy; others were commenting particular passages: – a low murmur of agitation crept through the house, like the rustling of leaves to a gentle wind, until the rising of the curtain stilled every voice, composed every muscle, and riveted the very *existence of the audience* (if I may use the expression) upon the scene.
>
> The theatres of other countries assemble *spectators*; but an *audience* is only to be found in a French theatre.[5]

The significance of *Hamlet* could only heighten the sense of expectancy within the Odéon. The keen attention, so different from the casual racket at Drury Lane, coupled with the far more appropriately proportioned auditorium, created a superior environment for the performance.

The text of this particular *Hamlet* could be bought in the theatre, each of the major plays in the repertory being printed separately in English, in French and in a combined edition.[6] The publisher claimed that each text conformed 'in every respect' with the production. The version represents about two thirds of the complete text, and the omissions are of two kinds: those reflecting contemporary English practice, and a series of additional cuts introduced either to meet the objections of the French censor and some possibly as concessions to French taste, or for the simple if misguided advantage of a shorter evening. Omissions usually made in England included Polonius's advice to Laertes, Reynaldo, the English Ambassadors, Fortinbras, much of the First Player's recitation and Hamlet's Hecuba reaction, the dumb show, even Claudius's prayer in Hamlet's presence: the play ended with the words 'The rest is silence'. A multitude of small cuts removed textual ambiguities, most of the sexual innuendo directed by Hamlet towards Ophelia, all references to incest; the question of Ophelia's suicide became more ambivalent, Gertrude less blameworthy, Claudius more so. To meet the demands of the censor Claudius and Gertrude were titled 'Duke' and 'Duchess' (a demotion largely ignored by the commentators), and the Priest was left out together with the discussion about the burial of suicides. *Hamlet*, both play and character, emerged as substantially more decorous and less complex than that of the full text; the contrast with Ducis's version, however, was startling.

Dumas dispensed with the aid of a translation. His recollections may stand for the shock, wholly pleasurable, felt by the members of the 'bataillon sacré des claqueurs de Shakespeare'.

It is hard to explain everything I felt once the curtain rose – the truth of the dialogue – of which I understood not one word, I admit, but whose sense I could gauge just from the inflexions and intonations of the actors; the naturalness of the gestures, which were intended solely to echo and support the ideas; the relaxed postures which added to the illusion, since they suggested that the actors were so intent on the business in hand that they had forgotten the public's presence . . . and in the very centre, the poetry, that Muse who presides over all Shakespeare's work . . . all this overturned every traditional theory of the theatre that I had acquired and allowed me to glimpse, as through a mist, that glittering summit where ideas, born of inspiration, could be enthroned.[7]

If few could equal Dumas's all-embracing exuberance, numerous accounts agree about the exceptionally absorbed atmosphere: the audience was fully as much a part of the experiment as the play and the actors. The flourish of trumpets which heralded the entrance of Claudius and Gertrude (played by Burke and Mrs Vaughan) led to a 'cordial' reception from the French part of the spectators; this turned to warm applause when it was realised that Hamlet was on stage. Kemble came forward and bowed, which evoked even greater applause before a profound and respectful silence fell on the house.[8] The episodes which caused greatest interest included every appearance of the Ghost, especially the exchange between the Ghost and Hamlet. The scene which aroused the most intense reaction during the first three acts was the Mousetrap scene, with its concentrated action and unclassical 'mélange de bouffonneries et de choses terribles'. Delécluze left both a sketch of how the actors were placed and a detailed description of the manner in which the episode was played. Delécluze's training and ability as an artist, coupled with his close dramatic and textual study of Shakespeare, make him a particularly reliable witness; he was by temperament a Classicist, and his criticism has the tone of informed objectivity.

At the back of the stage in the centre was the 'petit théâtre'; stage-left front were the two 'crowned assassins', stage-right was Ophelia on a kind of sofa, and between the two Hamlet lay sprawled on the floor propped on one elbow and leaning against Ophelia. Lying there against Ophelia's lap Hamlet 'held Ophelia's fan, with which he contrived, during the players' speeches, to follow the effect that their words were producing on the expressions of the king and queen'. (This use of Ophelia's fan was mentioned again and again; Dumas even identified the scene as 'la scène de l'éventail'.)

> He swivelled first towards the players to urge them on, then towards the king to uncover his secret and then to Ophelia to draw her attention to everything that was happening. The French spectators were most receptive to all these movements by Kemble, who played this passage with much intelligence and with a certain wholly English grace such as we have no conception of.
>
> But the interest grew. At the very moment when, on the stage within the stage, the poison was poured into the ear of the sleeping king, and when King Claudius and his wife seemed struck by the resemblance between this crime and the one they committed, Hamlet rapidly dragged himself right over to them and somehow riveting them to their seats cried out in a sparkling outburst of words such as only the English language can produce: 'He poisons him in the garden for his estate. His name's Gonzago; the story is extant, and written in very choice Italian: you shall see anon, how the murderer gets the love of Gonzago's wife!'[9]

It is perhaps significant that this climactic dramatic moment singled out by Delécluze and others was in prose. Then Claudius called for lights, and Kemble cried out 'Ah! Ah!' in the tones of a man triumphing in a difficult task – 'with all the ecstasy of the trick's accomplishment and the joy of the first achievement in the act of vengeance'.

The controlled force of Kemble's acting at this crucial turning point of the play drew round after round of applause from the audience. The scene is, obviously, far less dependent than many on the precise understanding of every word although, as Magnin pointed out in the *Globe*, Shakespeare's genius for the pictorial dramatic image makes it possible to follow and understand his plays without recourse to language. (The impact and influence of the Berliner Ensemble's Brecht productions in London in 1956 provide an analogy.) The scene was also, even in its rather attenuated form, a striking example of the way Shakespeare fused the tragic and comic modes within one short episode, demanding from the actor a correspondingly varied use of posture, gesture and inflexion. The classically-minded within the audience saw with mingled horror and fascination the spectacle of a Prince, in a tragedy, albeit within his 'antic disposition', violating all decorum by crawling about the stage. Voltaire would have been disgusted. Such a style of acting had not always proved acceptable in England: J. P. Kemble had been admonished in 1783 for 'lolling, not only to say resting not only his arm,

9. Charles Kemble as Hamlet, Harriet Smithson as Ophelia, in *Hamlet*, act 3, scene 2. Lithograph by A. Devéria and L. Boulanger, from *Souvenirs du théâtre anglais à Paris*, 1827.

but in great measure his person on Ophelia's lap',[10] and even so late as 1814 Kean was described, with clear misgivings as to propriety, as exposing his 'derrière' to his mistress while crawling towards the King 'like a wounded snake in a meadow'.[11] Charles Kemble was somewhat more restrained in his acting than Kean. Nevertheless, the Romantics found the energy and physical detail of the performance enthralling, and responded as strongly as Dumas to its primary focus in Kemble. Charles Nodier, always liable to be swept away with enthusiasm at the theatre, kept whispering to Delécluze at the Ghost's entrances that it was better than *Orestes* – 'plus beau que l'Oreste des anciens'; at Kemble's *tour de force* he exclaimed loudly, 'There, at last, is the very essence of tragedy!' Delécluze recorded that the scene moved him to the very limit and that he found it in production, just as he had in reading, as original as it was noble. It was the capacity of the theatrical experience to match or surpass their already idealised concepts that so impressed the French.

Not every part of the play met with such overwhelming approval; and even in the recognisably great scenes such as the encounter between Hamlet and Gertrude there were elements which did not please. The more conservative of the French regarded the role of Polonius as absurd, and Hamlet's 'A rat? Dead, for a ducat, dead!' was another flouting of decorum. The first three scenes of act four were ruthlessly collapsed into some seventy lines with little more purpose than to provide an explanation for Hamlet's absence and subsequent return, and the interest shifted to Ophelia – a grave fault in the eyes of the Classicists.

A distinct murmur of shock and surprise greeted Harriet Smithson's first entrance in the scene of Ophelia's madness, as she came running into Gertrude's presence wreathed in black, with long wisps of straw scattered amongst her hair, and uttering the first plaintive notes of her song. Yet as the scene progressed, it is evident that the emotional surge of Harriet's performance was imprinting itself upon the audience's imagination in a rare and heightened way. One reason for this was the very unexpectedness of the effect. Chateaubriand had analysed the 'heart-moving madness of Ophelia', and suggested that in the depiction of this and the terror of Desdemona or the piety, tenderness and generosity which characterise Imogen 'the romantic takes the place of the tragic, and the picture appeals more forcibly to the sense than to the soul'.[12] For most, however, the play of *Hamlet* was known for the Prince, archetype of the self-torturing artist-hero, and for the Ghost and the graveyard; the role of Ophelia had not been anticipated to the same extent, while Ducis's Ophelia had practically nothing in common with Shakespeare's. Secondly, the stage business was very striking, although it was almost exclusively traditional: the straws, the way Ophelia spread her long black veil on the ground and, mistaking it for her father's shroud, scattered flowers upon it – these external actions stamped themselves upon the memory. But it is the accounts of Harriet's projection of grief and delirium which create so vivid an impression. If one can accept Berlioz's rather idealised and *post factum* account of Harriet's private exploration of the role, it was this aspect of her interpretation which she had prepared herself to offer. Without perhaps being fully in control of what she was doing, keyed up by the atmosphere and the sensitive reactions of the audience, she unleashed an almost overwhelming emotional force. This was achieved partly by using her extensive command of mime to depict in precise detail the state of Ophelia's confused mind; partly, as she had so often observed in Kean, by conveying the impression of an absolute identification with the role which was totally at variance with French classical acting.

Harriet's voice seemed to reach out and address each spectator individually. Instead of treating the songs as a sweetly pleasing musical

10. The Mousetrap scene, *Hamlet*. Lithograph by E. Delacroix, 1835.

11. Harriet Smithson as Ophelia in *Hamlet*, act 4 scene 5. Lithograph by A. Devéria and L. Boulanger, from *Souvenirs du théâtre anglais à Paris*, 1827.

65

interlude, she used the broken snatches to express Ophelia's distress in a far more realistic manner:

> How should I your true love know
> From another one?
> By his cockle hat and staff
> And his sandal shoon.

In the space of a few seconds her acting, and the 'anguish on features that were yet so young and beautiful', began to affect the audience to the heart, even those who did not understand the language. As with the Mousetrap scene, the power of the dramatic imagery is here less dependent upon a precise knowledge of what the words mean.

When Harriet made her first exit in this scene – 'Good night, ladies, good night, sweet ladies, good night, good night' – her blue eyes, opened so wide, 'so full of light and suffering', transfigured her.

We scarcely heard the words of her mournful songs – but we all heard and understood, in our souls, the heart-rending sobs, the utter despair which they revealed, the shuddering sighs of her impending collapse. There was utter silence amongst the profoundly moved spectators – and then at the first cry of madness, a great burst of cheering, the most enthusiastic that I have ever heard.[13]

Harriet, in the wings, was understandably confused by an audience reaction so foreign to her experience – so much so that she turned to one of the company standing nearby and asked, 'My God, what are they saying? Do they like it – or hate it?' The actor was able to reassure her that she had an immense success.[14] So, with a basket of flowers in her hand, she went back on stage for her last scene.

Passing suddenly from the most wrenching grief to a kind of convulsive joy, like the sardonic laughter of a dying man, she offers flowers to those around her, whom she no longer recognises, and sings, without being aware that she is singing, words whose frivolity forms the most melancholy and theatrical contrast with her actual condition . . . This description is much too cold to give an adequate idea of the painfully intense pantomime of Miss Smithson.[15]

The element of mime referred to by Moreau was also emphasised by Delécluze: 'The most remarkable feature of her acting is her "pantomime": she adopts fantastic postures; and she uses the "dying fall" in her inflexions, without ever ceasing to be natural, to great effect.' That comment 'without ever ceasing to be natural', coming from the fastidious Delécluze, is significant in the light of later suggestions that Harriet impressed by means of melodramatic excesses. The scene was judged to convey both poetry and reality; it was at once 'heart-rending

12. The mad Ophelia, *Hamlet*, act 4 scene 5. Lithograph by E. Delacroix, 1834.

and graceful, simple and sublime'.[16] By the time Harriet spoke the final words, 'And peace be with all Christian souls, I pray heaven. God be with you', there was hardly a dry eye in the house, and men reportedly stumbled out of the auditorium unable to watch further.

The success was indeed immense: for Shakespeare, for the English style of acting, for Kemble, and for Harriet Smithson. She began the evening as an attractive, useful but inconsequential walking-lady, at least in the eyes of the general public. She completed it as a tragic actress of note. The impact of that influential *Hamlet* was clearly due as much to her as to Kemble, perhaps because the fifth act, the Graveyard scene excepted, seemed absurd to most people, thus ensuring that much of the emotional climax of the play remained associated with Ophelia. As the audience filed out into the foyer at the end of the evening, the dispute between the Classicists and the Romantics was rousingly engaged on the subject of Shakespeare. In terms of acting, though, Kemble and Smithson drew everyone's praise. 'It was the first time that I saw in the theatre,' recalled Dumas, 'real passions, giving life to men and women of flesh and blood.'[17] Dumas spoke with a voice charged with the energy of Romanticism. Yet even many of those critics and commentators who maintained Voltaire's view of the barbarous Shakespeare gave credit to Harriet's performance. As for the French actors, the naturalism shown by the English company was a revelation. Mlle Mars, who was not noted for her humility and whose acting of the madwoman in Soumet's *Emilia* was now unfavourably, if unfairly, compared with Harriet's Ophelia, attended every performance of the English theatre, where tears were real tears, and where acting signified truth rather than artifice. Mlle Mars's admiration for Harriet's acting and her many acts of generosity towards her form one of the more unexpected tributes to Harriet's achievement. Mlle Mars had been a member of the Théâtre-Français since 1799; she was forty-eight, supreme in comedy, and with a finely developed instinct for self-preservation which other actresses, managers and writers learned to fear. Perhaps her public friendship for Harriet came about more easily because the other, an Irishwoman, could never be a true rival.

There were many English spectators present who were delighted and flattered by the positive response to the production. The English press later adopted a distinctly sceptical tone in reporting Miss Smithson's new-won fame, tending to attribute it to French lack of discrimination, misunderstanding of the language, and susceptibility to a pretty face and figure. None of these qualifications carries much weight. The French critics were fully as demanding in their standards as the English, rather more so in many cases, and far from inclined to allow lightly that English theatre was superior to their own whatever their attitude to Shakespeare. Their knowledge of the English language naturally varied, but there is a remarkable unanimity in this instance between those with a close understanding and those with none. While Dumas may have been overwhelmed by powerful action and gesture, the more objective analyses of Moreau, Magnin, Delécluze and many more suggest a sensitive and acutely critical awareness of what they were seeing and hearing. Harriet was certainly attractive, and no doubt the more so because her kind of beauty was relatively unfamiliar; yet the emphasis of commentary is always on the theatrical image, of the actress in character, rather than on her personality. It is interesting to have a contemporary English reaction to that first performance from Lady Granville, who describes with an air of surprise how her emotions overcame her critical judgment:

Tell Hart that the English theatre is une vraie manie. Appony and Girardin roar over Miss Smithson's Ophelia, and strange to say so did I. Mlle Mars is jealous of her. She is very handsome and has deep feeling, with the vulgarest pronunciation and gesticulation. The Odéon is full every night to the roof. With all this 'Umlet' puzzles them and they laugh when the Queen drinks and everybody dies.[18]

By 'vulgar' gesticulation, Lady Granville may have been reacting against the realistic portrayal of madness; 'vulgarest pronunciation' is harder to interpret: provincial? unrefined? One senses that even 'deep feeling' has connotations of vulgarity.

For Harriet, the unaccustomed attention was wonderfully gratifying. The criticisms published over the succeeding days were almost uniformly favourable, at least to her and Kemble if not invariably to the play or the production as a whole. The *Figaro*, for instance, noting the extent of touching grief and truth in Harriet's acting, refers to the extraordinary transformation which has converted her from a young woman of average ability into an actress 'such as we no longer possess in these days', explaining the change as caused by something supernatural at the heart of Shakespeare.[19] The immediate result of so much acclaim was the announcement of *Romeo and Juliet* for 15 September. There was no longer any reluctance on Kemble's side to entrust Juliet to Harriet. Although it was not a role she had often played – or been allowed to play – she had recent experience of it, performing it at Margate in August *en route* to Paris.

Romeo and Juliet, like *Hamlet*, was presented in a severely cut version, with the ending supplied by Garrick. The principal addition involves the revival of Juliet in the tomb after Romeo has drunk the poison but before his death agonies, a situation which gives rise to some long-drawn-out and pathos-ridden exchanges between the lovers. (Berlioz, who was moved to passionate protest at the assassinations practised by obscure hacks against Molière and Shakespeare, let alone against Mozart, Weber or Beethoven, considered Garrick's dénouement an 'inspired discovery'.) The play as given ended with the death of

13. Harriet Smithson as Juliet, *Romeo and Juliet*, act 2 scene 6. Lithograph by A. Devéria and L. Boulanger from *Souvenirs du théâtre anglais à Paris*, 1827.

Juliet, and the general tenor of the omissions, amounting to more than half the play in terms of number of lines, was to soften the more explicit sexual references and to increase the emphasis on the two principal parts, wisely in view of the company's restricted talent. For once the woman's role became as important as the man's, and the emotional climax rested on Juliet's act of self-sacrifice.

Again the theatre was full, though not quite so packed as for the two preceding nights. Delécluze thought the audience contained a larger proportion of students of English, and described the atmosphere as more serious. The play's plot was reasonably familiar in France; there was a Ducis version, closer to Shakespeare than his *Hamlet* but still very much an adaptation. There was the added interest of seeing how

14. Charles Kemble as Romeo, Harriet Smithson as Juliet, in *Romeo and Juliet*, act 3 scene 5. Lithograph by A. Devéria and L. Boulanger, from *Souvenirs du théâtre anglais à Paris*, 1827.

Kemble and Smithson would compare with the rendering of Crescentini and Mme Pasta in the Théâtre-Italien's production of Vaccai's opera, *Giulietta e Romeo*, given its Paris première the same day.

Romeo and Juliet was only marginally less well received than *Hamlet*; there was some criticism of the supporting actors, and the Odéon administration was blamed for the poverty of the stage settings. In an age when décor was becoming increasingly important, it is remarkable how striking an effect the English theatre achieved with minimal assistance in that area. Audience and critics alike were highly appreciative of Kemble's and Harriet's acting. There were a few minor reservations: Delécluze felt that the successive stages in the death agonies of the couple were shown in too detailed and realistic a manner. But what caused a momentary hesitation in the minds of the more traditionally inclined was a source of fascination for the warmer-blooded Romantics, who recognised in these performances an image of the kind of theatre and art they themselves longed to create. To see Kemble and Smithson was a passport to a new country, long imagined but now suddenly and indisputably present. Delacroix commented that the *pavé* of the whole quarter vibrated as the carriages came rolling up to the Odéon. 'Our actors have gone back to school and stare wide-eyed. The consequences of this enterprise are immeasurable. Miss Smithson has created a sensation in the roles of Miss O'Neill.'[20] Sainte-Beuve, who was gradually replacing Nodier as the guiding critic of the Romantic movement, saw the event as a crucial moment in the general campaign.

This play of Shakespeare's was not only a noble spectacle, it was an instrument of war. The enemy – the Absolutist literary establishment – was bombarded from the vantage point of Juliet's balcony; and we were filled with the hope of scaling with Romeo, in defiance of the unities, that lofty and forbidden stronghold of emotion and delight. But why, oh why, on the day when every obstruction was so abruptly overturned and the breach gaped wide open, was there no one, practically no one, who could be found to enter?[21]

While Shakespeare as revealed in those nights at the Odéon became a catalyst for the French Romantics, Harriet as Ophelia and as Juliet became for a while their figurehead and symbol. When Stendhal reported early the next year that four young poets had presented translations of *Romeo and Juliet* to the Théâtre-Français, he presumed that the charming Miss Smithson was the muse to whom they owed their inspiration, and credited her acting for ensuring a good reception for French tragedies founded upon Shakespeare.[22] For Ferrard de Pontmartin she was 'a vision, a dream of Thomas Moore, an enchantment'.[23] Jules Janin was later to call her 'the first passion, the first enchantment, the first love of modern drama'.

Harriet's image as the mad Ophelia, illustrated as in the lithographs by Devéria and Boulanger, by Ducarme and by de Valmont, could be seen in all the bookshop and printshop windows. The conjunction of beauty, forlorn love, madness and premature death was irresistible. Her own appearance is elusive; more than many actresses of the time, she seems in these vignettes to recede into the part she is supposedly playing. The most striking pose of the woman herself is an engraving after a portrait by Dubufe, taken probably in 1828. Here, for once, Harriet is presented as more tangible than in the lithographs, even sensuous, rather than an image of idealised fragility, for all the air of utter stillness

15. Charles Kemble as Romeo, Harriet Smithson as Juliet, *Romeo and Juliet*, final scene.
Lithograph by Francis, 1827.

16. Harriet Smithson. Mezzotint by G. Maile after a painting by C. M. Dubufe, *c*. 1828.

and passivity. Her braceleted wrists serve to draw attention to the pure whiteness of her bosom, shoulders and neck: the head is half turned, and the sweetly naive face is quite expressionless. The mouth is full, the forehead high, the hair luxuriant with a semicircle of ringlets framing the face with just a hint of disorder. But the central feature is undoubtedly the pair of large eyes which are raised and gaze into a distance we cannot see. It was Harriet's eyes which had been celebrated in London:

Oh! tell me not of sorrow's seal,
It *chills*, but cannot quench the soul;
Say not life's cup no sweets reveal,
There's still some brightness in the bowl.
Can all be dark that life supplies?
Whilst earth can boast of SMITHSON's eyes.[24]

In the Dubufe portrait there is a confidence, an awareness of her beauty, that is lacking in other studies: for instance, a drawing by Achille Devéria of much the same time, shows Harriet clothed from toe and wrist to neck and topped by a kind of giant befeathered tam-o'-shanter, looking as though she has come to pay a social call and has long ago run out of conversation. In the latter she is presented as a sweet, shy girl; in the Dubufe as a woman of mystery.

The *Figaro* commented that for as long as Miss Smithson appeared at the Odéon, 'tout le quartier St Germain comprend ces mots anglais: I love you!'[25] For a few weeks almost every number carried some allusion to her. She even became the model for a Parisian fashion: a coiffure 'à la Miss Smithson' was introduced, a coiffure 'à la folle', consisting of a black veil with wisps of straw tastefully interwoven amongst the hair.[26] Known as 'La Belle Irlandaise', Harriet was socially admired and lionised. A lady who had known her in Ireland and England commented that

her personal appearance had been so much improved by the judicious selection of a first-rate *modiste* and a fashionable *corsetière*, that she was soon converted into one of the most splendid women in Paris, with an air *distingué* that commanded the admiration and the tears of thousands . . . as I now looked at her, it struck me that not one of Ovid's fabled metamorphoses exceeded Miss Smithson's real Parisian one.[27]

The Irish musician George Osborne recalled meeting Harriet at a public ball,

and while walking with her leaning on my arm, we were stopped by Mlle George, the great French tragedienne, who took my other arm, making me look like an urn with two handles as we paced up and down the room. Many were the winks and nods I received, one gentleman loudly remarking, 'look at that monopoliser of tragedy'.[28]

There was one man who received the full force of the Shakespeare performances in a more personal and idiosyncratic way. Hector Berlioz had been in the audience for that first night of *Hamlet*. It began what he described as 'the supreme drama' of his life. He was overwhelmed both by Shakespeare and by Harriet – or, more accurately, by Harriet in Shakespeare.

17. Harriet Smithson. Lithograph by A. Devéria, *c.* 1827.

The impression made on my heart and mind by her extraordinary talent, nay her dramatic genius, was equalled only by the havoc wrought in me by the poet she so nobly interpreted. That is all I can say.

Shakespeare, coming upon me unawares, struck me like a thunderbolt. The lightning flash of that discovery revealed to me at a stroke the whole heaven of art, illuminating it to its remotest corners. I recognised the meaning of grandeur, beauty, dramatic truth. At the same time I saw the absurdity of the French view of Shakespeare which derives from Voltaire:

That ape of genius, sent

76

By Satan among men to do his work

and the pitiful narrowness of our own worn-out academic, cloistered traditions of poetry. I saw, I understood, I felt . . . that I was alive and that I must arise and walk.[29]

Berlioz was twenty-three. For nearly six years he had been living in Paris, first as a reluctant medical student, then, with the grudging acquiescence of his father who even on occasion cut off his allowance, studying to become a composer; since August 1826 he had been enrolled at the Conservatoire. He had already experienced one intense and painful encounter with the idea of an unattainable love, centred upon a girl six years older than himself, Estelle Duboeuf, whose image he never discarded. Now, under the double blow of Shakespeare and Harriet which affected him like an illness, he scarcely slept, but wandered through the streets of Paris and over the surrounding countryside hardly conscious of where he was. As he came out of the Odéon that first time, 'shaken to the depths by the experience', he vowed not to expose himself a second time to the flame of Shakespeare's genius. But he was unable to put up even a token resistance.

Next day the playbills announced *Romeo and Juliet*. I had my pass to the pit. But to make doubly sure of getting in, just in case the doorkeeper . . . might have had orders to suspend the free list, I rushed round to the box office the moment I saw the posters and bought a stall. My fate was doubly sealed.[30]

The contrast with *Hamlet* only served to accentuate the impact of the second tragedy upon Berlioz's febrile mind:

to steep myself in the fiery sun and balmy nights of Italy, to witness the drama of that immense love, swift as thought, burning as lava, radiantly pure as an angel's glance, imperious, irresistible, the raging hatreds, the wild, ecstatic kisses, the desperate strife of love and death contending for mastery – it was too much. By the third act, hardly able to breathe – as though an iron hand gripped me by the heart – I knew that I was lost.[31]

Even at this early stage, there is an aura of public drama attached to Berlioz's absorption in Harriet's Shakespearean image. The memoirs are necessarily adjusted with hindsight, though Berlioz writes so vividly that he recaptures the immediacy of the passing moment. Reviewing them years later, Ferrard de Pontmartin recalled attending the very same performances and having his attention diverted from the stage to one of his neighbours:

On our right, in the same row of the pit, I saw a young man whose appearance, once seen for three minutes, was unforgettable. His thick shock of light auburn hair was tossed back and hung over the collar of his appropriately threadbare coat. His magnificent Marmorean, almost luminous, forehead, a nose one might have supposed carved by

18. Sketch for the Capulets' tomb. Watercolour drawing by A. Devéria, 1827.

Phidias' chisel, his fine and slender curved lips, his slightly, but not too, convex chin, his whole delicacy of mien which seemed to spell the ascetic or the poet, created an ensemble which would have been a sculptor's delight or despair. His was the ideal profile for a medallion or a cameo. But all these details vanished at the sight of those wide eyes, a pale but intense grey, fixed upon Juliet with that expression of ecstasy which the Pre-Renaissance painters gave to their saints and angels. Body and soul alike were wholly absorbed in this gaze.[32]

Ferrard de Pontmartin gives the moment a complex perspective which seems to belong more to art than to life. For Berlioz, there was no distinction between the two. Harriet, as Juliet and as Ophelia, had inescapably become a part of his imagination.

6 'La Belle Irlandaise'

The third Shakespeare tragedy to be given by the English theatre was *Othello* on 18 September. The public interest was as high as before: it took an hour for the queues stretching from under the portico and out into the *place* to be admitted. But the chorus of praise for the two previous productions was not repeated. The inferiority of many of the supporting actors was more apparent in *Othello*: no one less suitable than Egerton could be imagined as Iago – 'gros, gras, rubicond, sans mouvement, sans physionomie'; Kemble, apart from isolated sections such as the scene where Iago awakes Othello's jealousy, seemed rather wooden, expressing a cold hatred rather than the turmoil of love and anger as though he had too much English and too little African blood in his veins.[1] Harriet herself was less effective as Desdemona and handicapped by the heavy cutting of her role; the willow song, familiar through Rossini's use of it in *Otello*, was omitted much to the critics' regret. The business of the handkerchief was thought absurd, and the last act especially offensive, in French classical terms: if the general slaughter at the close of *Hamlet* approached the ludicrous, the stifling of Desdemona by Othello was blatantly savage, and Kemble compounded the horror by taking his time about it (the *Courrier Français* clocked him at more than a minute)[2] and then adding two gratuitous *coups de grâce* with his dagger. Women ran out, men averted their eyes, even Mlle Bourgoin, tragedienne of the Théâtre-Français and very much a woman of the world, seemed appalled.[3] The domestic nature of the incident increased the sense of disgust: 'A woman in bed between the sheets, faced by a monster who embraces her twice before suffocating her, as she begs in vain with pleas and tears, will always be an intolerable spectacle.'[4] Yet the general attraction was sufficient for *Othello* to be repeated a week later for Kemble's last performance to an audience which included the Duchesse de Berry. For all the expressions of

19. William Abbott as Cassio in *Othello*. Lithograph by A. de Valmont, 1827.

distaste, the energy and violence of *Othello* struck a responsive chord among the Romantics, since it clearly shared the tone of paintings such as *Scènes des Massacres de Scio* and *Mort de Sardanapale*, and pointed to the subject matter of the dramas of Dumas, Hugo and Vigny.

Not dead? not yet quite dead?
I, that am cruel, am yet merciful;
I would not have thee linger in thy pain.

20. Charles Kemble as Othello. Lithograph by A. de Valmont, 1827.

Charles Kemble returned to London, and his place at the head of the playbills was taken by Miss Foote. Although Maria Foote had a high reputation as a comic actress, it was her beauty and a fame brushed by scandal which drew audiences to see her. Like Kean, she had lately found herself in court, though in her case it was as the offended party; she brought a successful action for breach of promise against Hayne, who had offered to marry her – in spite of the existence of her two children by Colonel Berkeley – and then thought better of it. These adventures added a piquancy to her performances in *The Belle's Stratagem*, *The School for Scandal*, Mrs Centlivre's *The Wonder* and Mrs Cowley's *The Weathercock*. On 4 October the English theatre transferred to the Salle Favart on the other side of the Seine, a move which was probably to its advantage since, although the stage was smaller, the location was more fashionable and convenient. Laurent, whose original application to use the Salle Favart had been refused, most probably for fear that the Théâtre-Italien's receipts might suffer, now undertook to finance both enterprises, and the two companies sometimes performed on the same night. On 8 October, in response to numerous pleas in the press, Shakespeare replaced comedy and farce and, with Abbott playing Romeo, the Parisians had the opportunity to compare Maria Foote to Harriet as Juliet. Harriet was tactfully attending the performances, sharing a box with Mlle Mars at the latter's invitation: according to Lady Granville, 'every Frenchman's heart leapt from his waistcoat at seeing such a sight'.[5] The French thought Miss Foote lovely, and found it difficult to decide between her and Harriet in point of beauty; many an *élégant* might be seen wandering in the Champs-Elysées and sighing 'How happy could I be with either!'[6] As Juliet, the balance of criticism was slightly in Harriet's favour. Delécluze, whose opportune version of Luigi da Porto's *Giulietta* had by this time been published, accompanied by translations of several scenes from Shakespeare's play with a commentary on the style and language, preferred Harriet's interpretation for its qualities of youthful freshness and purity, whereas Miss Foote seemed too experienced, too much the woman of the world. The *Quotidienne*,[7] the *Corsaire*[8] and the *Journal des Débats*[9] all thought Harriet superior in the tragic scenes while praising both the actresses as equally moving.

Harriet was by now sufficiently established as an attraction in her own right to be given increased responsibility within the company, which had been strengthened by the addition of Chapman but which lacked anyone else of real ability. The vehicle chosen for her was

21. Théâtre des Italiens. Engraving, early nineteenth century.

Rowe's she-tragedy, *Jane Shore*, a creaking Augustan digest of Tudor sources written 'in imitation of Shakespeare's style' but closer in spirit to Beaumont and Fletcher. The subject matter was well-known in France, because it formed the basis of Andrieux's *Léonore*, and of Népomucène Lemercier's version which was given by the Comédie-Française with Talma as Richard: during 1824 there were three *Jane Shores* in Paris. Rowe's play has limited merit and, as was pointed out in the *Mercure de France*, resembles nothing so much as one of the colder French tragedies.[10] But it offers a strong and central part to an actress and a forceful last act. Even the language, which at times resembles an evangelical tract in its pious exhortations, or strains uncertainly for weight in lines such as: 'My feeble jaws forget their common office' achieves towards the end an effective simplicity – or at least a simplicity that can be made effective:

> Then all is well, and I shall sleep in peace.
> 'Tis very dark, and I have lost you now.
> Was there not something I would have bequeathed you?
> But I have nothing left me to bestow,
> Nothing but one sad sigh. Oh, Mercy, Heaven!

In this role Harriet enjoyed a huge popular success, and it was entirely through her brilliance that the English theatre maintained a hold on its audience. As Jane Shore she reduced the spectators to floods of tears. Once again Lady Granville felt obliged to apologise for her emotional reaction.

I must own I roared, but then it is because she is natural and feels deeply, though vulgar and ungainly. When taxed with this, 'Mais vous pleurez, Madame l'Ambassadrice,' I said, 'Yes; so I should if I saw my housemaid die,' and they said, 'Ah, que c'est joli.' But do not think I influence them. They are enchanted with themselves for having found out Pasta and Miss Smithson. 'Elles sont de notre création. Il faut venir à Paris.'[11]

Lady Granville makes an interesting juxtaposition with her use of 'natural' and 'ungainly'; perhaps she recognised the appropriateness of the latter quality to the part but disliked the inelegance of the effect. Her comments both endorse the general tenor of the French criticisms and provide an explanation for Harriet's lack of acceptance in London.

The *Mercure de France* printed a caustic commentary on the public's taste for Rowe's 'Classical' tragedy, and described how the 'Romantic' crowd stood shivering on the Place Favart for an hour in the cold and wind before filling the auditorium in the twinkling of an eye when the doors opened. There, to the supposed question 'Were you at the

22. Harriet Smithson in *Jane Shore*, act 5 scene 3. Lithograph by A. Devéria and L. Boulanger, from *Souvenirs du théâtre anglais à Paris*, 1827.

Comédie-Française yesterday?' the reply came back, 'Can one possibly go to the Comédie-Française? No, it is only English tragedy which stirs the emotions.'[12] The combination of a naturalistic technique with the ability to project emotion and draw forth an equally strong emotional response was suddenly within Harriet's capacity, and she obviously answered to the needs of the moment, for there was for a short interval little in the current French repertory which provided similar opportunities. Macready recorded that when Harriet uttered the words:

> 'Alas! I am wondrous faint:
> But that's not strange; I have not eat these three days,'

'a deep murmur, perfectly audible, ran through the house – "Oh, mon Dieu!"'[13] It is clear from the context that Macready regarded the reaction and the acting which provoked it as somewhat unrefined, a common opinion of his where other people's performances were concerned. The critics, while conscious of the limitations of the play, praised Harriet in almost extravagant terms. Duviquet in the *Journal des Débats*, for instance, called her 'the beautiful and sublime interpreter of Rowe' and wondered how a young woman could both portray physical weakness so naturally and yet combine it with a strength of spirit and a technique which did not falter for one syllable.[14] Five minutes after the fall of the final curtain, people were still sobbing in their boxes.

In the course of the English season Harriet's *Jane Shore* was performed more often than any other play. During the late autumn, when she and Abbott virtually carried the company, she added other major roles, Belvidera (another study of madness) in *Venice Preserved*, and Mrs Haller in *The Stranger*. *Jane Shore* retained its appeal, however, and an extract was even given at the Théâtre-Français when the English company were included in the programme for Baptiste's benefit.

The English were especially popular with their French theatrical colleagues. A short farce, *Anglais et Français*, was written by Bayard and Wailly (Wailly was later to be a co-librettist with Barbier for *Benvenuto Cellini*) and performed by a cast which included actors from the Odéon company. The plot revolves around a young Frenchman, Eugène, in love with an English girl. He disguises himself as an Englishman, though scarcely knowing one word of the language, and flees from Paris pursued by a friend of his family, M. Deschamps. The young Frenchman meets an Englishman, Sir Richard (played by Abbott) who is in love with a French girl and who, conveniently for the plot, speaks fluent French. Sir Richard convinces M. Deschamps that the inarticulate Eugène is Irish, and takes his place as a Frenchman to further his own suit. All is resolved, and the two international marriages promise increased harmony between the French and the English. This piece of polite nonsense, full of topical references, was given several repetitions and was a pleasant compliment to the English company generally and especially to Abbott. If only Harriet had learned to speak French, it might have served as a model for integrating her into a French cast and play.[15]

Another and much more substantial compliment arrived in November, when a handsome volume entitled *Souvenirs du théâtre anglais* was published, with an introduction and detailed commentary by Moreau, and a series of lithographs by Achille Devéria and Louis Boulanger.[16] Of the twelve major illustrations, three are of scenes from *Hamlet*, five from *Romeo and Juliet*, two from *Othello* and two from *Jane Shore*, and of these nine depict incidents in which Harriet featured. The poses are clearly identified, either by act and scene or by quotation and commen-

23. Charles Kemble as Romeo, Harriet Smithson as Juliet, in *Romeo and Juliet*, final scene. Lithograph by A. Devéria and L. Boulanger, from *Souvenirs du théâtre anglais à Paris*, 1827.

tary, and it is reasonable to regard them as evidence about the visual element in the productions: they are 'souvenirs' of what happened, rather than imaginative responses to text or performance. The moments chosen of themselves provide indications as to what were considered the key scenes and images within the plays, several of which had already been the subject of lengthy analysis and discussion in the various critiques. The episodes from *Hamlet* are the play within the play, Ophelia's madness, and Hamlet and Horatio in the graveyard with the solitary Clown of the Odéon production. Among the *Romeo and Juliet* illustrations, the Tomb scene is particularly powerful, and reflects the graceful realism of the interpretation which struck the

24. Charles Kemble as Othello, Harriet Smithson as Desdemona, in *Othello*, act 5 scene 2. Lithograph by A. Devéria and L. Boulanger, from *Souvenirs du théâtre anglais à Paris*, 1827.

French spectators so forcibly: Juliet is sprawled, her back to the audience, in Romeo's lap; Romeo is half sitting, half lying, his head lolling forward; Juliet has one arm round his neck, while her left is stretched out groping for his right hand. Moreau's comment stresses, without wholly approving, the detailed naturalism of the actors' depiction of the pain and convulsions which preceded their deaths. The second *Othello* scene is the murder of Desdemona: Desdemona, her breast half exposed, lies with one hand raised in weak defence, while Othello, in a long white robe and necklaces of coloured beads, stands threatening her with pillow upraised. Of the book's last image, a sketch of Jane Shore lying dead, Moreau wrote: 'Theatrical illusion cannot go further than this.' These lithographs and engravings, along with other contemporary prints, gave the dramatic images of the Paris season their first concrete extension into a related but distinct medium.

The English season was due to close at the end of December. In fifteen performances at the Salle Favart receipts had been 59,473 francs and the profit 10,110 francs. According to Donaldson, Harriet's salary was twenty-four napoleons a week – more than Abbott at twenty, and three times as high as the next member of the company.[17] These figures probably refer to the second phase of the season; it is unlikely that Harriet could have negotiated so substantial a salary in advance of her success. After years of being undervalued, and with heavy family commitments, it is not surprising that she relished her comparative affluence and wished to remain in France rather than return to Drury Lane, where, it was rumoured, she would appear as Juliet opposite Edmund Kean's son Charles.[18] Meanwhile, Daniel Terry was staying in Paris: he was an old friend of Abbott and a sound actor (as well as an adapter of Scott's novels for the stage), and he agreed to help extend the repertory by appearing as Lear and Shylock. This decision led to a critical failure. The version of *King Lear* was Tate's adaptation, the supporting cast and *mise-en-scène* were poor, and Terry's forte was in character parts: he had insufficient technique or passion to overcome the audience's apathy. Harriet was *ravissante*, but for most the production lacked distinction. A few saw through the shadows to Shakespeare. Antoni Deschamps brought the evening he had shared with Alfred de Vigny to mind:

> J'aimais surtout le roi Léar et Cordélie!
> Les autres sont des fous, mais lui c'est la folie!
> Alfred, souvenez-vous . . .
> Et nous deux, à l'aspect de si grandes douleurs,
> Dans le vaste Odéon nous étions tout en pleurs;
> Et nous disions après, l'âme encore enivrée:
> Nous ne reverrons plus une telle soirée.[19]

The Merchant of Venice was less successful than *King Lear*. The season meandered on, largely on the strength of *Jane Shore*, but in the absence of famous names to reinforce the company, the series was brought to a temporary close.

Harriet had more than earned a benefit and on 3 March 1828, after all the necessary permissions had been granted, she received public recognition of her newly found status. Three companies contributed to a varied and unusual programme: the English theatre played three acts of *Romeo and Juliet*; the Théâtre-Français, including Mlle Mars, gave Andrieux's comedy *Le Manteau*; while Sontag and the Théâtre-Italien performed the second act of *Il Barbiere di Siviglia*. The *Quotidienne* named Smithson, Mars and Sontag as 'les trois grandes puissances dramatiques de Paris'.[20] The house was full, with crowds outside unable to obtain places. The audience included the Duchesse de Berry, the Duc and Duchesse d'Orléans, the Duc de Chartres, the Prince de Saxe-Cobourg; the Duchesse de Berry presented Harriet with a magnificent Sèvres vase, the King sent her a purse of gold.[21] Abbott, always the epitome of tact, came forward when the curtain rose for *Le Manteau* and made a short speech of thanks to the Paris public for their great encouragement to a talent 'qui a grandi sous ses yeux', a phrase which neatly complimented both parties; the public responded by prolonged applause and calls for Miss Smithson. Finally, M. le chef des choeurs announced that police regulations forbade any actor to make a reappearance. A loud voice roared out from the right of the balcony, in a strong Provençal accent, 'The rule doesn't apply to foreigners, these are English and Italian actors!' However, the law could not be waived, and the public outcry slowly subsided.[22] Harriet, buoyant upon this great wave of approval and acclaim, might be forgiven for an act of *folie de grandeur*: on her carriage she ordered to be painted the device 'My kingdom for a horse'.

In his speech Abbott had announced that a new series of English plays would begin on 7 April, and he travelled to London to make the necessary arrangements. He was able to secure Macready for an initial three weeks, at a weekly salary of a hundred pounds. Macready agreed to begin with *Macbeth*, which he had been acting at Drury Lane since his return from America. Macbeth was one of Macready's favourite characters and certainly one of his most finished realisations. The play had never before been given in France in English; Geoffroy's reaction to Ducis's filtered version had been one of affront by a 'foreign and grossly savage concept of tragedy, intended for Northern hordes'.[23] Public expectation reached the level of the previous September, and once again the social and intellectual world gathered at the Salle Favart.

The production was something of a disappointment. The elements of the grotesque, which seized the imagination when read in the study, appeared either flat or ridiculous on stage. Much of the responsibility for this disappointment lay with the *mise-en-scène*. The English company had to make do with the scenery from the Italian operas, which could not at this time stretch to suitable settings for either the heath or Macbeth's castle. There was no thunder, no lightning, no music to accompany the witches; the final battle was a tame affair contested by a paltry foursome. The indecorous language retained its capacity to astound French taste; the ingredients of the witches' cauldron were greeted with an exclamation of 'Oh mon Dieu! quel mélange!' Yet Macready's quality survived to impress many of the more discerning. It would be impossible to

depict a character better, and, at the same time, to command an audience's attention more forcefully. Above all, he seized hold of the spectators' imaginations, and his whole style of acting is calculated to heighten this faculty . . . His delivery is completely natural, and simple, with no hint of chanting. The lower register of his voice is rich and clear, like Talma's.[24]

Macready was not unanimously admired. Stendhal reported to the *New Monthly Magazine* that the *Macbeth* was not liked because of Macready's somewhat wooden and over-technical approach to the part: 'he holds himself as if the pit were full of painters'.[25] Macready was admittedly inclined to overwork the held pose; Edward Fitzgerald once wrote that Macready 'looked well enough in Macbeth, except where he *would* stand with his mouth open (after the witches had hailed him), till I longed to pitch something into it out of the Pit'.[26] But Stendhal's comment distorts the general sense of pleasure which Macready's acting gave; he always liked to be of a minority in his critical opinions.

Harriet played Lady Macbeth. The role was not especially suited to her talents, demanding greater strength and energy than she could easily command. In the earlier scenes she had several striking moments, but neither in the banquet scene nor, more surprisingly, the sleepwalking scene could she create the required effect. She may have been inhibited by the pressure of playing with Macready, who had a name for thoughtlessness, even ruthlessness, in professional matters. Fanny Kemble, fully capable of looking after herself on stage as elsewhere, later recorded that Macready was

not pleasant to act with, as he keeps no specific time for his exits and entrances, comes on while one is in the middle of a soliloquy and goes off while one is in the middle of a speech to him. He growls and prowls, and roams and foams about the stage, like a tiger in his cage, so that I never know what side of me he means to be; and keeps up a perpetual snarling and grumbling like the aforesaid tiger, so that I never feel sure that he *has done* and it is my turn to speak.[27]

To this general uncertainty, which fits strangely with the suggestions of a too-technical approach but which emphasises how much this was the age of the solo, bravura performer rather than the ensemble, was added the threat of physical violence. Fanny Kemble, expecting the worst as

Desdemona, imagined that in Lady Macbeth she must be immune, only to be

astonished and dismayed when, at the exclamation 'Bring forth men-children only', he seized me ferociously by the wrist and compelled me to make a demi-volte or pirouette such as I think that lady did surely never perform before.[28]

Macready pinched her black and blue and almost tore the point lace from her head.

Harriet had appeared with Macready before, at Drury Lane and in Ireland, but never in such an important role. Kean, a profligate in private life, was infinitely more considerate to women on stage than the rigorously respectable Macready, who became so emotionally identified with his part that he could not answer for himself. To act with Macready was to enter into competition, not partnership; Harriet found little encouragement from him to break new ground.

Macbeth was given three times in all. A more successful impression was created by Macready's other part on this visit, as the hero in Knowles's *Virginius*. Macready had played the original role at Covent Garden in the first production in 1820. The piece, although of little literary value, was well constructed and offered a carefully structured series of intensely emotional scenes to actors who were sufficiently controlled to avoid bathos. For the French Romantics it provided an interesting example of a historical drama fashioned upon the Shakespearean model – indeed, most of the more vivid incidents seem to echo moments from *Titus Andronicus* or *Coriolanus*. Virginius publicly kills his dearly loved daughter Virginia to save her from the clutches of the dissolute Appius, an action which deprives him of his sanity; in the last scene this is restored when, after strangling Appius with his bare hands (off-stage), he is confronted with the urn bearing his daughter's ashes. Macready won a stirring response: Paulin Duport's review in the *Réunion* had to be supplemented by comments from his friends, since he was so moved that he could not steel himself to watch the action continuously.[29] Harriet was appropriately cast as Virginia, which called for the expression of a young girl's deep affection towards both her father and her first love, and for the portrayal of abused innocence. This role, which Harriet had played in Dublin with Macready, was comfortably within the range she had explored as Ophelia, Juliet and Desdemona, and she was able to contribute fully to the play's effect.

Hot on Macready's heels came Kean. Inevitably, comparisons were

25. William Macready as Virginius. Engraving by T. Hollis after a painting by H. Tracey, 1850.

made, and these were mostly to the latter's disadvantage. Kean was approaching the end of his career; indeed, the French were anxious to have a chance to see him before he died: disease, alcohol and fatigue were steadily obscuring his genius. He opened with *Richard III*, followed by *Othello, The Merchant of Venice, Lear, A New Way to Pay Old Debts*, and Payne's *Junius Brutus*, with Harriet supporting him as Elizabeth, Desdemona, Portia, Cordelia, Margaret and Lucretia. Kean's tendency towards inconsistency of interpretation was more marked than ever, and his vocal powers, never his strongest attribute, were failing. But occasional moments and passages could still excite an audience who admired, for instance, his prolonged climactic fight with Richmond. *Othello* still provoked resentment by its final scenes. Vigny declared that he blushed to write for a people whose reaction to Shakespeare, *Othello* and Kean was the most vulgar buzzing that the ignorant Parisians had ever given vent to in a theatre.[30] The part in which Kean most nearly lived up to his fame was Shylock, which he acted four times. *The Merchant of Venice* had met with indifference earlier in the year when Terry stressed the comic element, and neither the character of Shylock nor the play as a whole had been properly conveyed. Kean's Shylock was a man dominated by hatred, and the critics could at last applaud the actor 'in all the beauty and fullness of his talent'.[31]

Towards the end of June Kean departed; his memory would be revived in Paris by Frédérick Lemaître in Dumas's play, and by a more immediate legacy in the sardonic laugh acquired in imitation of him and Kemble by the actor Bocage. Macready returned to take his place and after repeating *Virginius* gave another Knowles play, *William Tell*, before bringing the season to an appropriate close with two performances of *Hamlet* and a final, triumphant *Othello*. The enthusiastic reception of *Othello* was not only a tribute to Macready's acting but an indication of the change in the French appreciation of Shakespeare over the nine months since Kemble played it at the Odéon. Harriet had perfected her understanding of Desdemona, and the truth of her silent acting in the fifth act made an important contribution. Now, in deference to French taste, Othello drew the bed curtains before setting to work with the pillow; Magnin suggested that this would be a more appropriate action for Desdemona to carry out, as though she were attempting to make a protective barrier[32] (a piece of stage business later adopted for a production at the Haymarket). In the aftermath of the murder Macready surpassed himself, and at the curtain he was cheered and demanded for twenty minutes. When Abbott appeared to explain that the police would not allow a stage call, Macready was hauled into the orchestra by a group of young spectators and hoisted on to the forestage where a laurel wreath landed at his feet.[33] Recalling the Porte-Saint-Martin fiasco of only six years before, one might take this moment as the apotheosis of Shakespeare in France, and the confirmation and consolidation of the new perspectives that Kemble and Smithson had first revealed in *Hamlet* and *Romeo and Juliet*.

The enthusiastic and acutely critical response to the English season is readily apparent. Delacroix sardonically described it to Hugo as a general invasion:

Hamlet raises his ghastly head, Othello whets that murderous dagger of his, so subversive of all dramatic law and order. Who knows what might happen next? King Lear will tear out his eyes before a French audience. It would befit the dignity of the Academy to declare all such foreign importations to be incompatible with public morality. Farewell to good taste![34]

The Shakespeare plays gave a rude and immediate shock to the prevailing system; it is less easy to assess the more enduring effects. Charles Nodier, throwing down the Romantic gauntlet in the *Mercure de France*, called the season one of the events of the epoch, one of those events whose importance can only be appreciated by what results from them.[35] In terms of the debate about Shakespeare, about his significance for and influence on French literature and art, the importance of the English theatre had been to some extent gathered up in and superseded by Hugo's Preface to his play *Cromwell*. *Cromwell* itself had been completed by the end of September 1827, after which Hugo addressed himself to the task of writing the Preface. He read it at the Arsenal, and published it with the play in December. The reality Hugo sought in the theatre, he argued, was not that of the plain mirror, offering a simple reflection, but a concentrating force, an intensifying flame, such as had been offered in drama only by Shakespeare. The direct line between the English performances and the Preface is impossible to establish, although Mme Hugo's *Victor Hugo raconté par un témoin de sa vie* suggests a connection; but Hugo's examples of contexts where the grotesque and the sublime meet – Hamlet and the gravediggers, Macbeth and the witches – were at least given concrete expression during the season. (Hugo may have been indirectly responsible for the general disappointment with the performance of *Macbeth* by raising expectations about the effect such a scene should have.) Vigny's first reaction

26. Alexandre Dumas. Lithograph by A. Devéria, c. 1829-30.

was to prepare a translation of *Romeo and Juliet* with Emile Deschamps, which was accepted by the *Comité de lecture* of the Théâtre-Français as early as April 1828. Vigny proceeded to translate *The Merchant of Venice* into *Shylock*, and *Othello* into *Le More de Venise*. Dumas, fired by the sudden illumination, gathered together the plays of the great dramatists and laid out their works

like corpses on the operating table, and, scalpel in hand, night after night probed into their very heart and life-blood . . . to discover the secret of the mechanism which gives life to the nerves and muscles, the skill through which the self-same framework of human bones becomes clothed in different forms.[36]

The immediate results of these literary dissections were *Christine* and *Henri III*.

The French actors and critics sensed in the style and technique of the leading English actors qualities which could be imitated and assimilated to advantage. At the very beginning of the season the *Courrier Français* wrote:

[it] is absolutely essential – and this is Mlle Mars' opinion too – that our actors borrow from the English the proper and reasonable manner of behaving on the stage as though they are in a drawing-room. In our tradition, when five or six characters are on stage at once, they form a semicircle in front of the footlights, and all too often someone who is not speaking peers towards the boxes, which destroys any kind of illusion. In England, the actors come and go on the stage. When there is no need for them to take part in the dialogue, they retire to the rear, in other words they behave as people in the salons of Paris and London behave.[37]

Delécluze noted how effective this greater naturalism was in *Romeo and Juliet*, when Romeo was standing beneath Juliet's balcony. 'The lovers were at the back of the stage, wholly preoccupied by their roles and paying no attention to the public. Kemble never turned his head once towards the footlights, and although Juliet has frequent asides, she never once glanced at the spectators.'[38] The English actors identified themselves much more closely with their roles than was the custom in France. When Garrick gave his mimed impersonations in private salons on his Paris visits in the 1760s, Grimm remarked on the total absorption: 'when he has once really grasped the role, he ceases to be Garrick, and becomes the character which he has assumed'.[39] For the French spectators, Harriet did not impersonate or portray, she became Ophelia, Juliet, Desdemona.

These more naturalistic patterns of movement and positioning, and conventions of stage demeanour, were accompanied by a much more intense portrayal of emotions, particularly the strong emotions, and a far more detailed expression of physical feelings. The *Pandore* urged Mlle Bourgoin to cry properly as they cry in the English theatre, without worrying about spoiling her dress or her pretty face.[40] When Soulié's *Roméo et Juliette* was played at the Odéon in June – a free adaptation with the couple already married when the play begins and the interest centred on the lovers' deaths – Lockroy and Mlle Anaïs were inevitably compared to Kemble and Miss Smithson; Lockroy in particular was judged to have modelled his death scene on the English production. *Faust* (in a version by Béraud, Merle and Nodier) opened at the Porte-Saint-Martin in September with Frédérick Lemaître as

27. Charles Kemble as Romeo, Harriet Smithson as Juliet, *Romeo and Juliet*, act 3 scene 5. Lithograph by A. Devéria and L. Boulanger, from *Souvenirs du théâtre anglais à Paris*, 1827.

Mephistopheles and Marie Dorval as Marguerite; Mme Dorval was supposed consciously to be imitating Harriet: 'in the mad scene one can detect Miss Smithson even in certain vocal inflexions. Marguerite's dishevelled hair is borrowed from Jane Shore.'[41] The resemblance did not strike Berlioz, who merely commented that Goethe's work had been profaned. The distinctive quality of the English style of acting was its 'truthfulness'; its fault, arguably, was truthfulness extended to the point of excess, especially in the marking of the successive stages of, say, death by poison in a manner which emphasised the purely physical at the expense of the properly dramatic. It was an emphasis, however, which held undeniable attractions for the Romantics, and was wholly in keeping with the theatrical spirit of a painting such as *Mort de Sardanapale*. What was unprecedented was to see these extremes of realism in the enactment of more-or-less classical tragedy at the Odéon or the Salle Favart rather than in melodrama at the boulevard theatres. It was, in fact, the actors trained on the boulevards, Marie Dorval and Frédérick Lemaître, who would most successfully create the characters of the French Romantic dramas.

In terms of décor, the English theatre contributed nothing. The stage sets were taken from stock, and their inadequacies were often all too obvious. There was little comment on the costumes, which would have been provided by the principal actors themselves for the main characters. Visually the most important, if indirect, reflection of the performances was in the work of Delacroix, who showed a greater understanding of Shakespeare than any of his literary or theatrical contemporaries apart from Berlioz. His full series of lithographs of *Hamlet* would not be published until 1843, although a single lithograph of Hamlet and Horatio in the graveyard appeared in 1828.

Berlioz's winter had been made miserable by the after-effects of his exposure to Shakespeare and Harriet. He does not seem to have dared endure any further direct assaults upon his imagination, but he haunted the precincts of the Odéon, pacing within the arcade or observing from the shadows as Harriet entered the theatre for a rehearsal. On nights when the English company was not playing he would sit in a corner of the pit, pale, thin, distraught, easily identified by his mop of reddish hair, and from time to time as he watched some comedy by Picard a ghastly burst of mirthless laughter would be wrung from him. The more heartless mocked him and called him 'Le Père de Joie'.

Joseph d'Ortigue recorded these days of misery in the *Revue de Paris* in an article which was based on what Berlioz told him. 'If she could only understand a love like mine,' he sometimes exclaimed to his friends, 'she would fling herself into my arms and die spent by my embraces.'[42] Intimations of death were present from the very beginning of this passion, which for so long had no outlet. Only once was Berlioz able to express musically something of the feelings which possessed him:

It was on my return from one of these wanderings (during which I looked like a man searching for his soul) that I came upon my copy of Moore's *Irish Melodies* lying open on the table at the poem which begins 'When he who adores thee' and, taking up my pen, wrote the music to that heartrending farewell straight off . . . This is the sole occasion on which I was able to express a feeling of the sort directly in music while still under its active influence. But I think I have rarely found a melody of such truth and poignancy, steeped in such a surge of sombre harmony.[43]

The precise date of composition of the song, *Elégie en Prose*, is uncertain. Written by a countryman of Harriet, the verses carry a delicate irony in view of the future course of events. Years later in London, Leigh Hunt told Berlioz that the poem was based on the love of Robert Emmet for Sarah Curran. At the time, in the circumstances of Harriet's fame and Berlioz's own comparative obscurity, they must have seemed an all too faithful echo of his apparently hopeless yearning:

> When he who adores thee has left but the name
> Of his faults and his sorrows behind,
> Oh! say, wilt thou weep when they darken the fame
> Of a life that for thee was resign'd!
> Yes, weep! and, however my foes may condemn,
> Thy tears shall efface their decree;
> For Heaven can witness, though guilty to them,
> I have been but too faithful to thee!

After several months 'dreaming ceaselessly of Shakespeare' and of the 'fair Ophelia who had become the rage of Paris', and reflecting on the contrast between Harriet's dazzling image and his own reputation, Berlioz roused himself from lethargy and decided to speak to her through his music.

I resolved that though my name was unknown to her I would by a supreme effort make it shine so that even she caught a gleam of it. I would dare to attempt what no composer had attempted in France before: I would give a concert exclusively of my own works, at the Conservatoire. *I would show her that I too was a dramatic artist.*[44]

The concert took place on 26 May 1828, in the teeth of virulent opposition from Cherubini, and with some forced adjustment to the programme. Although it did not attract a large audience and barely paid its way, the concert certainly made Berlioz better known and incidentally taught him the many practical difficulties involved in promoting his own work. It may, too, have brought Berlioz's name to Laurent's attention; at the end of June he was discussing the possibility of making *Virginius* into an opera for the Théâtre-Italien. So far as its intended effect on Harriet was concerned, however, the event might just as well not have taken place.

Harriet was entering an arduous and distinctly frustrating phase of her life. Hailed as a great tragic actress, she could not decide, or could not secure, the right place to pursue her career and consolidate her success. Various possibilities for a future extension of the English theatre in Paris were being explored. Meanwhile, she and Abbott and the slightly tattered remnants of the company went to Rouen and Le Havre where they were joined by Kemble, who offered Harriet an engagement at Covent Garden. With hindsight, she would have been

wise to accept his terms immediately: £20 a night for twenty performances, with a benefit, and a 'very handsome engagement for three
years, to commence the season after that positively'. Price had twice
invited her to return to Drury Lane. But France, the land which had
'warmed into life that talent' which in her own country had 'shrunk into
obscurity from the chill of bitter neglect' and brought her fame and
profit, seemed infinitely more attractive, and there was the prospect of a
tour to include Bordeaux, Brussels and Rotterdam before Harriet was
due to reopen in Paris.[45] For a while she thought that Europe lay at her
feet.

These ambitious plans did not materialise. Kemble accompanied
Harriet as far as Paris, to appear with her in *Venice Preserved* and
Hamlet. The signs were ominous. *Galignani's Messenger* feared that as
for 'that comfortable-looking gentleman who acted the King, and some
others of the subordinates, never did a Parisian Theatre exhibit a group
who "imitated humanity so abominably"'; the director was advised to
select a more worthy company, 'or we can predict for them nothing but
failure and disgrace'.[46] There were several brief engagements in towns
like Orléans, Blois, Tours, Nantes; there was a fortnight in Bordeaux.
But the tour became increasingly precarious. Harriet fell out with
Abbott about the level of her salary, placing too high a premium on her
value to the company. Interest waned, and when she and Abbott made
their way back to Paris they found that arrangements for a further
season there had run into problems.

In the course of this winter of 1828–29, Harriet must have become
acutely aware of Berlioz's infatuation with her. Although she was
seldom free of her mother's and sister's company and was additionally
insulated from the Parisian world by her imperfect French, she could
scarcely escape hearing from someone that Berlioz's passion was growing ever more intense. It is not clear at what point he began to write to
her; he received no reply. Drawn by some fatal magnet, he even found
himself living opposite her: his apartment at 96, rue de Richelieu faced
hers on the corner of the rue neuve Saint-Marc, so that he always knew
when she returned home in her carriage and could watch for the
moment when she extinguished her light.

For a while during January and February Berlioz's hopes of a more
sympathetic response rose. An Englishman, Turner, who was known to
Berlioz, was also involved in organising Harriet's business affairs now
that she no longer had confidence in Abbott. Whatever the facts,

Berlioz was led to believe that Harriet was only waiting for her mother to be out of the way before seizing the chance to talk about Berlioz with Turner. On 2 February he wrote to his oldest friend, Humbert Ferrand, that he was in a frenzy of joy:

Ophelia is not so distant from me as I thought; there is some reason that I cannot be told for a while which makes it impossible at this moment for her to declare herself openly.

But, she has said, *if he truly loves me*, if his love is not of the kind which it is my duty to treat with scorn, a few months of waiting will not be able to wear down his faithfulness. Oh, God! If I truly love her! . . .[47]

Berlioz persuaded himself that 'Ophelia' – this was the first time that he had so referred to her in his letters – had arranged for Turner to accompany her to Holland, so as to be able to talk 'much and often' about him. Suddenly, the darkness and storms of the past months vanished, and in the succeeding calm and sunshine Ophelia's love, or the prospect of it, multiplied his creative faculties a hundredfold: he urged Ferrand to send him the proposed revison of the *Francs-juges* libretto as soon as possible. Already his mind had leapt forward to the idea of marriage, and the problems of obtaining his parents' consent. He had written to his sister Nanci the previous year, describing the kind of woman he wished to marry, perhaps hoping to prepare the way for the coming shock. He wrote a declaration of love to Harriet, and entrusted it to Turner to be delivered to her in Amsterdam. His heart and imagination strove to come to terms with the intensity of his anticipated happiness: 'O dear friend! O my heart! O life! All! All!'

The days passed, and Harriet's departure was postponed. Berlioz was in torment, believing that he could have no reply until the letter was handed over in Amsterdam, and so paradoxically forced to long for the absence of his beloved.

Abruptly, the elaborate fantasy which Berlioz had built up disintegrated. Unable to wait longer, he sent Harriet a note in English begging for a single word in reply, only to find that she had expressly forbidden the servants to receive any communication from him. Harriet had agreed to take part in a benefit for the poor at the Opéra-Comique on 25 February; Berlioz, hoping once again to advance his cause through his music, had arranged for his Waverley overture to open the programme. In his memoirs, he recalls arriving at the theatre for a rehearsal at the very moment that the English actors were running through the Graveyard scene:

I came in just as the frantic Romeo was bearing Juliet in his arms. My glance fell involuntarily on the Shakespearean scene. I gave a shriek and fled, wringing my hands.

28. Harriet Smithson; 'dessiné d'après nature'. Lithograph by Langlumé, *c.* 1828.

Juliet saw me and heard my cry. She was afraid. Pointing me out to the actors who were on the stage with her, she warned them to beware of that 'gentleman with the eyes that bode no good'.[48]

Later, Harriet confessed that various friends had warned her about Berlioz, indicating that he was epileptic and mentally unbalanced.

Certainly his behaviour on this occasion provided some alarming evidence, if only of uncontrollable emotion.

On the night of the performance, Berlioz left the theatre the instant the overture was finished, not risking a further exposure to the sight of Harriet as Juliet. Instead, he took advantage of her absence to go and talk to M. Tartes, the manager of the furnished apartments where Harriet was staying. All Berlioz's forebodings were confirmed. M. Tartes reported the course of a bleak conversation which culminated in Harriet stating, in a tone and manner which said infinitely more than the words themselves – 'Oh, monsieur, il n'y a rien de plus impossible.'

Various explanations of the impossibility of Harriet returning Berlioz's love were advanced. M. Tartes, so Berlioz reported, believed that Harriet had last year refused, with inexplicable brusqueness, an extremely brilliant offer of marriage. The reason might be that she was already engaged to someone in London, even secretly married. Such an idea only made her the more precious to Berlioz. He went to hear Beethoven's Seventh Symphony, and the suffering which Berlioz sensed lay behind it strengthened his admiration for the other's genius, and spoke to his own anguish.

Back in his apartment, he turned to Moore – 'Ireland, always Ireland!' – whose melodies brought tears to his eyes. In the street his eyes rested upon a torn playbill:

aujourd'hui mercredi
   Rom
  And Jul
         tragédie de Shak
précédée de *Waver*   verture
  par M. Hec   lioz
 Le rôle de Juliette sera   thson
   pour la dernière
         son départ
 Le spectacle sera terminé
    La Fiancée

Berlioz watched as the light in Harriet's room was put out, and pictured her happiness at the thought of returning to the person she loved.[49] He was playing all the parts in this imaginary scenario. He planned to rise early and leave the house before the hour of her announced departure.

I had been lying since the previous evening crushed, moribund on my bed, when at three in the afternoon I got up and went mechanically to the window and looked out. By one of those malignant freaks of fate, at that precise moment I saw Miss Smithson get into her carriage and drive off on her way to Amsterdam.[50]

Harriet had been in correspondence with Kemble at Covent Garden. 'Alas for Paris!' she had written in January, 'I regret to say that there appears at present but little chance of our theatre opening for some months.'[51] By now it seemed that her long-delayed departure might be the end of an episode.

7 The *idée fixe*

Harriet might have expected to be received with a measure of interest and generosity on her return to London. However, the publication the previous autumn by both *The Times* and the *Theatrical Observer*[1] of a private letter in which she showed a clear preference for France did her cause no good. A substantial sector of the press, having failed to uncover her talent when she was at Drury Lane, seemed eager for the chance to confirm their previous judgment. The newspapers seemed equally sceptical about her foreign triumphs as about an unidentified illness which had afflicted her in Amsterdam and which was delaying her début at Covent Garden. As the *Dramatic Magazine* explained, 'after having refused the hands of several Princes, Dukes, and an innumerable number of commoners; after having caused a dozen suicides, and about twice as many duels, after having drawn tears from the Dutchmen's eyes, fast as the medicinal gum flows from the Arabians' trees',[2] Harriet prepared to make her first appearance at Covent Garden. It was decided she should do so in *Jane Shore* which she played on 11 May, with Egerton as Gloster and Kemble as Hastings. It was not a judicious choice. Covent Garden was enduring a disastrous season at the box-office; in spite of, even because of, the praise given it in Paris, the outmoded *Jane Shore* was not likely to be either a critical or a popular success, and so it proved. The *Theatrical Observer*, still loyal to Harriet, declared that Miss Smithson 'by her performance of last night, fully justified the encomiums which have been lavished on her'.[3] Most of the other reviewers had been prophesying disaster; they declared that the French, incapable of appreciating the finer nuances of English declamation, had misjudged and overvalued Harriet, and searched hard for evidence to prove their forecasts right. The house at least cheered Harriet's first entrance. The receipts, no doubt swelled by curiosity, were higher than for *Hamlet* the previous week, but slumped to a very low £122 on 14 May, the second night.[4]

Theatre Royal, Covent-Garden.

The Public is respectfully informed that
MISS SMITHSON
will have the honour of appearing this evening, in the character of JANE SHORE.

This present MONDAY, May 11, 1829,
Will be acted, the Tragedy of

JANE SHORE.

Duke of Gloster, Mr. EGERTON,
Lord Hastings, Mr. C. KEMBLE,
Sir Richard Ratcliff, Mr. HORREBOW, Sir Wm Catesby, Mr. RAYMOND
Dumont, Mr. EVANS, Belmour, Mr. DIDDEAR,
Captain of the Guard, Mr. Shegog, Porter, Mr. Atkins,
Derby, Mr. Mears, Messenger, Mr. Irwin,
Jane Shore, Miss SMITHSON,
(Being her first appearance at this Theatre)
Alicia, Miss LACY.

With, 12th time, a New Divertisement, (taken from the BALLAD) called

AULD ROBIN GRAY.

The MUSIC composed and selected by Mr. WATSON.
Principal Dancers....Mr. D'ALBERT, *(From the King's Theatre)*
Mesdames BEDFORD, VEDY, ROUNTREE, RYALS, GRIFFITHS, THOMASIN, EGAN,
SHOTTER, KENDALL, F. MARSHALL. Masters JOHNSON and HARVEY.

After which will be performed *(for the 17th time)* a New Musical Tale of Romance, called The

DEVIL'S ELIXIR

OR, THE SHADOWLESS MAN.

The Overture and Music composed by Mr. G. H. RODWELL.
Francesco *(a Capuchin)* Mr. DIDDEAR,
Count Hermogen, *(his Brother)* Mr. WOOD,
Nicholas *(the Bell Toller)* Mr. KEELEY,
Gortzburg *(Demon of the Elixir)* Mr. O. SMITH.
The Shadow King, Mr. PURDAY,
Oldburg and Stormworg *(his Agents)* Mr. HENRY and Mr. TETT,
The Lady Aurelia, Miss HUGHES,
Ureka *(her Attendant)* Miss GOWARD.
In act II. a PAS de TROIS, by Mesdames BEDFORD, EGAN and THOMASIN.

The Scenery will be shewn in the following Order :

The Mystic Cavern of the Shadow King.   GRIEVE.
Francesco's Cell.   Finley
The RELIQUARY CHAMBER in the SILVER PALM TREE MONASTERY.   T. Grieve
The Exterior of the Monastery, and its Domains. (T.Grieve)—The WOODMAN's HUT. T.Grieve
The Castle of Hartzmere, & Forest in the distance. W. Grieve
The GRAND CHAMBER in the Castle of Hartzmere.   T. Grieve
The Interior of the BELFRY in the Monastery.   W. Grieve
THE SHRINE OF ST. ANTHONY,
Whose falling Ruins cause

THE DESTRUCTION OF THE DEMON,

And shew
The Monastery on the Silver Palm Tree Lake,
the Interior BRILLIANTLY ILLUMINATED.   Grieve

The Farce of MASTER'S RIVAL, performed last Saturday for the 2d time at this Theatre, was received with shouts of laughter and unanimous applause—it will be repeated Tomorrow & Thursday.

THE DEVIL'S ELIXIR: or, The Shadowless Man,
continuing to be received with rapturous applause, will be repeated on Wednesday & Friday.

Miss PATON
will on Saturday perform the character of *Rebecca,* in the Opera of THE MAID OF JUDAH,
which she will repeat twice a week till the end of her Engagement.

Madame VESTRIS
will perform Tomorrow, *Madame Germance* in the popular Piece of HOME, SWEET HOME.
and on Wednesday, *Elizabeth,* and *Victoire,* in
THE SUBLIME AND BEAUTIFUL, and THE INVINCIBLES.

Tomorrow, will be revived MILTON's Masque of

COMUS.

With new Scenery, Dresses and Decorations.
Comus, Mr. C. KEMBLE, First Spirit, Mr. DURUSET, Second Spirit, Miss H. CAWSE.
Brothers, Mr. HOLL and Miss J. SCOTT,
Chief Bacchants, Mess. PHILLIPS, WOOD, B. TAYLOR, G. STANSBURY, ISAACS, PURDAY]
Lady (with 'Sweet Echo,') Miss HUGHES, Bacchantes, Miss FORDE, Miss GOWARD, &c.
Pastoral Nymph, Miss BYFIELD, Sabrina, Miss CAWSE,
Euphrosyne. Miss COVENEY, *(her first appearance on this stage.)*
With, 10th time. HOME, SWEET HOME.
After which, 3d time, the Farce of MASTER'S RIVAL.

On Wednesday, (21st time) the musical Piece called THE SUBLIME AND BEAUTIFUL.
With (57th time) THE INVINCIBLES.
In both which Pieces Madame VESTRIS will perform.
To conclude with, 18th time, the new Musical Tale of Romance called THE DEVIL'S ELIXIR.
Printed by W. REYNOLDS, 9, Denmark-court, Strand.   VIVAT REX.

29. Playbill, Theatre Royal, Covent Garden, 11 May 1829.

Harriet next gave Juliet, with Kemble as Romeo. Some critics remained dismissive, but there is a noticeable, if at times slightly grudging, shift towards approval on the part of several others. *The Examiner*, which had assumed a particularly incredulous attitude towards Harriet's 'indispositions' and been severe on the selection of *Jane Shore*, now described her performance in Juliet, taken as a whole, as 'by many degrees the best we have seen since the days of Miss O'Neill . . . with all her defects, she is the best tragic actress now in London'.⁵ The *New Monthly Magazine* honoured her with a long and thoughtful analysis in the two roles above, and when she played Belvidera for her benefit, although condemning her recitation, praised 'the superiority of her silent acting' as 'the noblest we have seen on the English stage since Mrs Siddons left it'.⁶ This element of pantomime, so often referred to in the accounts of the Paris performances, was also stressed by the *Theatrical Observer*: 'When at last worked up to an agony of despair, her imagination borders on phrenzy, she exhibited a picture of conflicting passions which could not be surpassed – it reminded us of Mrs Siddons in the zenith of her glory.'⁷ Two weeks later the same journal was pleased to record that 'our contemporaries are beginning to make the *amende honorable* to Miss Smithson; one or two who prophesied her total failure in *Juliet*, have acknowledged her excellence in the part, and thereby, falsified their own predictions'.⁸

Harriet never received the consistent praise, let alone the adulation, in England that she had become accustomed to in Paris. Yet there is sufficient informed criticism from 1829 onwards to indicate that she returned to Covent Garden a very different actress to the beautiful but rather colourless walking lady who had left Drury Lane two years before. References to Miss O'Neill and Mrs Siddons were not lightly conferred; Harriet's boldness in action was compared to that of Kean. The area where she was most often judged to have failed was her declamation: she was accused both of 'false emphasis, mispronunciations, provincialisms', and of a wooden and automatic style of recitation. Horace Smith's analysis of the erratic brilliance of her acting seems to fit the evidence and to show a sensitive insight into Harriet's pattern of development:

Up to the moment when the effect is to be produced she is tame and feeble; but at that moment she starts into energy of voice and manner with the utmost promptitude and decision, flings into the words the whole soul of an impassioned woman, seems attired in sudden brightness, and absolutely dazzles the imagination by her brilliant rapidity of action and picturesque variety of attitudes. Then her voice, scarcely audible before, becomes at once strong and tremulous with passion, her eyes, lately bent on the ground, flash with indignant fire, and the pretty awkwardness of her carriage gives way to postures which are eloquent and which flash on us as the boldest which enthusiasm can justify. She seems to have two voices – almost two natures, her acting is one long paradox; yet its excellence (as real excellence must do) a thousand times outweighs its deficiencies.

Its explanation seems to us to be this: that the actress, endowed with fine capacities for her art, had formed an unfortunate style of recitation, by which they were obscured and beneath which they were frozen; that her feelings and her powers had been roused from their protracted slumber by the excitement of the Parisian applause and the calls of the higher station she was required to occupy; but that the influence of habit, though broken, is still so far unsubdued as to prevail yet, except where the immediate exigencies of the situation, and the passion awakened by them, overmaster it, and returns again when the tumultuous emotion subsides.[9]

In Paris, Berlioz had eyes only for the accounts of Harriet's 'immense success'. He was living a solitary life, 'wandering the streets at night, obsessed by a piercing grief' as though his breast had been branded.[10]

When Covent Garden closed for the summer Harriet embarked on a lengthy tour of the provinces: her continental reputation ensured that she was in high demand, initially at any rate. Cheltenham, Gloucester, Leamington, Liverpool, Manchester, Hull, Glasgow, Carlisle, Dumfries, Newcastle, and Edinburgh were among her engagements. Her repertoire was in striking contrast to the roles she used to play. It lay now almost exclusively in tragedy: Juliet, Desdemona, Lady Macbeth, Jane Shore, Belvidera, Isabella, Imogine in *Bertram*, with less regular appearances as Mrs Haller, Portia, Lydia Languish or in the occasional afterpiece. At Liverpool she acted with Kean, who performed for her benefit: the full house included the French consul and his family. In Newcastle, the people were more interested in the rival attraction of Ducrow's circus. In Carlisle and Dumfries she attracted large crowds and glowing notices. Glasgow brought her into renewed contact with Frank 'Schemer' Seymour, who had acted for her father at Ennis and was shortly to be ruined when his theatre burned down uninsured. In Edinburgh, Macready's least favourite venue, the houses were very thin; but Christopher North saw *Jane Shore* which convinced him that Harriet was 'an actress not only of talent but of genius – a very lovely woman'.[11]

It was a hard way to earn a living after the rewards of Paris. Macready, indisputably the greatest actor in England since Kean's decline, was touring the country simultaneously to Harriet. At Bristol, where his own father had been a popular and respected manager, he was reported to have played to a house of only £11 which, since his terms were for a third of the receipts, would not even have covered his expenses. Theatre everywhere was in sharp decline, and political and social unrest predominated. The cost and fatigue of travel by coach or ship, the endless round of lodgings and hotels, the constant attention to details of publicity and the drumming up of support for a benefit night which decided the profit or loss of an engagement, soon soured any attraction that Harriet might have found at first in the unaccustomed respect and curiosity of an English audience. In February she was back in Dublin, where she played for one week at the head of the bill and then stayed on to support Macready in *Virginius* and *Macbeth*. This was a more distinguished engagement: the programme was backed by Cooke as William in Douglas Jerrold's *Black-eyed Susan*, and there was a good production of Pocock's *Rob Roy Macgregor*, with Macready as Rob Roy and Harriet as Helen (she had been the first Diana Vernon in Soane's Drury Lane version).

Harriet had no desire to continue touring the provinces longer than necessary. She was hoping for a more permanent position in London or Paris. There had been mention of a leading part in a new play by Knowles, but this had not materialised. In 1828, Kemble had offered her terms for Covent Garden. Whether or not Harriet expected this offer to be renewed, two factors had intervened to alter the situation. First, Covent Garden's debts had risen to such an extent that its creditors had foreclosed, and it was only as a result of a public subscription during the summer that the theatre was able to reopen at all. Secondly, Charles Kemble decided to introduce his daughter Fanny to the stage, and in spite of Abbott as a less than inspiring Romeo she made her début as Juliet on 5 October 1829 to great enthusiasm. Her next part was Belvidera: another in Harriet's main repertoire. Fanny Kemble would undoubtedly have preference over Harriet in that line of parts; besides, she was much less expensive – she and her father agreed not to draw their salaries during the worst of Covent Garden's troubles. At Drury Lane, Price was also coming under increasing financial pressure, and Miss Phillips had taken over Harriet's roles. When Harriet received an unexpected offer to return to Paris she accepted, even though it was to join the Opéra-Comique, and with her mother and sister set out on the long and expensive journey from Dublin.

As Ophelia and Juliet, Harriet still occupied a central place in Berlioz's imagination. The period since he had first seen her and encountered Shakespeare had been one of astonishing activity for him during which, in the intervals of being prostrate through grief, he was responding vigorously to a series of intellectual and aesthetic experiences and at the same time entering upon a highly productive phase of composition. After the thunder bolt of Shakespeare came the almost equally great shocks of Beethoven, whose Third and Fifth Symphonies were given their first Paris performances in the spring of 1828, and Goethe, who with Virgil completed Berlioz's pantheon. Delacroix's series of lithographs on *Faust* had been published in 1827, to be followed by Gérard de Nerval's translation: Berlioz, spellbound, read it again and again. Goethe's protagonist, restless, aspiring, passionate, intellectual, doomed, held vivid attraction as a type of the heroic artist-genius. The poetic drama's structure and variety of form spoke fully as strongly to Berlioz, and he contemplated a number of musical responses which culminated at this time in his *Huit Scènes de Faust*, published about the end of March 1829. He was also working on settings for Moore's *Irish Melodies*, translated for him by Gounet. Forming in his mind was his first major work, the symphony which became the *Fantastique*.

The *Mélodies Irlandaises* appeared in the first part of February 1830. Shortly after composing the *Elégie en Prose* which completes the sequence, Berlioz had found himself plunged once more into the anguish 'of an unending and inextinguishable passion'. Harriet was still in London, so he believed –

and yet I think that I feel her all around me; all my memories revive and unite to destroy me; I hear my heart beat, and its thudding shakes me like the vibrations of a steam engine. Every muscle in my body throbs with pain . . . Vain! Frightful!

Oh! ill-starred one! if she could comprehend for a moment all the poetry, all the immensity of such a love, she would fly to my arms, she would die in my embrace.[12]

The terms Berlioz uses here and elsewhere in his letters, while naturally not necessarily corresponding to his actual feelings, are highly evocative of the image he had constructed around Harriet and in place of her. One needs constantly to recall that he had as yet never spoken directly to her, that he had scarcely ever heard her speak except from the stage in the character of Ophelia and Juliet: his was a passion which had been conducted within the confines of his own theatrical imagination. The nature of that passion has something in common with that of Baudelaire's Samuel Cramer: Cramer, when finally confronted with the actress La Fanfarlo 'dans la splendeur radieuse et sacrée de sa nudité', asks her to become Colombine for him, the Colombine who has driven him mad 'avec son accoutrement fantasque et son corsage de saltim-banque!'; and La Fanfarlo's maid is sent off to the theatre to fetch her mistress's costume, with an instruction not to forget the rouge.[13] Berlioz, like Cramer, was in thrall to an idea. Harriet's very inaccessi-bility served to increase her attraction for him, just as Estelle Duboeuf at a remote eighteen could be the more fervently worshipped by the twelve-year-old Berlioz because she was unattainable. Harriet was Irish, famous, chaperoned, indifferent, possibly even bespoken, abroad. Iconographically, she was a tragic, doomed figure – borne senseless in Romeo's arms, lying cold in the Capulets' tomb, fainting with hunger and neglect, drowned beneath a willow, buried with Yorick in the graveyard at Elsinore.

Early in March, on the anniversary of Berlioz's last glimpse of Harriet as she set out for Amsterdam, the sense of doom was even more strongly present in his heart's outpouring to Hiller:

Oh! Ill-starred one! How I once loved you! I write shuddering that *I love you*! . . . If there is another world, shall we find each other again? . . . Shall I ever see Shakespeare? Will she be able to recognise me?

Will she understand the poetry of my love? . . . Oh! Juliet, Ophelia, Belvidera, Jane Shore, names that hell repeats without ceasing.

Then, at the end of the letter, he foresees that 'Henriette Smithson and Hector Berlioz *will be reunited* in the oblivion of the grave'.[14] They had hitherto only been united by the shared experience of the theatre.

In Berlioz's letter to Ferrand of 6 February, Harriet is clearly iden-tified with the process of composing his long-projected symphony: 'I was on the point of beginning my major symphony (Episode in the life of an artist), where the development of my hellish passion must be painted; I have it all in my head, but I can write nothing.'[15] In the space of a few weeks the block was removed. Berlioz was enabled to continue with the *Fantastique*, and the haunting image of Harriet was tempor-arily exorcised. On 16 April he could inform Ferrand that he had just written the last note of the symphony, and that he was in the process of being healed.

The person who partly effected the cure was, unsurprisingly, a woman, Mlle Marie Moke, known as Camille. She was a virtuoso pianist with whom Berlioz's friend Hiller was in love at a time when all three were teaching music part-time at a Paris school. Hiller had told Camille about Berlioz's infatuation with Harriet; Berlioz used to carry

30. Marie Pleyel (Camille), formerly Marie Moke. Lithograph by Jacolin after M. Alophe.

messages between Camille and Hiller. Camille found Berlioz, with his growing reputation and romantic aura, decidedly interesting and something of a challenge. Before long Hiller found himself supplanted in her affections and, after weeping bitterly when Berlioz confessed, he put a brave face on the situation, shook his rival warmly by the hand, and left for Frankfurt.

Camille proved a refreshing contrast to the ephemeral Harriet, and gave Berlioz the fresh and flattering experience of being the pursued rather than the pursuer. Camille was an excellent musician, being judged by some superior as a pianist to Liszt. She was sophisticated, quick-minded, vivacious and extremely attractive. She was almost as tall as he was, wrote Berlioz to his sister Nanci, 'with a slender, graceful figure, wonderful black hair and great blue eyes which at times shine like stars and then cloud over like someone's on the point of death when she becomes possessed by the demon of music'.[16] She was, in fact, not unlike Berlioz in her subordination of everything to her art. Camille and her mother were fully in control of the relationship, and Berlioz was soon being assessed as a potential husband. In June he wrote to his father asking for, and receiving, permission to marry Camille whom he called first Corinne, after Mme de Stael's heroine, and later, the final Shakespearean accolade, Ariel.

In the course of Harriet's eclipse, her reputation was also blackened. Berlioz was told 'frightful truths' about her which could not possibly be doubted, and which reinforced his sense of relief when he finally, as he thought, laid her image to rest both by the completion of the *Fantastique* and by the transference of his passion to Camille. In d'Ortigue's account, dictated by Berlioz in 1832, a friend passed on 'une calomnie absurde' about Harriet.[17] The shock caused Berlioz to disappear from Paris for two days. While the friend scoured the city, including the morgue, Berlioz was lost in the countryside, stretched out in the moonlight on a scatter of hay listening all night long in a semi-conscious daze to the grazing animals' bells and scaring the partridges which came to feed at his feet, then sleeping throughout the next day in a ditch near Sceaux, overcome by hunger and fatigue. When he returned, he refused to answer his friends' anxious questions, but 'six months later, the symphonie fantastique was written'. According to Berlioz's letter to Edouard Rocher of 5 June it was Camille who revealed all Harriet's 'infamies' to him.[18] Now he was able to be sorry for Harriet, and to despise her, and with clinical detachment delivered a judgment which is brutal, chillingly egotistic when one considers how innocently passive the object of his admiration and scorn had been, and yet convincingly apt. 'She is an ordinary woman, endowed with an instinctive genius for expressing that anguish of the human soul which she has never felt, and incapable of conceiving the boundless and noble love I honoured her with.'[19]

The unsuspecting object of these remarks was fulfilling a bizarre engagement at the Opéra-Comique. She had reached Paris towards the end of March, an arrival which perhaps prompted Camille to invent the 'infamies' to ensure there would be no challenge to herself from that direction. On 10 May Harriet made her début as Cécilia in *L'Auberge d'Auray*, a comic opera by Moreau and d'Epagny with music by Carafa and Hérold. It was anticipated that the role would be a dumb one; in fact, in a rare variation of the genre, the part required Harriet to speak English while all the remaining dialogue, spoken and sung, was in French. It was an awkward compromise, since Harriet's style of acting did not blend easily with that of the rest of the cast, and the *Journal des Débats* thought that the piece and the theatre alike made an unsuitable setting for her talent.[20] Even so, she pleased her admirers, who still talked of 'the truth, the soul, the simplicity of her acting'.[21] The situation was immaterial: 'Her talent gives it interest; and, though she speaks in a strange tongue, she is never unintelligible.'[22] 'C'est la nature, c'est le désespoir vivant!' exclaimed Boulay-Paty in the *Constitutionnel*, 'I have never experienced such emotion.'[23] Juste Olivier, a young poet from Switzerland who became a close friend of Sainte-Beuve and who had travelled to Paris to gain experience of the artistic and literary world, was moved almost in the Berlioz mode.

At last! I have seen an actress! No, I saw a woman, a wife, a mother. I saw Madame Smithson in *L'Auberge d'Auray*. She is an English actress who does not know any French and who plays a role in this piece, or rather, she is the whole piece itself.[24]

Olivier gnawed at his handkerchief and returned to suffer deliciously all over again a few days later. Although receipts languished, *L'Auberge d'Auray* was repeated frequently until mid-June, when the theatre closed abruptly: Ducis and Saint-Georges, the directors, absconded and Harriet found herself marooned, not only without a job but without having received any payment for her previous performances.

It was not a good moment to try to extract sympathy or even attention from the relevant ministry. Charles X's intransigence was forcing the growing political unrest to crisis point. 'I was finishing my cantata,' Berlioz recalled, 'when the revolution broke out.'[25] He dashed off the final pages 'to the sound of stray bullets coming over the roofs and pattering on the wall' outside his window. Dumas sent his servant off to the gunsmith's to collect his double-barrelled gun and two hundred cartridges, strode about Paris with the mob and, according to his own report, raided the factory at Soissons for La Fayette and returned to

115

Paris in triumph with several thousand pounds of gunpowder. Berlioz emerged from his retreat on 29 July with the orchestral score of the Cantata to be submitted for the *Prix de Rome* complete.

He was crossing the courtyard of the Palais Royal when he heard the sound of his own music: a chorus of a dozen or so young men were singing the 'Chant Guerrier', one of his arrangements of Moore's *Irish Melodies*. Berlioz joined forces with them and later in the day found himself exhorting a crowd of thousands, hot from the barricades, to roar out the 'Marseillaise'. It was both a musical and somewhat theatrical revolution.

It was also efficient. After three days Louis-Philippe, seconded by La Fayette brandishing an outsize tricolour, was accepted by the people, and the Academy was able to turn its attention to the *Prix de Rome*. This was the fourth time that Berlioz had entered, and on this occasion he was determined to give the academicians no chance to find fault with his composition. He tactfully observed the traditional musical conventions in his Cantata and duly won first prize. This official recognition delighted his parents, confirmed his reputation, and gave him a measure of financial independence. It also required him to spend two years in Italy. Berlioz did everything he could to have this clause waived, but his request was refused.

Before leaving Paris, Berlioz wished to arrange a public concert. He was never easily satisfied about the conditions in which his works were performed or about the quality of the performers, but even so 1830 had been a singularly unfortunate year for him in this respect. The projected concert at the Théâtre des Nouveautés where the *Fantastique* should have been given its première never took place because Berlioz, wishing for a performance on a 'really grand scale', engaged an additional eighty players to swell the ranks of the resident orchestra, and it was found quite impossible to accommodate them all on stage – the violins alone could only just be squeezed into the pit.[26] At the *Prix de Rome* prizegiving, disaster of a different kind overtook the *Mort de Sardanapale* Cantata. Once Berlioz was assured of the prize and therefore of public performance at the ceremony by a full orchestra, he rewrote the finale to include a musical description of the climactic bonfire, where Sardanapalus orders everything to be put to the torch rather than live to admit defeat. This section had caused a considerable stir at rehearsal. However, when the moment arrived the horn-player missed his cue and the failure was passed down the line to the bass-drum which should have been the signal for the 'final explosion'. 'The violins and cellos went on with their futile tremolo; otherwise, not so much as a pop.'[27] The third musical catastrophe followed on 7 November. Berlioz's fantasy on *The Tempest* was included in a benefit performance at the Opéra. Musically, everything for once promised well. An hour before the doors were due to open a freak storm burst over Paris and made the streets virtually impassable; the fantasy was played to an almost empty house. To compensate for these reverses, a concert was organised for 5 December at the Conservatoire, to include both the rehabilitated Cantata and the *Fantastique*.

The relationship between the *Symphonie Fantastique* and Berlioz's passion for Harriet is so well-known that it became for a while fashionable to disparage or minimise it. It is patently absurd to suggest that the Symphony is strictly autobiographical, a kind of musical illustration to the programme notes, or that the *idée fixe* is somehow the equivalent of Harriet, distilled and translated into a musical idiom. On the other hand, it is impossible to ignore that the initial experience around which the *Episode de la Vie d'un Artiste* is formed was, according to Berlioz, the volcanic love that the object of the artist's adoration instantly inspired in him together with the painful resolution of that love; or that Berlioz himself on repeated occasions associated himself with the figure of the artist and the idealised Harriet with the figure of his beloved. 'At present, my friend,' he wrote to Ferrand,

this is how I have woven my story, or rather my history, whose hero it will not be difficult for you to recognise.

I suppose that an artist endowed with a vivid imagination, finding himself in that state of mind which Chateaubriand has painted so admirably in René, sees for the first time a woman who is the realisation of beauty and enchantment that his heart has invoked for so long, and falls madly in love with her.[28]

The programme underwent many revisions, as did the Symphony itself. In life, Berlioz became obsessed not so much by a woman as by the image of a woman, a dramatic image lent force by the supreme art of Shakespeare and intensity by a highly charged occasion and performance. The *Fantastique* was, in part, Berlioz's artistic response to Shakespeare, to Beethoven and to Goethe but with a focal point of intense personal experience which was no less real for having been relived and explored so far entirely within the mind. The paradox lay in Berlioz making the experience so public in a number of ways: the original moments had themselves occurred in public and been observed by others; Berlioz's subsequent behaviour, acting the role of the artist suffering from acute love-melancholy, was noted and

31. Illustration to 'Fantômes', *Les Orientales* by Victor Hugo. Lithograph by L. Boulanger, 1829. (Photo Bulloz.)

described by his contemporaries; he himself, in letters and the subsequent memoirs, or in accounts given freely to writers like d'Ortigue and Janin, constantly gave the experience a particular verbal shape. The *Fantastique* and its accompanying programme was itself a different kind of public statement, not least in form – an early exploration of music drama to be given fuller treatment with the completion of the *Roméo et Juliette* Symphony.

The concert on 5 December was Berlioz's first undisputed success, in spite of sparse reviews. The *Fantastique* was cheered, the *Marche du supplice* encored: Spontini called it prodigious; Meyerbeer and even

Fétis were enthusiastic. Liszt, whom Berlioz had met for the first time the day before, hauled him off to a celebratory dinner, claiming precedence over Camille herself. Mme Moke was suitably impressed by Berlioz's new status and shortly after gave permission for her daughter's marriage to take place at Easter 1832. As Berlioz wrote to Ferrand, 'It is my music which has extracted consent from Camille's mother! Oh! my beloved Symphony, I shall owe Camille to her.'[29]

While Hamlet returned to life, the wretched Ophelia still languished in Paris. On 15 August she wrote to Louis-Philippe, who as Duc d'Orléans had been a regular attender at the English theatre, to ask for his intervention on her behalf so that she might be paid what was owed to her by the former directors of the Opéra-Comique from Ministry of the Interior funds. Her style was unrestrained: she had travelled one thousand miles accompanied by an aged mother and an invalid sister both of whom were, had been from very childhood, dependent upon her professional exertions for support; the late directors had disappeared 'having spent in the most extravagant luxury' the produce of her labours; having no father or brother to protect her she was denied her just claim, seven thousand four hundred francs earned at the expense of her health from over-exertion and the loss of her time for five months. Her plea for justice to the fountainhead was to no avail. As Queen Elizabeth or Jane Shore she could bring tears to an audience's eyes; but on the letter is only pencilled the laconic and final comment, 'Le Ministre n'a pas d'argent pour cet objet.'[30]

The theatrical community came to her rescue, and official sympathy was sufficient to make the Opéra available for a benefit. It took place on the evening of 5 December, a few hours after the triumph of the *Fantastique*. The suggestion sometimes advanced that Berlioz chose this particular day for his concert in order to humiliate Harriet is false, for a number of reasons caused a postponement from the original date of 28 November. One of these was the illness of the singer Maria Malibran, whose willingness to take part was another indication of Harriet's high reputation among her fellow professionals. Her friends put together a glittering programme: Taglioni danced, Malibran and Lablache sang in a *scène de chant* introduced into *L'Ours et le Pacha*; Firmin and Mlle Mars appeared in Etienne's *La Jeune Femme Colère*. Harriet herself took the role of the deaf-mute Fenella, with Nourrit as Masaniello, in Auber's opera *La Muette de Portici*, a work that was something of a landmark in Romantic theatre, as much for its subject, a rising against tyranny, as for any musical innovation – a performance in

32. Setting for *La Muette de Portici*, by Ciceri, 1828.

Brussels sparked off the Belgian revolution. It was also a visual *tour de force*, with settings by Ciceri and a spectacular eruption of Vesuvius. Harriet, although her pantomime remained a little emphatic for French taste when divorced from the context of Shakespeare, was generously applauded on this rare appearance at the Académie Royale de la Musique, and the evening was well-attended. According to the *Journal des Débats*, the receipts amounted to fifteen thousand francs, a 'proper compensation' for the losses she had undergone.[31] The profits, obviously, were very much less. The *Courrier des théâtres* reported caustically that Lablache was only asking a thousand francs for his contribution: 'Pourquoi pas la recette? Entre artistes . . .'[32]

At the end of a year which had seen the apparent conclusion and sublimation of Berlioz's feelings for Harriet, he left Paris for his home in the provincial peace of La Côte Saint-André, a first stage on his reluctant journey to Italy. Camille and her mother wrote to him once at La Côte, but when he at last reached Rome and settled in to the Academy he became increasingly disturbed by the lack of news. In early April he travelled to Florence, so as to be well placed for a rapid return to Paris should the need arise, and there he waited in a turmoil of anxiety. In a wood beside the Arno he read *King Lear* for the first time; in the cathedral he gazed on the corpse of a young married woman, held her hand, would have embraced her if he had been alone, and thought of Ophelia – Shakespeare's Ophelia. Then at length the infamous letter from Mme Moke arrived.[33]

Camille, to whom he was engaged, who had first declared her love for him and implored him to return it, was to marry wealthy, middle-aged M. Pleyel, head of a firm of piano-makers. Berlioz's mind grew dark with thoughts of death. He conceived elaborate schemes of revenge. He would disguise himself as a lady's maid, obtain entrance to the Moke household, present a letter from some fabricated notable, and shoot first Pleyel and Mme Moke before revealing his identity to Camille and administering the *coup de grâce*. The conception is reminiscent of one of Dumas père's hastier dramas. The maid's outfit was ordered from a French milliner's, the double-barrelled pistols loaded, phials of strychnine and laudanum purchased in case of misfires; and to bring an end to his own life when the triple slaughter had been accomplished. Berlioz, whose ability to attend to his musical affairs in the midst of other preoccupations was remarkable, also made some revisions to the score of the *Fantastique* and sent a copy to Habeneck so as to secure his reputation for posterity. Then he launched himself towards Paris. At Genoa he discovered that the disguise had been left behind when there was a change of carriage, and a substitute set was hastily run up. By this time his frenetic behaviour had understandably attracted the notice of the Sardinian police, who took him for a revolutionary and insisted that he travel via Nice rather than Turin. When the Corniche was reached the driver stopped to secure the drag to the carriage wheels and Berlioz experienced an almost overwhelming compulsion to fling himself over the precipice and into the sea. The driver sprang back into his seat, the moment passed, the fever began to subside.

Berlioz wrote a letter of explanation to Horace Vernet, the director of the Rome Academy, asking for advice, and continued his journey to Nice.[34] In the letter he recounts a rather more literal return to life, in which he lies on the beach vomiting salt water after being apparently fished out of the sea. Whether the ritual suicide attempt was real or imaginary seems immaterial. Vernet's calm reply, and the balmy atmosphere of Nice, completed the cure. Berlioz wandered about the orange groves, swam in the sea, wrote the *Roi Lear* overture, made love to a girl on the shore (his first sexual encounter since an excursion with

33. Hector Berlioz. Painting by E. Signol, 1832.

Camille to Vincennes), corresponded voluminously with his family and friends. The episode, which he himself could refer to as the 'little comedy', was over. In spite of the therapeutic value of the violent bout of activity and Berlioz's subsequent irony at his own expense, it seems likely that he was deeply hurt by the behaviour of Camille. She had not been a remote image like Harriet, but a close companion and lover, a gifted musician who shared his interests and the delight at his blossoming career, and a woman whom he had longed to marry and to make part of his family. The humiliation, too, was a particularly public one. Vernet recommended work and art as the remedies for an afflicted mind, and Berlioz made his way back to Rome.

Harriet had decided to return to England in the New Year. She contacted her agent about possible engagements and, after being detained at Abbeville because of her sister's serious illness, reached Boulogne where she found a reply waiting for her. Her letter to William Kenneth of 15 February reveals something of the problems that her life as an independent actress entailed:

I take shame to myself for not having bestowed sufficient attention in explaining to you *my views* otherwise I should have saved you the trouble of applying to any minor theatre in London as nothing could possibly be more diametrically opposed to my inclination or taste, at the same time acknowledging my respect for the undoubted Talent which supports those Establishments – neither did I for an instant contemplate travelling so many hundred miles in search of *money* to Scotland or poor Ireland!! the performers who gain any in either place are very fortunate and very limited in number.

With regard to America I am delighted at your proposition as it meets my views & I wish you could arrange my Engagements there to commence about the beginning of June next, if you think it a good season for theatricals, of which you are the best judge and you will be pleased to direct your answer to this place Poste Restante as before with your advice & accept dear Mr Kenneth the sincere acknowledgements of
    yours truly – Harriet C Smithson
The offer of the Exeter managers is not sufficiently liberal for my acceptance but I agree to the proposal made to me last year by the manager of the Wisbeach Theatre (of which you can remind them) provided you could make a little tour for me in the same direction.
I believe Mr Manlys Theatres lie in that route if so please to write & remember me to him on the kindest terms. – my mother & sister desire their best regards to you and Mrs Kenneth. I would willingly go to Exeter for the third of each night & half of my *Benefit*.[35]

Whatever Harriet's inclination and taste, it was not long before she was compelled to swallow her pride and return to the minor theatres. After a series of provincial engagements in 1831 in places such as Norwich, Bristol, Lincoln and Liverpool as well as a visit to Mr

Manly's theatre at Nottingham where she was hailed as 'one of the very first actresses of the present day',[36] she found herself back at the Royal Coburg theatre in January 1832. Harriet still had influential patrons. The Duke of Devonshire, who had perhaps seen Harriet act at Buxton and knew of her Paris triumph from his sister's letters, was reported to have given her £50 for a benefit ticket. His diary for 29 February records a visit from 'poor Melpomene Smithson, whom I promised to go to Coburg and see act and then was obliged to throw over and said much to her'.[37] But such generosity could not disguise the unsatisfactory nature of the engagement. Davidge, a member of the original Coburg company and lessee since 1825, had additionally acquired the New City Theatre in Milton Street, Cripplegate, and trundled his actors to and fro in hackney carriages furnished as dressing rooms so that they could appear in both theatres on the same night. There is no evidence that Harriet was reduced to such extremes, but she certainly played in both places in roles such as Jane Shore (not, of course, in Rowe's tragedy, but in a melodrama founded upon it) or Belvidera (in a burletta founded on *Venice Preserved*). Even though Kean himself had acted at the City, an appearance there could only harm Harriet's standing.

In June her fortunes took a turn for the better, when she joined the company at the Theatre Royal, Haymarket, possibly through the Duke of Devonshire's kind offices. The season was not especially distinguished, nor did she receive much critical attention, but the standard of acting and production was appreciably higher and the repertory more in line with her ability. Kean had been engaged for a limited number of appearances and Harriet played opposite him as Queen Elizabeth in *Richard III* for her début on the Haymarket stage, and later as Portia, Desdemona and Cordelia. (When *Hamlet* was given, she took no part; she never played Ophelia in England.) She also acted frequently in comedy, taking Julia in *The Rivals* and the Widow Belmour in Murphy's *The Way to Keep Him* for the first time. However, when Knowles's *The Hunchback* was introduced, Miss Phillips was given the role of Julia. This was a disappointment in view of Harriet's previous expectations of a part in a new Knowles work, for there were few enough fresh plays available for a serious actress to make her mark in: Fanny Kemble had played the original Julia in the spring at Covent Garden, another reminder to Harriet that she was blocked from further advancement there. If she was disillusioned with London theatre and London critics, there was good cause. Even the Duke of

Devonshire, wrote *The Age*, could not make Miss Smithson an actress; 'she was a passable sentimental actress some years since at Drury Lane, and she is now grown too fat to be so any longer'.[38]

More and more actors were looking to foreign tours to restore their fortunes and reputations. America was, for obvious reasons, the most favoured destination, but Harriet had her family to consider. France was closer, and she always felt more at ease on the Paris stage than anywhere else. Mlle Mars had been acting at Covent Garden during the summer, and may have encouraged her in her ambition. That autumn Harriet made the courageous but hazardous decision to go back to Paris and attempt to set up an English theatre on a permanent basis under her own management.

It would be hard to construct less auspicious circumstances for such a venture. Harriet had had ample opportunity to observe the habitual complications of theatrical management in Paris during the frustrating months of 1830, to say nothing of the fruitless negotiations of 1828–29. Paris, like London earlier in the year, had been suffering from a severe outbreak of cholera. The political situation remained volatile, with the Duchesse de Berry's escapades in La Vendée providing all the necessary drama for the season. The Parisian audience, warm towards Harriet herself, had, with the one exception of *Jane Shore*, shown marked interest only for Shakespeare and for the leading English actors, while the critics had been consistently harsh during 1827–28 about the weakness of the general company and the *mise-en-scène*. Yet for a season of any length as late in the year as November when the Drury Lane and Covent Garden companies were under contract there would be little chance of securing supporting players of much quality. As for starring names, Harriet failed to make sure of a single leading actor: Macready, the obvious and ideal choice, turned down her initial proposals; Kean, in any event a doubtful asset in his decayed state, was not available. The hard bargaining required to make people commit themselves did not come easily to Harriet; she had to leave for Paris without either a leading actor or anything novel by way of repertory, though there was talk that *The Hunchback* would be presented later.

Harriet returned to her former lodgings at 1, rue neuve Saint-Marc before moving to the Hôtel du Congrès in the rue de Rivoli, and plunged into negotiations for a theatre. There is a note of desperation in her letter to Thiers, the Minister for the Interior, asking for a moment's audience with a postscript saying that she would be obliged if the meeting could take place 'le plus tôt possible'.[39] The meeting was arranged, and permission given for the English theatre to open at the Théâtre-Italien. Harriet, who like Laurent in 1827 already had actors under contract, breathed a sigh of relief and decided to begin with *Jane Shore*.

This was probably inevitable, considering that only Harriet of the company had any reputation in Paris, but it was a stale and predictable selection which seemed to ignore the dramatic revolution which had taken place in Paris since the days of *Hamlet* in 1827. An audience that had seen Dumas's *Henri III et sa Cour, Christine, Antony* and *La Tour de Nesle*; Vigny's *Le More de Venise* and *la Maréchale d'Ancre*, and Hugo's *Hernani* and *Marion de Lorme* could hardly be expected to master much excitement about a revival of Rowe.

On 7 November, Berlioz arrived in Paris. He had left Rome with the director's special leave six months early, spent some time at home composing and copying the orchestral parts of his completed mono-drama, *Lélio*, and now intended to arrange a few concerts before proceeding to Germany where he was due to pass a further year under the terms of the *Prix de Rome*. Finding his former apartment in the rue de Richelieu taken, he was moved by an impulse to take rooms in the house opposite which he had gazed at so forlornly from his bedroom window. 'Next day', he wrote in his memoirs,

meeting the old servant who had for many years been housekeeper to the establishment, I asked what had become of Miss Smithson and whether she had heard any news of her. 'But sir, didn't you . . . She's in Paris, she was staying here only a few days ago. She left the day before yesterday and moved to the rue de Rivoli. She was in the apartment that you have now. She is director of an English company that's opening next week.' I stood aghast at the extraordinary series of coincidences. It was fate. I saw it was no longer possible for me to struggle against it . . .

A believer in the magnetic attractions and secret affinities of the heart would find in all this some fine arguments to support his theories. Without going so far, I reasoned as follows: I had come to Paris to have my new work (the monodrama) performed. If I went to the English theatre and saw her again before I had given my concert, the old delirium tremens would inevitably seize me. As before, I would lose all independence of will and be incapable of the attention and concentrated effort which the enterprise demanded. Let me first give my concert. Afterwards I would see her, whether as Ophelia or as Juliet, even if it killed me; I would give myself up to the destiny which seemed to pursue me, and not struggle any more.[40]

It would seem as if Harriet, too, drawn inexorably towards the theatres of Paris, was in some way subject to these magnetic attractions and secret affinities of the heart, and to a destiny which appeared to pursue her.

8 Episodes in the life of an artist

Jane Shore was performed on 21 November 1832. It is hard to assess the precise nature of the disaster which overtook Harriet's first venture into management. The English language *Galignani's Messenger* described the audience as 'fashionable and, considering the earliness of the season, numerous',[1] a rather obvious euphemism for sparse; the hostile *Courrier des Théâtres* claimed that the house had been papered, and that despite the zeal of bought applause 'the British production thoroughly bored everyone'.[2] The *Artiste*[3] and the *Journal des Débats*[4] called Harriet's acting sublime, especially in the fifth act where her beautifully pathetic playing affected the spectators as powerfully as ever.

At the box-office, the effect was totally inadequate. Harriet on her own, for all her ability to move an audience to tears, could no longer fill the Salle Favart. In a long article in the *Artiste* the following year there is a detailed analysis of the public's fickleness in failing to support 'one of the finest talents of the era', 'a poetic actress, a woman of passion and tears, an actress of sharp and finely perceived emotion'.[5] Among the reasons advanced were, first, the volatile political situation: the Duchesse de Berry had been smoked out of her hiding place in Nantes and discovered to be pregnant, while Louis-Philippe had narrowly escaped an assassination attempt as he rode across the Pont Royal. Secondly, and more practically, the English theatre lacked the well-directed and sustained publicity campaign, the spate of articles, translations, anecdotes which had been so conspicuous during the 1827–28 season. Harriet's naivety, her retiring temperament and poor command of the language made her quite unsuited to the job of organising favourable publicity and influencing the Parisian response. She needed someone like Abbott to advise her.

Southerne's *Isabella* was announced to follow *Jane Shore*, but postponed because of Harriet falling ill. Whether this was a diplomatic

127

indisposition to gain time and sympathy or an understandable reaction to the prospect of financial ruin, the result was to increase the crisis, for no performance could usefully take place without her and she remained responsible for the company's salaries. After several announcements and postponements, which did nothing to help her cause, the next production was given on 5 December. The result was much the same as before. Maurice of the *Courrier des Théâtres*, to whom Harriet had astonishingly sent a complimentary ticket and who had been strenuously urging the English to take the *paquebot* while the weather was still fine, called the evening 'Mademoiselle Smithson toute seule'; he then soured this somewhat dubious compliment by attributing to her a 'mérite vulgaire' and wished the company 'Bon vent!'[6] In attracting Maurice's venom, Harriet was in good company; for years he pursued a bitter personal vendetta against Mlle George, and savaged the actor Samson because he refused to take out a subscription to the *Courrier*. But without any real success to set against this curt dismissal, Maurice's attitude was likely to prevail.

Berlioz was busily occupied in arrangements for his concert. The programme was to consist of the *Fantastique* followed by *Le Retour à la Vie* (later known as *Lélio*), the two works forming complementary parts of *Episode de la Vie d'un Artiste*. According to Berlioz, 'The subject of this musical drama, as is known, was none other than my love for Miss Smithson and the anguish and "bad dreams" it has brought me.'[7] To an important though indefinable extent the subject was also concerned with the effects of his relationship with Camille Moke; certainly it was in the aftermath of her rejection of him that he reassembled and organised the sections which comprise *Lélio*. Behind both images, perhaps, lies the figure of Estelle and the Dauphinois landscape in which Berlioz set her. The six parts of *Lélio* were in fact all reworkings of earlier compositions, though little had been heard in public: the finale, for instance, was drawn from the *Tempête* fantasia performed at the storm-wrecked concert at the Opéra. The accompanying text extends the series of episodes in the artist's life which had been provided as programme notes for the *Fantastique* in the form of descriptions of the hero's dreams. In *Lélio*, the artist is represented by an actor, who recites the soliloquies which link and introduce the musical sections.

The concert hall at the Conservatoire was made available. Habeneck agreed to conduct. For the role of 'mélologuist' Berlioz chose Bocage, the original Antony in Dumas's drama, Delaunay in *Marion de Lorme*, and most recently Buridan in *La Tour de Nesle*. Bocage's tall, thin

34. Pierce Bocage in Dumas's *Antony*. Lithograph, *c.* 1831.

figure, pallid complexion and melancholy eyes were well suited to the part of a romantic artist. The concert promised to have the same importance as a landmark in musical taste and opinion as had *Antony* and *Hernani* in the theatre. It was carefully prepared with articles in the press; even the rehearsals themselves attracted close interest. Berlioz had been warmly welcomed on his return from Rome by his fellow musicians, and instrumentalists vied with each other to form part of the impressive musical forces he was assembling. The chorus, 'too small',

129

was fifteen women and twenty men. The bills were on display twelve days in advance.[8] Never had Berlioz been in such a state of readiness, nor found such ideal circumstances to surround his work.

Two days before the concert, Berlioz was in the music shop of his publisher Schlesinger when the latter pointed out to him an Englishman named Schutter, who wrote for *Galignani's Messenger* and knew Miss Smithson.[9] Schlesinger persuaded Berlioz to give him a box for the concert and, perhaps envisaging some unusual publicity, suggested that Schutter invite Harriet to attend. Schutter arrived at Harriet's hotel on the day of the concert to find her in a state of 'profound despondency' about her financial predicament, and not especially disposed to spend the afternoon listening to music. Ironically, Harriet's sister, later so violently opposed to the association, encouraged Harriet to go along as a distraction, and an English actor who was with them was equally eager. 'A cab was summoned, and Miss Smithson allowed herself, half willingly, half forcibly, to be escorted into it.'

Berlioz's account in his memoirs is based, he states, on what Harriet later told him. At this point she did not apparently know that Berlioz was in any way involved; only when she read the programme which Schutter gave her in the cab did she discover that the concert was to be of Berlioz's work, and even then the symphony's title and the section headings were in themselves insufficient to warn her that she herself formed part of the subject. The concert had attracted the kind and quality of audience that had marked out events like *Hamlet* or *Hernani* as critical watersheds: Liszt, Chopin, Paganini, Hugo, Dumas, Vigny, George Sand, Heine, Gautier, Legouvé, Janin, d'Ortigue were among the spectators, many of them aware at first or second hand of Berlioz's involvement with Harriet. When she entered the stage-box, wrote Berlioz,

above a sea of musicians . . . she was aware of a buzz of interest all over the hall. Everyone seemed to be staring in her direction; a thrill of emotion went through her, half excitement, half fear which she could not clearly account for. Habeneck was conducting. When I came in and sat breathlessly down behind him, Miss Smithson, who until then had supposed she might have mistaken the name at the head of the programme, recognised me. 'Yes, it is he,' she murmured; 'poor young man, I expect he has forgotten me; at least . . . I hope he has.'[10]

A glance at the programme notes must have immediately begun to dispel that illusion:

The Composer imagines that a young musician, afflicted by that spiritual sickness which a famous writer has called the *vague des passions*, sees for the first time a woman

GRANDE SALLE DU CONSERVATOIRE DE MUSIQUE.

Dimanche 9 Décembre 1832, à une heure précise,

GRAND
CONCERT DRAMATIQUE,

Donne par M. Hector Berlioz.

PROGRAMME.

ÉPISODE DE LA VIE D'UN ARTISTE,
Symphonie fantastique, en cinq parties (1),
de M. *H. Berlioz.*

1re.   *RÊVERIES. — PASSIONS.*

2me.   *UN BAL.*

3me.   *SCÈNE AUX CHAMPS.*

4me.   *MARCHE DU SUPPLICE.*

5me.   { *SONGE D'UNE NUIT DU SABBAT.*
{ Messe funèbre burlesque.
{ Ronde du Sabbat.
{ *Dies iræ* et ronde du Sabbat réunis.

(1) Un programme détaillé de la Symphonie sera distribué dans la salle.

LE RETOUR A LA VIE.
MÉLOLOGUE, (mélange de musique et de discours) EN SIX PARTIES, faisant suite à la Symphonie fantastique; paroles et musique de M. *H. Berlioz.*
Le rôle parlé de l'artiste sera lu par M. BOCCAGE.

1re.   { MONOLOGUE DE L'ARTISTE.
{ *LE PÊCHEUR,* Ballade imitée de *Goëthe,* chantée, avec Piano seul, par M. A. DUPONT.

2me.   { MONOLOGUE DE L'ARTISTE.
{ *CHOEUR D'OMBRES* (avec Orchestre).

3me.   { MONOLOGUE DE L'ARTISTE.
{ *SCÈNE DE LA VIE DE BRIGAND.* Chant, Choeur et Orchestre; le capitaine, chanté par M. HÉBERT.

4me.   { MONOLOGUE DE L'ARTISTE.
{ *CHANT DE BONHEUR* (avec Orchestre et Harpe), chanté par M. A. DUPONT.

5me.   { MONOLOGUE DE L'ARTISTE.
{ *LES DERNIERS SOUPIRS DE LA HARPE.* Souvenirs (Orchestre seul).

6me.   { MONOLOGUE DE L'ARTISTE.
{ *FANTAISIE SUR LA TEMPÉTE,* (Drame de *Shakespeare*) pour Choeur et Orchestre.

L'Orchestre, composé de plus de **100** MUSICIENS, sera dirigé par
M. HABENECK.

Le Piano sera tenu par M. **FESSY.**

PRIX DES PLACES : Balcon, Stalles et Premières, 6 fr. — Secondes et Rez-de-Chaussée, 5 fr. — Parterre, 3 fr. — Amphithéâtre, 2 fr.

On trouve des *Billets chez* M. Réty, *au Conservatoire*; M. Schlesinger, *rue le Richelieu, n°.* 97 ; M. Pleyel, *boulevart Montmartre*; MM. Lemoine, *rue de l'Échelle*; M. Messonnier, *rue Dauphine*; M. Frey, *place des Victoires.*

LA SALLE SERA ÉCLAIRÉE.

VINCHON, fils et successeur de Mme. Ve. BALLARD
Imprimeur, rue J.-J.-Rousseau, No. 8.

35. Programme, Grand Concert Dramatique, 9 December 1832.

who possesses all the qualities of the idealised being that he has dreamed of in his imagination: he falls desperately in love. By a strange coincidence, the image of the beloved never appears to the artist's mind except in association with a musical idea, in which he finds the impassioned but at the same time refined and diffident quality which he attributes to the object of his love.

The occasion held certain affinities to the circumstances of Berlioz's *coup de foudre* at his first sight of Ophelia five years before. The public and theatrical nature of the setting, the heightened sense of expectation within the audience, were similar, with the added *frisson* that so many recognised in Harriet the original object of the artist-hero's passion, who instantly inspired in him such a 'volcanic' love: if any were in doubt, the long article in the *Revue de Paris* identifying the beloved with a 'célèbre Irlandaise' who took the role of Ophelia did everything but name her. Heine recalled seeing Berlioz for the first time that evening, adorned with a 'stupendous, antediluvian *frisure* or bristling mane which fell over his brows like a forest over precipitous rocks'; Heine's neighbour next pointed out to him the 'plump' and famous Miss Smithson, 'while Berlioz stared steadfastly at her alone, and when her glance met his, then he pounded away like mad on his kettledrum'.[11] Heine tactfully referred to 'la belle Anglaise' when the letter was published in Paris. The drum must be an embroidery on his part, but the public nature of the relationship was not. Harriet's very presence could be seen as part of the programme: the *Fantastique*, composed to transmute her tormenting image into art, had been first performed in her absence as an offering to Ariel; *Lélio*, conceived in the aftermath of Ariel's betrayal, was fortuitously associated with Harriet's reappearance. As Berlioz described it,

The brilliant reception, the passionate character of the work, its ardent, exalted melodies, its protestations of love, its sudden outbursts of violence, and the sensation of hearing an orchestra of that size close to, could not fail to make an impression – an impression as profound as it was totally unexpected – on her nervous system and poetic imagination, and in her heart of hearts she thought, 'Ah, if he still loved me!'[12]

Twice before Berlioz had thought to force himself to Harriet's notice by means of his music. Now, through chance as much as by premeditation, he achieved his purpose. It is not everyone who is wooed by a full orchestra.

If the *Fantastique* revived Harriet's memories of the passion directed at her in Berlioz's wild stares and tortured letters, Bocage in the role of the artist completed the process. In the fourth section the artist declares:

Oh, if I could only find her, the Juliet, the Ophelia for whom my heart is searching. If I could only drink from the cup of joy and sorrow which true love offers, and then one autumn night, lulled by the north wind on some wild heath, to lie in her arms and sleep a deep, last sleep . . .

Harriet, hearing these words spoken by Bocage, seeing in front of her, just next to the conductor, the artist who had written them, could not fail to believe that she remained the object of Berlioz's love. 'From that moment . . . she felt the room reel about her; she heard no more but sat in a dream, and at the end returned home like a sleepwalker with no clear notion of what was happening.'[13] Inevitably, Berlioz endows Harriet's response with the warmth and colour of his own imagination, almost as though he is creating a musical drama and finding the appropriate motif to complete the structure: the actress whose Ophelia and Juliet first aroused the series of images now receives them back transposed into another form. As art, the episodes have resonance, symmetry, and a sense of completeness. As life, the sequence obstinately refused to be resolved.

The next day, Berlioz wrote to his sister Adèle to describe the extraordinary success of the concert and added: 'I have won a quite different commendation, more unexpected, which is the subject of every conversation.' Harriet had sent him a message of congratulation: it was her first positive gesture of recognition, of interest, and it was enough. In return, Berlioz secured her consent to be introduced to her, and wrote:

If you do not wish my death, in the name of pity (I dare not say of love), let me know when I may see you. I beg you for mercy, and ask you sobbing on my knees for forgiveness!

Oh! Wretch that I am, I did not believe that I deserved all that I suffer, but I bless the blows which come from your hand.

I await your reply as I would the sentence of my judge.[14]

In the midst of this personal turmoil, each had demanding professional preoccupations. Berlioz was organising the repetition of *Episode de la Vie d'un Artiste* which had been spontaneously called for. Harriet was trying to secure the use of the Odéon in place of the Salle Favart, and on 11 December appeared as Jane Shore in a benefit for Samson at the Théâtre du Palais Royal. By 15 December they were meeting on entirely different terms, as Berlioz's distracted letter the following day reveals:

Adieu, I am so sad not to have seen H. Smithson this evening, that I cannot think clearly. I will not see her again until tomorrow. Yesterday evening was full of tears for *us*

36. Hector Berlioz. Drawing attributed to Ingres, *c.* 1832.

both. She has a deep and genuine sensitivity that I never suspected; I love her as on the first day, I think I am sure of being loved in return, but she trembles, she hesitates and does not know how to make up her mind: however will all this end?[15]

The tears and vacillations would become familiar motifs. It is difficult to construct the course of a relationship with much pretence to accuracy when only the records of one of the two remain, especially when that one is as mercurial, as extravagant in word and gesture and yet at times so acidly self-mocking, as Berlioz. Barzun implies that Berlioz took pity on Harriet, or that she appealed to him to extricate her from her crisis; 'Whether this predicament rekindled warmth of feeling in Berlioz, whether she made an appeal to him in her distress . . . the fact remains that by mid December the pair were deeply involved.'[16] These comments do not seem to take full account of the evidence of the letters, which suggest that apart from that one note of congratulation it was Berlioz who took the initiatives. Elated by the triumphant public reception of his music, he swiftly resumed his passion with all the ardency and anguish of before. Harriet, understandably, was at first more reluctant to commit herself. Berlioz after all had five years' start.

Harriet's chance presence in Paris, and her attendance at the concert and response to it, reawoke and reactivated the past. Stendhal and Berlioz have little in common temperamentally, but Stendhal's analogy in *De l'Amour* bears some relation to Berlioz's state of mind:

at the salt mines of Salzburg, they throw a leafless winter bough into some abandoned working. Two or three months later they bring it out covered with a deposit of shining crystals . . . what I call crystallisation is a mental process which sees in everything that happens new evidence of the loved one's perfections.

The first crystallisation was a process all the more complete because everything that happened was imagined, and so remained largely untouched by the intervention of Camille. Harriet's return caused the process to be renewed, but upon the foundation that already existed.

The factor which ensures that love will last is the second crystallisation, during which you realise every moment that you must either win her love or die. The very idea of ceasing to love is absurd . . . The stronger your character, the less is it subject to inconstancy . . . When the two crystallisation processes have taken place, and particularly the second, the original winter bough can no longer be recognised by indifferent eyes.[17]

For the two lovers, there was much ground to recross. Berlioz had both worshipped and reviled Harriet from a distance. She had been told that he was mentally unstable, epileptic; he had believed her to be promiscuous, and dismissed her as savagely as Hamlet had condemned Ophelia. Once Harriet had declared that there was nothing more impossible than for her to receive his proposals. Since that time, there was the relationship and engagement to Camille Moke to explain. Berlioz had earlier written to Nanci to tell their father not to worry about Harriet's presence in Paris; now he hastened to reassure Adèle that his 'unexpected commendation' did not come from Mme Pleyel, whom he had seen the other day 'as one sees a stranger'.[18]

Berlioz's rapt devotion is revealed in a letter to Liszt, who was clearly and with good reason concerned about the effect of Harriet on his friend, most probably because he realised how incompatible the two were by nature and perhaps because he foresaw that Berlioz would never be content with a temporary liaison.

You gave me great proof of your friendship yesterday morning; but it would have been worth more to me if it had been on another subject. Since I left you, I have had a scene with H.S. which, were it not for you, would have drowned me in unalloyed happiness, a

37. Franz Liszt. Lithograph by A. Devéria, 1832.

frenzy no tongue can express; this joy, this fever of love, has been poisoned, but I drink it whole, were I to die at the end.

Everything about her delights and exalts me; the frank confession of her feelings has astounded me and driven me almost mad. I appeal to you, in the name of our friendship, not to repeat, *either to me or to others*, anything of what you have said to me. We have not yet come to marriage.

I will never leave her. She is my star. She has understood me. If it is a mistake, you must allow me to make it; she will adorn the closing days of my life, which, I hope, will not last long. One cannot hold out against such emotions for ever. I beg you, suppress all talk about this with Dumas, and with Hiller when he comes; even say the opposite of what you think, you must, I beg you on bended knee.

136

Yes, I love her! I love her! and I am loved. She *told me that* herself yesterday in front of her sister; yes, she loves me, but I speak of it only to you, I wish to keep my happiness secret, if it is possible. So, *silence!* There is nothing now which can separate us. She knows about the affair with Mademoiselle Moke, it was necessary to tell her everything; it was her, her, H.S. whom I was missing; my existence is complete, here is the heart which must speak to mine. Don't take pity on me because of what I am writing to you; you have to respect love and rapture when they are as deeply inward as those I am experiencing.

Adieu, my friend, you must understand today that my heart counts on yours.[19]

Even within this letter, a revelation of Berlioz's feelings for the living Harriet, one can sense the pressure of literary, dramatic, iconographical archetypes. Berlioz never referred to her by her English name: she is H.S., Henriette, Ophelia, Juliet. Lélio's reverie was to lie in his beloved's arms, 'lulled by the north wind on some wild heath' one autumn night, and sleep a deep, last sleep. Berlioz imagines that he is ready, like Romeo, to drink poison in order to possess his love. His passion, like Orsino's, can scarcely be withstood for long – though characteristically he appends a postscript to tell Liszt the rearranged date for his concert. Just as he charged off towards Paris equipped with disguise, pistols and poison to wreak revenge upon Camille and her associates, so he flung himself into the role of ecstatic but potentially star-crossed lover in a drama which fully matched the romantic demands of the sublime juxtaposed to the grotesque. For an observer, it was often hard to decide whether the genre was tragedy, melodrama or farce. On 26 December, to complicate matters, Harriet resumed her place within the Romantic imagination by playing the last two acts of *Romeo and Juliet* for a benefit at the Vaudeville: Antoine Fontaney watched her from his box together with Auguste Barbier, Alfred de Vigny and Marie Dorval.

Berlioz's descriptions of the precise state of his relationship with Harriet show an at least intermittent objectivity which enabled him to take part spontaneously in the joy or agony of the moment and yet to stand back and view his, or more rarely Harriet's, behaviour with a critical and often ironic detachment. Theatrical allusions abound, apart from the constant references to *Hamlet* and *Romeo and Juliet*. He recounts to her the vicissitudes of his life since the day he fell in love with her as though he were Othello; 'quanti palpiti', he exclaims, glancing at Rossini's *Tancredi* (who also, though unwittingly, killed the woman he loved); he narrates the strange circumstances which have brought the two lovers together as though they are the carefully contrived elements of a dramatic plot.[20] Joseph d'Ortigue in the *Revue de*

Paris compares Berlioz's passion for the unnamed but universally identified actress to that of la Marquise de Rxxx for the actor Lélio in Sand's story, adding the comment that Lélio ends by discovering the Marquise's passion and sharing her love. Art and life are deliciously, if dangerously, confused. Harriet plans another performance of *Romeo and Juliet* which Berlioz will attend – though he has agreed to avoid seeing her act as a general rule, since she wishes to be convinced that it is Harriet whom he adores, and not the roles she plays. After the tragedy, Berlioz will be 'le véritable Roméo' at the feet of his Juliet, ready to die, ready 'even to live' if she wishes it.

It was the business of living which caused the complications. As art, as a symphony or tragedy which had to be brought to a close, the structure was almost perfect, requiring only the apothecary's draught or Sardanapalus' conflagration to bring it to a satisfactory conclusion. Harriet and Berlioz, after gathering up the past in hours of sympathetic ecstasy – converse handicapped by her poor French and his halting English while gazing into each other's eyes,[21] Harriet's tears falling as freely as had the audience's at the sight of Jane Shore or Ophelia – began to take account of the present and future. If theirs had been an emphatically physical love, it might have been simpler for both. But initially it was an affair 'of the heart and the mind'. Berlioz comments on Harriet's reserve when they are together, and makes it clear that her love for him was less intense than his for her. Harriet's inclinations, temperament, upbringing, to say nothing of the close family scrutiny under which she existed, steered the relationship away from the physical. Harriet was not so gracefully beautiful as she had appeared five years before; she had lost her slenderness, her bloom. But the denial of physical passion made the goal of marriage all the more compelling for Berlioz, who by background and character was himself not in sympathy with temporary liaisons. He wished to possess Harriet completely, and began to see marriage as the only possible outcome for his long gestated love.

The forces which Berlioz had to overcome to achieve this end were immense. Apart from the disapproval of his and her friends, and Harriet's own tentative nature, there was the outright opposition of both families. Harriet was, according to Berlioz, tyrannised by her mother and younger sister; these two had a direct interest in preventing Harriet from marrying, especially from marrying a Frenchman who lived in Paris, and although in the present situation their financial dependence on her was precarious, their whole lives had for years been attuned to Harriet's professional engagements. Harriet allowed herself to be dominated by her sister, who delighted in tormenting her and Berlioz.

Berlioz's family was equally united in disapproval. Harriet, English, Protestant, an actress, in debt, older than Berlioz, had even less to commend her now than when she had been simply the unattainable star. Berlioz anticipated opposition, and was anxious to time his approach as tactfully as possible. Joseph d'Ortigue had made some indiscreet comments in his biographical article;[22] uncle Félix Marmion, Mme Berlioz's brother, had arrived in Paris, and would without doubt be reporting on the matter to La Côte Saint-André. A direct request to Dr Berlioz for permission to marry could not be delayed for long.

Meanwhile, Harriet still bore responsibility for the English theatre. After further negotiations, a small theatre in the rue Chantereine was made available – very far from ideal, since the stage was too cramped to accommodate the productions effectively, and the auditorium too small to help the budget. Harriet was still hoping to sign up Macready, but he demanded too high a fee: Thackeray used to refer to him as McGreedy. The first evening, 3 January, offered *The Weathercock* and *Bertram*, which at least showed more perception about current French taste, for Gothic drama still enjoyed a certain vogue. *The Stranger* was another rational choice; *Galignani's Messenger* considered that if the season had begun with this, all might have been well. In the second half of the month there were revivals of *Othello*, *Hamlet* and *Romeo and Juliet*, and *Henry IV Part I* which Archer had played at Drury Lane. The audiences became more fashionable, and writers like Vigny returned to watch Harriet in Shakespeare. As Ophelia, Harriet was judged to be in no way inferior to when she had gained her high reputation: 'She was what she always was, naive, captivating, melancholy, passionate.'[23]

The *Artiste* chose January 1833, the apparent nadir of Harriet's fortunes, to analyse the qualities which gave her so much distinction:

Miss Smithson is an admirable actress, not simply one of those tragic actresses who articulate distinctly and project well, but an artist. And what is rarer than an artist in the theatre? To a meticulous and deep observation of nature, a quality which especially distinguishes English actors, she combines something of that élan and sudden passion of the south which has few examples or models in England.[24]

It is interesting to receive through the medium of someone other than Berlioz the impression of what constituted Harriet's attraction at this time, not least the assessment that she was an artist. Berlioz was not simply living in the past, reviving out of pity memories distorted by time of a few freak performances. In spite of the box-office failure, Harriet retained her ability to communicate her art particularly through the medium of Shakespeare.

On 3 February Berlioz wrote to his father, asking for his consent to the marriage. Dr Berlioz had become reconciled to his son's musical vocation with great reluctance; for Mme Berlioz, 'actors, actresses, singers, players, librettists, and composers were creatures of abomination, marked by the Church's ban and as such predestined to everlasting fire'.[25] When her son had first announced his wish to become a musician, it caused her such pain that she even resorted to a formal curse, and refused to speak to him when he set out once more for Paris. Her attitude was widely shared: when Talma asked to be married in church, the curé at first refused unless he promised to give up acting altogether; Joanny changed his name when he went on the stage to avoid bringing discredit to his relatives. The Camille Moke episode would have reinforced these prejudices. Now Berlioz was contemplating marriage with another of the same breed, and an English and Protestant specimen at that: nothing could be more morally or socially undesirable. Berlioz was able to envisage the family reaction only too clearly. The tension he suffered between affection and loyalty for his family and the impulse of his heart is apparent throughout. He admits all the factors which must disqualify Harriet in his father's eyes from being a suitable match; he omits all eulogies, because they will serve no purpose coming from him. His case rests on the pain that he has suffered and on the enduring laws of nature, which can only be resolved in one way.

I am no longer an adolescent; I do not live under a single illusion. I have been embittered beyond my power to express by long drawn out sufferings and I am *fully determined to endure them no more*. The sole objective of my life was the love of Miss Smithson, and I have obtained it; from now on my life can either be completely happy, or come to an end . . .

My dear father, look at the choice you wish to make *coolly*, if that is possible; and let me know your decision soon. I wait for it calmly, whatever it happens to be.

I am sadly isolated from all my family, by my ideas, my nature, my position, my career; and all this now is only a natural consequence which should not surprise you at all. There is at least one sentiment which we have in common, and that is the strongest affection, and nothing will ever alter that on the part of your devoted and loving son.[26]

The pressure upon Berlioz increased while he awaited his father's reply. His sister Nanci wrote calling the affair a 'caprice', and Berlioz threatened that he would refuse to open any more letters if her next was in the same tone. Uncle Félix was wheeled into the attack, and he made an expedition to the rue Chantereine to have a sight of the enemy – as Portia:

> I wanted to see Miss Smithson yesterday. I went to the modest theatre . . . where she is now appearing, *faute de mieux*, and where she had made Hector promise not to go to see her, as a theatre unworthy of her talent. I was very curious to unravel the secret of this powerful charm which has played such havoc. She has in fact remarkable features, an exquisite sensibility of voice, and nobility of gesture. The theatre is so small that it is scarcely favourable to any sense of illusion. Miss Smithson is of necessity at a disadvantage; on this stage she does not even seem young. Without having my nephew's eyes or unique nature, I understood the impact this woman must have produced upon his artist's soul.[27]

Although professing understanding, Félix Marmion believed that family considerations should prevail and undertook to do everything he could to promote them, with little expectation of success. These attempts at persuasion only stiffened Berlioz's resolve. When his father's refusal of consent to the marriage arrived, he took steps to initiate legal action: he began the process of the *sommations respectueuses,* under which a son enjoins his father not to disinherit him in spite of the action that he intends to take. This process would take three months, and fresh anxieties crowded upon Berlioz who was in any event loath to be at odds with his family. Harriet might have to leave Paris, to travel to Germany or even England. His own financial affairs, always insecure, were complicated by the terms of the *Prix de Rome*, which technically required him to go to Germany before he could draw the next instalment of his grant. Berlioz's letters to his father become hysterical: 'If by losing my grant I find it impossible to follow her, or even if I don't lose it but she refuses to allow me to accompany her because we are not married, I shall blow my brains out.'[28] Dr Berlioz's arguments, however motivated, show considerable foresight. The one that especially riled his son was that he was wronging Harriet by marrying her, and that he would in time abandon her for someone else. Nothing, he insisted, could separate him from his Henriette: 'When I say that *I would do anything* to obtain her it is in every sense of the word.'[29] The more he was opposed, the more adamant he became to achieve the promised land of marriage which he endowed with a dangerously inflated idea of happiness.

At this juncture in the strained negotiations occurred a stroke of ill-fortune which radically altered both the course and the tone of the scenario. Harriet was busying herself with the preliminaries of a benefit evening for which many of the leading French performers had promised support. Returning from an appointment at the Ministry of Commerce, she was descending from a cabriolet when her dress became caught up; her foot slipped on the running-board and she fell awkwardly to the ground. Two passers-by came to her assistance and carried her in to her lodgings. Her leg was broken in two places just above the ankle.

It was a painful, debilitating and rather unromantic accident. Several English newspapers, in reporting the event, implied that the seriousness of the injury had been exaggerated to gain sympathy for Harriet's financial plight. The hopes of the Berlioz family rose, on the grounds that these different circumstances might encourage a change of heart. Indeed, some alteration in Berlioz's attitude does appear to have taken place, for he wrote to Rocher asking him not to continue with the *sommations respectueuses*; 'je n'ai plus besoin de me marier aujourd'hui'.[30] On 21 March, however, he was again urging him to proceed, a request which Rocher reluctantly refused:

Allow me one last thought, Hector. You are twenty-nine. You were called to an honourable career in an art which seemed bound to make great strides under the influence of your genius; and you are sacrificing all this future to a disastrous love which must stop you in your tracks, and wound you heedlessly while at the same time deflecting you from your true destiny and making you the most wretched of men.[31]

There was a most irritating accuracy in the arguments of Berlioz's friends and family. With Harriet confined to her room, most of the work required for the approaching benefit at the beginning of April devolved upon Berlioz, and he threw himself into the task as though wishing to offer a concrete proof of his devotion. The musicians responded to his requests. Liszt and Chopin played a piano duet, Chrétien Urhan and Trinidad Huerta gave solos on the *viola d'amore* and guitar. The singers from the Italian Opera appeared, Rubini, Tamburini, the two Grisis. As always, Harriet was well supported by her French contemporaries, and the companies from the Vaudeville, the Palais Royal and the Théâtre-Français gave their services, most notably Mlle Duchesnois, who appeared for the last time as Phèdre, and Mlle Mars. The latter's generosity took Berlioz by surprise; he commented that 'she behaved splendidly on this occasion; she gave money, rallied her friends, and did everything in her power to help "poor Ophelia"'.[32] The evening realised six thousand five hundred francs, which were used at once to pay Harriet's most pressing creditors. Another benefit performance at the end of the month contributed towards the individual debts of other members of the English company.

The months of spring and summer were frustrating for Harriet and Berlioz alike. Harriet's leg mended very slowly. It remained extremely painful and required repeated and expensive visits from the doctor: it was four months or so before she was able to walk without crutches and go for tentative expeditions, supported on Berlioz's arm, to the Tuileries. Confined to her room and for much of the day to her bed, she was subjected to persistent criticism of Berlioz from her sister, who fought fiercely to preserve Harriet from marriage. 'There is no end to the absurd slanders she invents to try and detach Henriette from me,' Berlioz wrote to his beloved sister Adèle, the only member of his family whom he continued to confide in during this period.

Happily all this has no effect; but think how much patience I possess not to have put an end to this *damned little hunchback* who pursues her own self-interest in the face of the whole world and has just declared openly to me that *if she were strong enough she would throw me out of the window.*[33]

These continuous attacks, allied to her money worries and her physical discomfort, sapped Harriet's resilience. Her lack of decisiveness disturbed Berlioz. Yet his attitude of defiance towards his own family's opposition remained as ominously resolute as Romeo's: 'Henriette Smithson will be my wife sooner or later, at whatever cost.'[34] At times he had to contend equally with his Juliet's wavering commitment.

There were also happy discoveries. Berlioz was clearly longing to convince at least Adèle, or a friend like Ferrand, that the picture each might have conceived of Harriet was false. In particular, he seems concerned to dispel possible prejudices on either's part about the moral standards of a woman who had been an actress since she was fifteen.

One day, my dear sister, I will write you a long letter with every possible detail about Mlle Smithson, on her truly unbelievable character and on the delightful discoveries that I make every day.[35]

You will learn that every opinion you could have formed about her is as false as possible. Her life is quite another story; and her way of seeing, of feeling, of thinking, is not the least interesting part of it. Her conduct, in the position where she has been placed since childhood, is quite incredible, and it took me a long time before I believed it.[36]

The close knowledge Berlioz acquired of Harriet during these months of unglamorous and wearing delay only confirmed the strength of his love for her.

Marriage, however, seemed as hard to achieve as ever, and financial worries weighed heavily on them both. Harriet refused to accept any money from Berlioz, who had little enough to spare at this stage although he managed to obtain a grant of a thousand francs for her from an official fund. He conceived wild plans for borrowing from his family, his friends, even money-lenders. His febrile state of mind is reflected in a letter to Hiller in which he bequeathes him all his manuscript music and asks him to be sure to keep the letter 'in case some definitive accident befalls me'.[37] Thoughts of suicide alternated with and often obliterated a sense of attainable happiness.

At the beginning of August Berlioz was ready to break with Harriet. The third *sommation respectueuse* had been served on Dr Berlioz on 5 June and there was nothing to delay the marriage except Harriet's indecision.

> I still exist in the same tortured and agitated state; perhaps I will see Henriette this evening *for the last time*; she is so wretched that it makes my heart bleed: and her irresolute and timid nature prevents her from knowing how to take the least decision. But that must come to an end; I cannot go on living like this.
>
> All this tale is sad and drenched with tears; but I hope that there will be nothing more than tears. I have done everything that the most devoted heart could do; if she is not happier and in an established situation, it is her own fault.[38]

Harriet could not bear the thought of the separation which Berlioz threatened as an ultimatum. An act of civil marriage was begun: Harriet's sister tore up the document. In despair, Harriet went so far as to accuse Berlioz of not loving her. His response was uncompromising: he poisoned himself in her presence with an overdose of opium.

> Frightful shrieks from Henriette! . . . sublime despair! . . . cruel laughter on my part! . . . desire to live again on seeing her vehement protestations of love! . . . an emetic! . . . ipécacuana! vomiting for two hours! . . . there were only two grains of opium left; I was ill for three days and I survived.[39]

So ran Berlioz's variation on Garrick's alternative ending: the revival of Romeo. He must have judged the dose to a nicety, in this acting out of the wilder elements in the *Fantastique*'s programme. Juliet, not surprisingly, was overcome with remorse at this violent turn of events. What could she do to make reparation? Berlioz told her. Still she hesitated, suggested a delay of a few months. This was too much for Berlioz, who had waited nearly six years already. He gave her one last chance. Either she allowed him to take her to the town hall a week on Saturday, or he would leave for Berlin. He steeled himself to break free from Harriet and 'live for those who love and understand' him.

An added complication had been introduced into the plot, an episode of intrigue, probably instigated by Jules Janin and other friends either to force Harriet to make up her mind or to distract and console Berlioz. An eighteen-year-old girl, beautiful, quite alone in the world, had absconded from some wretched monster who had bought her as a child, and now threw herself on Berlioz's protection. Whether she was genuinely in distress or hired to play the part, Berlioz rose to the challenge. He offered to take her with him to Berlin, and find her a place in the chorus with Spontini's assistance. He prepared to fall in love with her.

Whatever the intention, this bizarre underplot served to bring about the longed-for resolution. At last Harriet made up her mind. The waif was taken care of by Janin, and the engagement was announced. On 3 October in the British Embassy, Harriet Smithson and Hector Berlioz were married by the chaplain, the Reverend Luscombe. Liszt was one of the four witnesses who signed the certificate. Hiller and Heine were also in attendance: Hiller remembered it as a 'quiet, somewhat sad ceremony'.[40] Berlioz, warned to control his emotions, remained proudly calm, while Harriet could not keep back her tears. They left the city to spend their honeymoon at Vincennes, with the help of three hundred francs lent to them by the poet Thomas Gounet.

9 Berlioz's muse

In the peace of Vincennes, the first few days passed like an idyll. Berlioz had rented a little house to shield them from the inquisitive. On the wedding day, they celebrated in complete peace. Harriet's sister left them alone; there were no servants; they fetched their meal from the restaurant, and picked fruit for their dessert from the garden. 'Il faisait un temps délicieux, riant, doux, frais, superbe.'[1] Their happiness was complete.

With hindsight, it is painfully clear that most of the ills envisaged by the couple's families and friends took place in due course, and that neither temperamentally, intellectually nor perhaps physically were Harriet and Berlioz a suitable match. The same could be said of innumerable pairs of lovers. From the point of view of Berlioz's career, the marriage certainly from its beginning imposed a heavy additional strain upon him which, quite apart from the inevitable anxieties about money, forced him to spend long hours writing *feuilletons* or making arrangements for concerts, hours which might otherwise have been free for musical composition. For Harriet, living in Paris restricted her chances of pursuing her own career, although in the early months she expressed a wish, according to Berlioz, of being at last able to retire from the theatre.

To set these factors in perspective is the great content which marriage at first brought to them both. Berlioz could not believe that anyone could be so deliciously pure and good as his wife – a purity almost unbelievable in an actress of her years: it gave him every confidence for the future.[2] He was right to listen to the voice of his heart: the voice which 'so often deceives has this time told me only the truth', he wrote to Adèle.[3] Harriet was 'Ophelia herself' – not Juliet, she did not have the necessary fire of passion; she was tender, sweet, above all shy. He described to Ferrand[4] a scene which might serve as a subject for a painting, or a theatrical tableau, in their apartment at 1, rue neuve Saint-Marc, to which they shortly returned from their retreat at Vincennes:

Sometimes when we are alone, silent, she leaning against my shoulder with her hand on my brow, or in one of those poses more graceful than any painter has ever dreamed of, she weeps while smiling.

'What is the matter, my poor love?'

'Nothing. My heart is so full! I think of how you are paying such a price for me, that you have suffered everything for me . . . Let me cry, or I shall suffocate.'

And I listen to her softly crying until she says to me:

'Sing, Hector, sing!'

and I begin the Scène du Bal, which she loves so much.

Harriet was highly sensitive, but without any musical taste or education: Berlioz noted with astonishment that she enjoyed the most banal tune of Auber. Her nature was always modest; since her disastrous season as a director and the long convalescence after her accident she had grown even less confident. Berlioz wanted Vigny to reassure Harriet about her career, and on 23 October they visited his home and each wrote something for the Comtesse de Vigny's album; but Harriet now did not greatly enjoy going out to other people's houses, or attending the salons. She preferred to stay at home and read beside the fire on days when she did not accompany her husband to the opera. But she received Berlioz's friends in the evening: his cousin Alphonse Robert, the poets Emile and Antoni Deschamps, Vigny, Legouvé, Liszt, Chopin. Harriet warmed at once to Robert, a doctor, and went happily to dine at his house. It was a calm beginning to domestic life.

Professionally, there were several setbacks. While debts remained unpaid there was every reason for Harriet to look for work; Berlioz was not legally responsible for Harriet's debts incurred before the marriage, but he nevertheless assumed full responsibility, and Harriet was naturally eager to contribute. She received an offer to join an English company in Berlin, which would fit in well with Berlioz's plans: he was still under some obligation to spend time there under the terms of the *Prix de Rome*. However, another actress was signed up, and, although Berlioz wrote to Spontini to ask him to intervene, the offer was not

* Theme of the *idée fixe* as played by violins and flute in the first movement of the *Symphonie Fantastique* (bars 71–9).

38. Marie Dorval as Adèle in *Antony*. Lithograph *c.* 1831.

renewed.[5] There was also the possibility of a future engagement with Kemble. In Paris, Berlioz had for some months been preparing for yet another benefit evening aimed at reducing the burden of debt. This was an ambitious undertaking with an inordinately long programme which would have lasted until one o'clock in the morning under normal circumstances. The first attraction was to be Dumas's *Antony* with Marie Dorval and Firmin; next, Harriet as Ophelia in the fourth act of *Hamlet*; and then a concert, conducted by Berlioz, to include the *Francs-juges* overture, *La Mort de Sardanapale*, Weber's *Concertstück* (played by Liszt), a Weber chorus and, finally, the *Fantastique*.

The evening brought deep embarrassment to both Harriet and Berlioz. Marie Dorval, currently married to Merle but more significantly Vigny's mistress, was at the height of her fame and although she was sure to attract an audience, she was too close to Harriet in terms of acting style to be an ideal complement: the many references to Harriet in reviews of Dorval inevitably suggested an element of potential competition. In appearance and especially in personality, she could not have been more different. Small and fragile, but with liquid eyes and delicate yet sensuous features, Marie Dorval exuded vitality. 'Everything was passion with her,' wrote Sand, 'motherhood, art, friendship, love, indignation, religious yearning; and as she neither knew how nor wished to practise moderation and restraint, her whole existence was lived at a terrifying pitch and at an intensity which seemed impossible to sustain.'[6] According to Berlioz, Dumas and Marie Dorval distributed their allocation of tickets to ensure a strong claque for *Antony* and its leading lady. This was a standard precaution and not in any sense aimed at Harriet; Marie Dorval, who was in any case 'admirable' as Adèle, was loudly applauded and recalled many times. The interval which followed lasted nearly an hour. D'Ortigue blamed the delay on an actress who had washed her only dress that morning and was waiting for it to dry. When the curtain was finally raised, the restless audience had little inclination for a fragment of *Hamlet*, out of context and with Ophelia's supporting characters indifferently played by English amateurs. To make matters worse the evening was a Sunday, when the English community who might have cheered Harriet was disinclined to visit the theatre.[7] Harriet still could not move freely; she was lacking in confidence and had difficulty in raising herself gracefully after kneeling beside Polonius's shroud. She was not recalled even once. 'Every woman and every artist will understand what she felt.'[8]

The concert began. The overture was well received, and Liszt was superb in the Weber piece. Then the rot set in. Berlioz had little experience at this point of his career of conducting, and the second violins missed an entry in the orchestral introduction to *La Mort de Sardanapale*. Worse was to follow. The Théâtre-Italien was hired for the evening, and the resident orchestra came with the building; the musicians, disgruntled by an additional evening's work, were further irritated by finding themselves playing alongside reinforcements from the Opéra who were in fact being paid. The Théâtre-Italien musicians' contract did not oblige them to play after midnight. Berlioz had miscalculated.

Sure enough, on the stroke of midnight my worthy artists slipped out furtively under cover of the Weber chorus. Only the extra players, who were being paid, remained at their posts. When I turned round to begin the symphony, I found I had an orchestra of five violins, two violas, four cellos and a trombone.

The audience demanded the symphony. Someone in the gallery called out for the March to the Scaffold. Berlioz explained his predicament as best he could, gesturing to the depleted forces, and the audience filed out. The proceeds, though welcome, disappeared into the seemingly insatiable maw of debt, and both Harriet and Berlioz had to endure the further mortification of the press reports: Marie Dorval's triumph was widely noted, while Fétis, who had been publicly mocked by Berlioz in *Lélio*, seized his chance to comment that Berlioz's music 'positively drove the players away'.

Berlioz was determined to exact artistic revenge. He booked the hall at the Conservatoire for 22 December, and hired his own orchestra which did not include a single member of the Théâtre-Italien. Girard agreed to conduct. There was some danger that the receipts would not cover the expenses, but Harriet gave her husband every encouragement. The standard of musicianship was excellent, the receipts heartening, the public's response, especially to the *Fantastique* where the March to the Scaffold was encored, enthusiastic. 'All the poets in Paris'[9] were there, and Harriet was overwhelmed to receive congratulations from Vigny, Emile Deschamps, Legouvé, Eugène Sue, Hugo. For Berlioz, the praise of another musician meant even more, 'a man with long hair and piercing eyes and a strange, ravaged countenance', who seized his hand and uttered 'glowing eulogies': it was Paganini.[10] Soon after this meeting Paganini asked Berlioz to write a viola solo for him; the piece proved unsuitable for the immediate purpose, but eventually formed part of Berlioz's next symphony, *Harold en Italie*. The friendship with Paganini would have a marked effect on Berlioz's fortunes.

Relationships with the Berlioz family at La Côte were unhappy, apart from the unchangingly affectionate Adèle. Berlioz had to make tortuous arrangements with the postmistress so that he could send Adèle a portrait of Harriet without the rest of the family interfering.[11] His elder sister Nanci and his mother refused to write at all. Harriet was now pregnant, and Berlioz decided they should move from the rue neuve Saint-Marc to Montmartre, where she could spend the summer months more comfortably in what was still a village, and where he could count on more peace while remaining only half an hour's journey on foot from the centre of the city. So at the beginning of April they left for the 'mountain of Paris', crowned with windmills, where you can stand and see the whole city spread out before you. There they rented a four-room apartment – the salon once a *pavillon* built by Henri IV – with a large garden looking out to the north over the plain of Saint-Denis, for seventy francs a month.[12]

The house, which Utrillo painted and where he himself perhaps lived, was the quietest of country retreats. Berlioz and Harriet were

completely insulated from the world; they knew nothing of the rising of
13 April until they heard drums beating the call to arms at one o'clock in
the morning. Berlioz worked and worked, and complained only of the
incessant singing of the nightingales. The weather was so fine and the
landscape so green and beautiful that Berlioz imagined he was back in
Italy. Yet even in this apparent paradise a restless note can be detected
in some of his letters; for him, the artistic and the personal were so
complexly interfused that harmony and content in both were hard to
achieve, let alone sustain. Several wounds to his artistic affections made
him wretched to the point of tears, he confided to Liszt, and neither all
his powers of reasoning nor the arguments of his poor Henriette could
make him forget or overcome them. At times, his sense of pity for
Harriet seems to spring from the understanding that in time he must
inevitably cause her to suffer.

I would like to see you. Will de Vigny come? There is something gentle and affectionate
in his nature which I always find charming, but which today seems almost essential for
me . . . Why are you both not here? Tomorrow my mood will perhaps be changed . . .
Are we really playthings of the air? Is Shakespeare right? . . . Is Moore right when he
says: 'And false the light on Glory's plume, As fading hues of Even. And Fancy's flash,
and Reason's ray, Serve but to light the troubled way. There's nothing bright, but
Heaven.'

And I do not believe in heaven! It is terrible. My heaven is the world of poetry, and
there is a blight on each one of its flowers . . . So, come and see me, and bring Vigny
with you: I need you, I need you both . . . Why cannot I prevent myself from admiring
with so strong a passion certain works which are so fragile, after all, like ourselves, like
everything that exists?[13]

So his friends came to spend the day with Berlioz in the country,
Liszt, Chopin, Vigny, Hiller, Antoni Deschamps. 'We talked, discussed art, poetry, thought, music, drama, in other words everything
that constitutes life.'[14] Berlioz's artistic world of poetry was a place of
constant and urgent passion which made more demands upon him than
Harriet could ever do as herself, rather than as transfigured by
Shakespeare into Ophelia or Juliet. It was a world where she could
scarcely enter in her own person, and of which she never became fully a
part. Very soon she grew aware of the tension between the domestic
scene and the wider artistic and intellectual sphere which Berlioz loved
and needed. As her pregnancy developed, she became understandably
more jealous of Berlioz's presence. Her message to d'Ortigue to the
effect that she was 'encore au monde' and refusing to allow her husband
to sleep or even dine away from the house may have been more than
half-serious.[15]

39. Alfred de Vigny. Lithograph by A. Maurin, 1832.

Berlioz made great efforts to create a new career for Harriet. In April he was brooding over a grand musical project for the newly formed Théâtre-Nautique, a musical and dramatic piece in which Harriet would play the principal role. Strunz, a witness at their marriage, was the theatre's musical director. This particular idea was never realised, but Harriet did eventually accept the offer of a mimed role at the theatre. It was an awkward decision, since it entailed planning for a nurse for the baby, but the impetus almost certainly came at this time as much from debts as from Harriet's desire to return to the stage: at the end of July Berlioz had to apologise to Edouard Rocher for not repaying a five-hundred-franc loan, and expressed the hope that they would soon be afloat again either by means of Harriet's engagements or the concerts he was planning.[16] There were other creditors, too, who were demanding payment.

The later stages of Harriet's pregnancy were uncomfortable. She was old to be having her first child. She had been helped by an English neighbour, and Robert and his wife assisted by arranging for a wet-nurse. It was a difficult labour, but after forty hours, on Friday, 14 August 1834, at eleven o'clock in the morning, she gave birth to a son, Louis.[17] Harriet was overjoyed; Berlioz wrote to tell his father the good news, and received in reply a letter as favourable as he had hoped for. But it is in Berlioz's letter to Adèle, whom they asked to be godmother – Gounet was the godfather – that one can sense the depth of pride and love which Louis's arrival brought to his mother and father.

First, rest assured, our boy has been baptised. He isn't called Hercule, Jean-Baptiste, César, Alexandre, Magloire, but simply Louis. He doesn't cry at all in the daytime, but makes up for it at night, which his mother and nurse complain about a little. As for me, I remain peacefully in my room where I sleep without hearing a thing . . . He is delightful, very strong, with superb blue eyes, a chin with an imperceptible little dimple (by request of his mother, I add a note here to say that he has a very fine forehead, which is true), fair hair a little on the red side like mine was as a child, small pointed bits on his ears like mine, and the lower part of his face a bit short. (Second note by order of his mother; he has a fine strong body, his limbs are well-formed.) All these are features he shares with his father, sadly he has taken nothing from his mother. Henriette is totally besotted. She is quite recovered now; when I go to Paris she comes with her son and the nurse to wait for me half way down the hill of Montmartre, in a shaded walk where, seven years ago, I often came to gaze at Paris while dreaming of *her*. If someone had said to either one of us that in 1834 we would come and sit down *en famille* on these rocks . . .

Yesterday, as she was waiting for me there, several English women came by; the nurse was a few yards off with the little one. The women drew close to look at the baby whom they found gorgeous. (Third note by Harriet's order: a great many other French ladies and women of Montmartre stopped as well to admire Louis.) To all their questions phrased in bad French Marie opened her eyes wide without understanding a word; Henriette listened with delight to all their exclamations and asides, but couldn't restrain herself from answering in English, half laughing and half weeping, that he was only *five weeks old*, that he was *French*, that he had been *born in Montmartre* and that SHE WAS HIS MOTHER. She cried with pride when telling me this. It is the event of the day.[18]

So many of Berlioz's descriptions show Harriet as passive, leaning against his shoulder, gracefully posed with eyes abrim with tears, gazing adoringly at their delightful baby. If she could have stayed as he portrays her, tranquil, doting on her child, resting patiently in the shade until her husband–artist returned from the world of Paris, the idyll might have survived for longer. But circumstances, including probably Harriet's own aspirations, dictated otherwise. It must have been hard to put aside the working habits of eighteen years; nor was Harriet a natural mother. She loved to admire and adore, but the practical care devolved upon the nurse and the maid. In October the family moved back to Paris, to an unfurnished apartment in the rue de Londres. This took time and money to arrange and furnish, but it was a much more convenient base for the multitude of activities which Berlioz was forced to busy himself with, and easier for Harriet while she was going to rehearsals for the Théâtre-Nautique in the Salle Ventadour.

The season had opened with *Guillaume Tell* and among other productions was a ballet by Louis Henry, *Chao-Kang*, an early specimen of chinoiserie. Criticism was already severe on the enterprise, and *La Dernière Heure d'un Condamné* proved to be the last offering. It was a tragic mime in one act by Henry, which itself lends some interest to the event. Henry had trained originally as a dancer, turned later to the creation of ballets and pantomimes, and was one of the leading choreographers of the Romantic period, having success in Milan and Naples besides Paris. As early as 1816 he had been responsible for a three act ballet of *Hamlet* at the Porte-Saint-Martin. This particular work, however, in which he played the part of the condemned man, was an exercise of unrelieved gloom.

The single feature worth naming of this piece is the performance of Madame Berlioz, as the wife of the condamné, on which the agony and despair of such a situation is depicted with a fidelity and painful truth only within the reach of a perfect artiste . . . the picture . . . is one of unmitigated horror, and in the hands of a less gifted actress would be too harrowing for representation.[19]

Galignani's Messenger records that Harriet was called for at the conclusion; Berlioz was able to write a laudatory notice in the *Gazette Musicale*. But a mournful production like this was incapable of changing the fortunes of an already doomed season. The manager was forced to close, and Harriet received no money until the summer of 1835 and only then after Berlioz had brought a lawsuit.

Harriet underwent more than her fair share of management failures. As the months passed she grew increasingly bitter about her lack of fulfilment as an actress, believing that she was deliberately and unjustly neglected. She could not bring herself to attend the first night of *Chatterton* at the Théâtre-Français. Vigny had offered the couple a box, but Berlioz had to write and explain that Harriet did not wish to go, as she feared she would find the occasion too painful.[20] The sight of Marie Dorval as Kitty Bell would indeed have been a poignant one: the actress associated with her own eclipse as Ophelia at the ill-fated benefit, playing the part of an English romantic heroine which, in every respect but the language in which it was written, would have suited Harriet to perfection. Gautier even remarked on Marie Dorval's 'grâce anglaise'.[21] But the refusal to be present was tactless, and an ominous sign for the future.

It was doubly frustrating for Harriet to be unable to contribute to the family budget when she knew that her husband's musical career was being adversely affected, especially by the drudgery of journalism. During the summer he was contributing to four publications, *Le Rénovateur*, *Le Monde Dramatique*, *La Gazette Musicale*, and, since January, the influential *Journal des Débats* – this last was at least well-paid, and the support of the owners, the Bertins, was valuable in itself. But he had to spend much time away from home, at the concert or the opera, when what he wanted above everything else was leisure to write music. *Harold en Italie* had been well received at its three performances the previous winter; a new work, a symphony on a grand scale, was in his mind as well as the long-gestated plans for an opera – the only certain way for a composer to achieve material success in Paris was through the Opéra.

Harriet had for years supported her family as well as herself, and now that responsibility was foisted upon her husband. Her lack of fluency, even competence, in French persisted, blocking one avenue. No one felt inclined to risk another English season in Paris so soon after the setback of 1832. The alternatives were to seek work abroad, or to find a suitable vehicle in French with a dumb role.

In May, the Berlioz family moved back to Montmartre. The garden was huge, the cost of living lower, and perhaps Berlioz found it easier to try to separate his family life from his other interests; it may, too, have been an attempt to encourage Harriet to settle down in a more placid atmosphere. Louis's arrival had improved relationships with La Côte Saint-André. Adèle, of course, was the first to send presents, but Mme Berlioz had softened: a trunk arrived with pots of jam and a selection of Prosper's old toys for his little nephew Louis; some much-needed linen was promised, and Dr Berlioz sent money. Out of loyalty to Harriet, Berlioz refused to be the first to write to Nanci since it was she who had broken off the correspondence; in due course Nanci was persuaded to write a conciliatory letter. But the wounds sustained during the months of courtship remained. Berlioz wrote to Rocher warning him, if he needed to correspond about the costs of the *sommations*, to address his letter *chez* Schlesinger, to avoid upsetting Harriet.[22]

During the summer of 1835 Harriet and Berlioz contemplated a tour of America, but lack of certainty about the offers she could expect, as well as Louis's age, persuaded them against so drastic and expensive an upheaval. Berlioz probably needed little persuading. From his account to Adèle one senses that it was Harriet who was the more enthusiastic.

Truly it is she who needs courage, for after all I am busy, I produce, am active, have distractions; but she is plagued all day by servants who rob us, becomes almost mad with anxiety at the least little illness of the child, finds herself surrounded by a world for which she was never fashioned and which does not even speak her language, and has to remain inactive when she is conscious of a great talent which could enrich us if circumstances were different – one must admit that her attacks of despair are fully justified.[23]

From time to time there was even talk of a tour to England. Meanwhile Berlioz had made various approaches to his friends to persuade them to create an opening for Harriet. The concept of a dumb role was not then as peculiar as it sounds today. There had been a distinct fashion for them in a variety of genres, as Cooke's Frankenstein or Fenella in *La Muette de Portici* exemplify, as well as Harriet's own roles in *L'Auberge d'Auray* and *La Dernière Heure d'un Condamné*. Hugo agreed to search, but it was a difficult commission: most of the suitable dramatic situations had been already used and marred.[24] Nothing emerged, and Harriet's hopes were yet again unfulfilled.

If there had been no opportunities whatsoever, Harriet might have reconciled herself more gracefully to retirement. But in March 1836 she was invited to appear at the private theatre at the Hôtel Castellane. She decided on Ophelia, as it was relatively simple to arrange the *mise-en-scène* and to cast the other roles. Before a select and glittering audience of three hundred, Harriet enjoyed the kind of success she knew in her first Paris season. 'Never has the great tragédienne found nobler inspiration, never was so true a sensibility expressed in such a poetic and fresh manner', reported the *Quotidienne*.[25] Harriet was recalled on stage, and everyone asked why such an original talent, which had contributed so much to French drama, had no permanent place in Paris.

Among Harriet's sadnesses of 1836 was the death of her sister. As Berlioz wrote to Adèle, 'We are much closer to those we love the more sacrifices we make for them, and Harriet had made sacrifices for her sister all her life long.'[26] Now, when she longed to continue acting for her own sake, she could not. In September she was in correspondence with Butler, whose wife she had known in Montmartre, about the terms required by the shareholders of the Salle Ventadour if they let the theatre to an English company, and she enclosed an estimate of the expenses with her translation annexed. Perhaps she nourished a faint expectation of appearing with them, but the enquiry was not pursued. The letter is in her more plaintive vein, with a final prayer from the bottom of her heart 'that your decision whether *for* or *against*, may be for your ultimate welfare' and an apology for putting Butler to the expense of double postage.[27]

That September the Berlioz family moved back to the city to a different apartment in the rue de Londres. On 15 December Harriet gave her last public performance in a Paris theatre, at a benefit at the Théâtre des Variétés for the great Frédérick Lemaître. The faithful Dumas had arranged for Harriet to appear. Once again she chose to play Ophelia. But if this role provided an appropriate *envoi* for Harriet, it did not suit the tone of the evening which was heavily weighted towards vaudeville. In the *Journal des Débats* Janin, Harriet's most fervent admirer, advised her never again to act except in a complete play. His notice reads like a valediction:

I cannot let the occasion pass without referring to a woman of great talent who is abused without compassion or respect. This woman is Miss Smithson. She is noble, she is beautiful, she is intelligent. We owe to her, to her first of all, our understanding of Shakespeare in the theatre.[28]

Berlioz made a last attempt to conjure a complete drama for Harriet from among his friends. One of the salons he visited regularly was that of Marie, Comtesse d'Agoult; he had introduced Liszt, who was to become her lover, to her. George Sand, who was also for some time a very close friend of Marie d'Agoult, had earlier urged Liszt to introduce her to Berlioz, and clearly believed him to be an important artist, though her admiration was not unbounded: 'I was obliged to go to Berlioz's concert,' she wrote, 'for a thousand reasons . . . I dressed with all the gaiety of a whipped dog.'[29] Berlioz decided that Sand might be persuaded to write a suitable drama; certainly, she was one of the swiftest and most prolific writers of the day, though neither a natural nor particularly successful dramatist – one might have imagined Dumas far more likely to manufacture something to the purpose. Berlioz went to work in a distinctly roundabout manner. Marie d'Agoult wrote to George Sand, 26 March 1837: 'Berlioz–Alcibiades is forming in the secrecy of his heart a wish that he does not dare expose to you; it involves a drama in which there would be a role almost entirely pantomimic for his Aspasia.'[30] She commented later, sharply, that Aspasia seemed possessed with a mania to appear on stage. Neither woman, equally strong-minded and self-possessed, would have much sympathy for so passive and helpless a figure as Harriet. Sand replied that she would do what she could, but would have no leisure before the end of the summer. She was at Nohant and was heavily committed, first with finishing *Mauprat*, and then to working on *Les Maîtres Mosäistes*. Berlioz maintained his oblique approaches; by May, Liszt and Marie d'Agoult were staying at Nohant, and both were enlisted to make sure that the promise was not forgotten.

Harriet was keeping her hand in with another appearance, this time as Jane Shore, at the Hôtel Castellane. Excusing herself from rehearsal because of a heavy cold, Harriet exclaimed with slightly more irony than usual: 'Nothing but crosses, every kind of Cross except the indispensable one for our Tragedy, perhaps you will condescend to speak about it today and also to banish the blooming cocoa trees and clear blue waters of the lake from Shoreditch.'[31] But her efforts, according to Janin, brought her 'les honneurs de la soirée'[32] and could be cited as current proof for the poetic truth of her acting. Janin may have been responsible for securing some minor involvement for Harriet in the spectacles mounted to celebrate the wedding of the Duc d'Orléans to the Princesse Hélène on 30 May. Some weeks later a chevalier of the Duchesse delivered a complimentary message and a present of five hundred francs.[33]

On 20 June, confident at last that Sand was amenable, Berlioz wrote to her to convey Harriet's gratitude ('Harriet asks me to tell you that in writing for her you give her air and life') and went on to outline the central dramatic idea:

The idea is new: it involves finding some context within a French drama for an English woman who speaks French with difficulty and with an accent that must be justifiable, or who does not know sufficient French to express certain ideas and who therefore speaks in her mother tongue while at the same time having recourse to pantomime to help her occasionally. There is certainly some terrible drama inherent in the inability to communicate or in the false interpretation of language or of a word; you will find it, I feel sure, and in writing about it you will create a fine and beautiful work . . . Besides, you will be giving a helping hand to a great artist who has too much cause for despair and whose suffering is wholly worthy of your sympathy.

As for the theatre which will mount the piece, I think there will be an embarrassment of choice.[34]

The 'terrible drama' inherent in the situation might have been drawn in every detail from Harriet's own life. Sand certainly sketched out a play during the summer. In September, the newspapers announced a play by her called *Les joies du coeur perdues*, and Berlioz hurriedly wrote to enquire whether this was the promised work.[35] From the fragments which remain, it seems more likely that it was intended for, if anyone, the actor Bocage, Berlioz's Lélio, who had arrived at Nohant in June to persuade Sand to write a play, and whose Byronic good looks had diverted her attention from the distant plight of poor Aspasia.

While Harriet's career faded into memories, Berlioz, at an enormous cost of nervous energy, slowly became established as the one indisputably great and innovative French composer of his generation, though his contemporary reputation remained a subject of controversy and he never achieved lasting financial security. In April 1837 he was given a commission from the state to compose a Requiem, to be performed at the commemoration ceremonies for those who died in the 1830 Revolution. Enemies within the administration effectively blocked the scheduled performance, but at least the Requiem existed, and when General Damrémont was killed at the siege of Constantine in October, Berlioz contrived to have the work selected for the state funeral; it was given triumphantly on 5 December at the Invalides.

The first performance of *Benvenuto Cellini* took place at the Opéra on 10 September 1836. The opera had been completed over eighteen months before, thanks to financial assistance from Legouvé; the intrigues and machinations that preceded and accompanied its production would furnish a libretto, and in fact did provide d'Ortigue with material which he used in a book.[36] Yet although the orchestra massacred the score and the leading tenor helped to sabotage the work's reception, enough was achieved to indicate that Berlioz had infinitely more to contribute both musically and dramatically than the current box-office attraction, Meyerbeer. Berlioz collapsed under the nervous and physical strain, with persistent headaches and acute sore-throat; Harriet and Louis were each ill as well. But he roused himself to conduct a concert in the Conservatoire on 16 December, the second of two he had organised that winter, with a programme to include both the *Fantastique*, and the *Harold en Italie* Symphony.

Among the audience was Paganini, by now very ill from cancer of the larynx. He had attended the disastrous first night of *Benvenuto Cellini*, and been shocked by its rejection, declaring afterwards that if he were the director of the Opéra he would commission three more works, pay for them in advance, and 'get a very good bargain out of it'. This evening was his first chance to hear *Harold en Italie*, which he had originally instigated by asking Berlioz to write something especially for him. After the programme Paganini came up to Berlioz and told him through the medium of his son Achille that never in all his life had he been so affected by any concert. Then he seized Berlioz by the arm, dragged him back on to the platform, and there knelt and kissed his hand.[37]

Two days later, with Berlioz back in bed with a chill and fatigue to add to his earlier maladies, Achille called and left a letter from Paganini:

With Beethoven dead, only Berlioz can make him live again; and I who have heard your divine compositions, worthy of a genius such as yours, humbly ask you to accept, as a token of my homage, twenty thousand francs, which Baron de Rothschild will remit to you on your presenting the enclosed,

Believe me ever your most affectionate friend, Nicolo Paganini.[38]

Harriet came into the room and, seeing the expression on Berlioz's face, misinterpreted his emotion; instinctively she assumed that yet one more blow had fallen upon them. When she realised the extent of their good fortune she rushed into the next room to fetch Louis: 'Come here, come with your mother, come and thank God for what He has done for your father!'

And my wife and son ran back into the room and fell on their knees next to the bed, the mother praying, the wondering child beside her joining his little hands together.[39]

The public expression of Paganini's homage meant a great deal to Berlioz. His princely gift also became a public gesture, reported and commented on in all the newspapers and journals, and not always favourably. Many believed that Paganini was merely the channel for a gift from another source. For Berlioz and Harriet, the gift meant the repayment of all their debts and security for the immediate future. Shortly after, Berlioz received further financial help in the shape of an official post at the Conservatoire library which involved him in a largely honorary capacity. At last he could concentrate on his music without distractions. He would 'give up everything else and write a really important work, something splendid on a grand and original plan, worthy to be dedicated to the glorious artist' to whom he owed so much.[40] In the end, he decided on the idea of a 'symphony with chorus, soloists and choral recitative on the sublime and perennial theme of *Romeo and Juliet*'.

Berlioz's evocation of the months of composition, from late in January to the beginning of September 1839, seems to echo the white heat of the artist–hero Cellini's struggle, striving to complete the casting of Perseus, ready to pour everything that he has already created into the perfecting of the new masterpiece.

Oh, the ardent existence I lived during that time: I struck out boldly across that great ocean of poetry, caressed by the wild, sweet breeze of fancy, under that fiery sun of love that Shakespeare kindled. I felt within me the strength to reach the enchanted isle where the temple of pure art stands serene under a clear sky.[41]

One might have supposed that with the removal of financial anxiety and the realisation of the long-anticipated idea of Berlioz being freed to steep himself in creative work, Berlioz and Harriet might have achieved an equilibrium between artistic fulfilment and domestic happiness. There is a hesitant, melancholy letter from Harriet to Adèle, composed in uncertain French which she refused to allow her husband to correct, and written during the time when Berlioz could sense the completion of his symphony. She recounts taking Louis to see Adèle's portrait, and how, when he finally came upon it, he clapped his hands and called 'C'est elle! c'est elle!!' She added, ominously, 'Je n'ai pas pu m'empêcher de verser quelques larmes en le voyant; parce que *Dieu seul sait si dans ce monde nous nous rencontrons plus.*'[42] Perhaps the tension between idealised image and the reality of Harriet as wife and mother was too great; there is a certain incongruity in that vignette of Harriet kneeling with Louis and praying at the bedside – it seems to belong to the scenario *L'Auberge d'Auray* or *La Dernière Heure d'un Condamné* rather than to the world of Shakespeare and Berlioz. Emile Deschamps was supplying the text for *Roméo et Juliette* – 'un libretto pour une symphonie!' – turning into verse the detailed scenario which Berlioz supplied to him. He concluded a letter which accompanied his latest contribution: 'Merci toujours et tous mes hommages aux pieds de madame Berlioz qui a été votre première et véritable muse.'[43] In terms of art, the story should end here.

161

10 The tragic dénouement

On 8 September 1839 Berlioz completed *Roméo et Juliette*, and dedicated it to Paganini. The first performance on 24 November was prepared for with long and detailed press articles, especially by one from Jules Janin in the *Journal des Débats*.[1] This caused Berlioz some embarrassment with his family in La Côte, for it referred to his early struggles as a penniless composer in Paris in a way that Dr Berlioz found deeply offensive. For Berlioz, the evening was a triumphant vindication, a success as emphatic and widely acclaimed as *Benvenuto Cellini* had been the reverse, in the presence of his most distinguished contemporaries. Balzac, so Berlioz told his father proudly, remarked, 'C'était un cerveau que votre salle de concert!'[2] The Symphony was repeated twice more in rapid succession, an almost unheard of stroke of daring. Present at the third performance, as forcibly struck as Berlioz had been by Kemble and Harriet in Shakespeare's play, was Richard Wagner. The work was the culmination of Berlioz's first phase as a composer.

Meanwhile, his life with Harriet began to atrophy. There were many reasons, and many faults, or misunderstandings, on either side. One major source of friction and sadness to them both was the still uneasy relationship with Berlioz's family in the Dauphiné. Berlioz's love for Adèle, and hers for him, never altered, and she was the first member of the family to make Harriet feel welcome and accepted, beginning with messages of affection in her letters and later making the effort to go to Paris to see her. But when Adèle became engaged to M. Suat, a lawyer, she assumed that her brother would attend the wedding celebrations: she had to suffer disappointment. Hector and Harriet could not travel south together, for either Harriet was too nervous of her reception, or more probably he did not dare expose her to the real or imagined slights of the family connections; and without Harriet he could not or would not go. The explanation that he gave Adèle for not visiting at least his father (his mother had died in 1838) was the constant pressure of work and family responsibility. The vehemence with which he expresses himself reveals how strongly he regretted the separation:

I do not leave Paris because I could not, without madness, leave it . . . I am not alone, I have a wife and son, and *you do not know what it is* to have to struggle every day for the necessities of life for you and yours . . . Your last letter made me very angry and that is the reason why I am only replying today . . . don't send me any more sermons, there is nothing more absurd.[3]

In his memoirs, he comments that it was at Harriet's insistence that he remained in Paris.[4]

There were plans for Dr Berlioz to visit Paris, or for Louis to go and stay with him in La Côte Saint-André; Adèle was arranging to come to Paris, and she could take Louis back with her. But although Adèle came and stayed happily – as did her elder sister Nanci Pal on a later occasion – excuses were always found to postpone the one visit which might have helped to draw the family closer together. When Berlioz finally made the journey home in September 1840, it was without either Harriet or Louis. Afterwards, he wrote to his father:

Henriette is deeply touched by the wish you have expressed to get to know her; have no doubt that we should seize with great eagerness any chance to come *all three of us* and spend a month near you, as soon as it presents itself.[5]

The opportunity never arrived, or was never made. Berlioz did not take Louis to meet his grandfather until the boy was thirteen, by which time there was no possibility of Harriet accompanying them. The irony is that by temperament Harriet, or at least the Harriet of 1833, seems wholly compatible with the Berlioz family, especially Adèle, and far more suited to the calm life of a provincial town than to the ferment of Paris.

Louis, whom both parents adored, was himself a cause of constant friction. There was little question that he was closer to his father. Harriet's imperfect French cannot have eased her relationship to him as he grew older. But even during Louis's early years there is more than a hint of proprietorial pride in Berlioz's descriptions of him: 'He is so sweet, so intelligent; but his almost exclusive preference for me often sends his mother into tears. However, he is beginning to love us both a little more equally.'[6] Yet Berlioz had a thousand preoccupations which prevented him from attending to the boy's upbringing with much consistency, and Harriet found herself unequal to the task. Louis grew increasingly unmanageable, so that even Berlioz had to apologise for his behaviour to the rest of the family.

Harriet's domestic failings, both as mother and housekeeper, increased her own discontent and were a constant source of irritation to her husband. Berlioz's letters refer to several problems with servants, one of whom detested Harriet so strongly that she secretly encouraged Louis to reject his mother. In September 1839 Harriet felt herself threatened by a madwoman who lived in the next door apartment, had conceived an antipathy for 'cette méchante anglaise', and who made life miserable by rapping on the wall and shouting threats through the partition.[7] Harriet took Louis to stay with some English friends until the unfortunate woman left, but Berlioz's description seems to imply a certain exasperation at Harriet's hypersensitive reactions. Madness seemed to cling to Ophelia; in Montmartre, one of her few friends had been Mme Blanche, whose husband kept an asylum, but Harriet shrank from visiting her because of all the patients wandering about the rooms and grounds.

Harriet's career had come to an end, beyond any thought of revival. This factor, more than any other, contributed to her feeling of isolation and resentment, for she never became reconciled to it. Berlioz transposed her image into other forms, she could be known as his muse, she delighted in his success and pleaded with him to risk everything to advance the cause of his music – he always paid tribute to her loyal encouragement in this respect; but her own yearning for fulfilment remained unsatisfied. It was limited comfort to be a resonant memory, a point of comparison, a historical episode: because she had come to success so late in her career she had never grown weary of it, nor learned to distrust the outward forms of fame. She believed that she had been spurned unjustly in England because of her popularity in France. Yet because she had embraced France, and married Berlioz, her career in the theatre had been restricted. If she had been a dancer like Fanny Ellsler, or a singer like Maria Malibran, or even a more versatile linguist like the Italian actress Ristori, there might have been simple solutions. As she was, her only outlets were towards a husband and a son who were beginning to grow away from her.

Harriet's accumulated bitterness made her increasingly dependent on her husband, and alarmingly possessive about him. Berlioz, in pursuit of his Ophelia, had shown himself to be tireless and single-minded; he expended amazing resources of patience and stamina to persuade Harriet to marry him. Now, in middle age, he found himself the object of a relentless and slightly absurd pursuit. His love for Harriet endured, but it had grown less intense and took the form of affectionate gratitude and respect. Her feelings for him had been slow to arousal; he considered she did not have sufficient passion to be truly Juliet, in life. But as she grew older and conscious that her beauty was rapidly vanishing she experienced an ardour for him that he had failed to awaken before, and which he could no longer reciprocate.

Harriet grew more and more demanding of Berlioz's time. Her health was poor during this period; there is a stream of references in his letters to an abscessed tooth, a heavy cold, tonsilitis, pleurisy. The wish for attention and affection is wholly understandable. But Harriet also became unreasonably and jealously suspicious, subjecting him to close cross-questioning and rummaging through his letters for incriminating evidence. Berlioz spent much of his time of necessity around and about in Paris, attending concerts, the opera, meeting musicians and singers. His friend Legouvé suggests that Berlioz gave Harriet ample justification for her jealousy.[8] Yet there is no other indication that Berlioz was lightly unfaithful at any time, and no gossip to that effect in the press. He himself states that he had given Harriet no cause for her suspicions at this stage. It is much more likely that Harriet's possessiveness and nagging, her opposition to any plan that would take Berlioz away from Paris and her side, helped to precipitate the affair that she dreaded.

The woman whom Berlioz turned to was Marie-Geneviève Martin, known as Marie Recio, a mezzo-soprano (and an indifferent one) at the Opéra. In a letter to Ferrand of 3 October 1841 which significantly makes not even a passing reference to Harriet, Berlioz expressed his sense of inward despair at the phase which his life, and marriage, had reached:

I seem to be going downhill at alarming speed; life is so short! For some time I have noticed that a sense of its ending is often with me! so with a fierce appetite I find myself snatching rather than plucking the flowers that I can reach as I slide down the rugged pathway.[9]

Berlioz said nothing to his sisters about the growing rift, though a comment to Nanci, 'Henriette never goes out, and I am hounded by her because I am always out'[10] implies more overt disagreement. However, uncle Félix Marmion, who once visited the Salle Chantereine to inspect the actress who had stolen his nephew's heart, reported to Nanci the true state of affairs:

Henriette has come back to the rue de Londres, almost cured in body but still very upset in mind and above all at heart. Yesterday I stayed there for an hour to listen to all her grievances but with interest, I assure you, never has she been so original. What a curious nature and, one might say, a privileged one! It was a mixture of trifles, tears, sarcasm, memories, I don't know, in the end it was both comical and pitiful. Oh, the poor woman! Her youth and beauty are gone without recall, she knows that well and has no illusions in that respect, although she still has, I think, a great need for love.[11]

What was most deplorable in Marmion's opinion was Harriet's inept management of the household and, worse, of Louis, who was being used to deflect attention from the problems between mother and father.

Berlioz took action to resolve the crisis. It was time for him to further his career abroad: various posts in Paris for which he had been a candidate, notably that of Director of the Conservatoire in succession to Cherubini, were denied him, and although he had embarked on *La Nonne Sanglante* for the Opéra, Scribe was being dilatory over the libretto: in any case Berlioz did not seem fully involved in the project, perhaps because it smacked too much of an attempt to manufacture a popular success. Harriet was wholly opposed to his leaving Paris; so, without informing her, he made secret preparations for two concerts in Brussels, smuggled a trunk and all the necessary music out of the house, and left – with Marie Recio.[12] The subterfuges required were extensive. He arranged to keep the names of the proposed singers out of the newspapers, in case Harriet spotted Marie's name; he was obliged to supply all the musical parts for each concert: they weighed five hundred pounds, and he had to hire a postchaise to transport them as they could not be entrusted to the embryonic railway system. He made his escape, and left a letter behind for Harriet to tell her what was happening.

From Brussels he went as far as Frankfurt where he found his contacts unprepared; he deposited the music there and returned to Paris to placate Harriet, taking up residence with her again in the rue de Londres while he organised an immense concert and completed his plans for the long-awaited tour to Germany. 'Harriet takes her situation very badly,' he told Nanci, to whom he confided more as his relationship with Harriet deteriorated, 'but I hope to leave her in a more reasonable frame of mind than I found her in on my return from my first trip.'[13] This time Berlioz meant to travel alone, but Marie Recio proved no more amenable than Harriet and he was forced to give in to her. It was a decision which brought him considerable social and artistic embarrassment: Marie could never be relied on not to say something tactless; worse, she demanded to take part in his concerts. Berlioz, who admitted that she sang like a cat, did not lightly make compromises when his music was at risk, and by gradual degrees he managed to limit her participation. 'Sympathise with me,' he implored Morel, 'Marie insisted on singing at Mannheim, Stuttgart and Hechingen. The first two times it was tolerable, but the last . . .'[14] He even tried once to leave her behind, but she was too resourceful and soon caught up with him again.[15] At one point he thought to ease an awkward moment by referring to Marie as his second wife. It was an ominous experiment.

Harriet was not neglected materially. Berlioz took pains to send her money in addition to transferring to her the royalties for his arrangement of *Der Freischütz* at the Opéra (two hundred and thirty francs a performance).[16] She needed money, but it was Berlioz's presence that she longed for. 'Mother is very sad because she hasn't had any letters for a month', Louis wrote to his aunt Nanci. 'She cannot sleep, every day she expects a letter that doesn't arrive; I do not know where my father is.'[17] Adèle had kindly offered to have Harriet to stay at Saint-Chamond during Berlioz's absence, but she had not been able to accept. Her wistful regret is only too apparent in Berlioz's later comment: 'Henriette often talks to me about your peaceful and contented home; she is envious of it.'[18]

There was nothing peaceful or contented about the rue de Londres household where Berlioz returned in the summer of 1843 in an attempt to live with Harriet once more. She became increasingly strident; at some point she also took to drinking brandy heavily, partly no doubt to hide her unhappiness, perhaps partly to seek relief from her habitual ill-health.

Berlioz was clearly coming under pressure from Marie as well as from Harriet. George Osborne blamed the whole situation on an 'uncontrollable jealousy' of the lady who eventually became Berlioz's second wife.[19]

One evening after dining with me, we conversed on the usual painful subject, and as I saw but one remedy, I frankly told him of it. Much to my surprise he sat down and wrote a charming letter of adieu to the lady, which he left at her lodgings when walking out with me. Next day he told me that he had gone back to the house, took the letter from the servant and tore it up, his courage having failed him.

Again, one is struck by Berlioz's need to discuss endlessly 'the usual painful subject' with his friends, as well as by his dilemma whether to let Harriet or Marie go. Legouvé, not a wholly reliable raconteur, tells a story which, however, can only have come from Berlioz. At some later stage Harriet, staying in Montmartre, answered a ring to find a young and elegant woman at the door enquiring for Madame Berlioz. 'I am

Madame Berlioz', replied Harriet. The question was put again, with the same reply. The other's crushing retort was: 'No, you are not Madame Berlioz; you mean the old Madame Berlioz, the abandoned Madame Berlioz, but I am talking about the young, the pretty, the adored Madame Berlioz.' Legouvé presumed that the instigator of such an abominable act had been turned away; Berlioz replied that he could not bring himself to do it, because he loved her.[20] Whatever the accuracy in detail, these two anecdotes from close and trusted friends indicate the strength of Marie Recio's attraction for Berlioz, and of his painful commitment to her. All his relationships were intense.

If he could not turn Marie Recio away, equally he could not lightly abandon Harriet. The mutual agony was as prolonged and stormy as one of Strindberg's grimmer scenes. Berlioz poured out his heart to Nanci.

I hired an apartment in the country, she stayed there a fortnight and on her return my torment has begun again. An existence like this is impossible, there are shouts and abuse and curses and recriminations so revolting, so absurd, that they would drive me demented if I didn't know the cause of this lunacy. A by now ingrained habit, for drinking spirits, because I must tell you everything, fuels this state of madness. To crown it all, that itself is to my mind a subject of insuperable disgust – as you will understand. If you saw the confusion, her state of dress, her abandonment of every care for her appearance! It isn't just that she can't even keep an account of our expenses. She gets up in the middle of the night when she knows me to be asleep, comes into my room, shuts the doors, and starts shouting abuse at me for three hours on end sometimes till daybreak; the next day she asks me to forgive her, swears she loves me, that I could trample her under foot without affecting her love; and in the evening it all begins again. Truly, it's unbearable.[21]

In August Harriet went to stay in the country, at Sceaux, while Berlioz was away, to see if she could come to terms with her drinking. Berlioz wrote to her to encourage her, and Harriet's replies indignantly declared that she was cured. But when Berlioz arrived at the house without warning and went to her room, he found her in the most deplorable state, scarcely capable of speech; there was a glass on the table and the stink of spirits permeated the place. 'It's awful,' he told Adèle, 'she's become vast. They say spirits make you fat, and here is the proof.'[22]

After the autumn of 1844, Harriet and Berlioz lived apart. From this moment Berlioz had two households to maintain, that of Harriet – she eventually moved back to Montmartre – and that of Marie and her mother with whom he spent most of his time. Harriet remained at Sceaux through the autumn, pleading to be allowed to live with her husband again. He wandered Paris in freedom, working ten times harder than normal. A different *Hamlet* threatened to trouble him, with the arrival of Macready and Helen Faucit for a short season. 'Oh, I cried this morning . . . thinking of Hamlet, of Ophelia, *of all that is no longer,* of all that has become, has almost become, like poor Yorick.'[23]

Louis's presence was a comfort at first. He was placed *en pension* in Paris, but was free to visit his mother every Sunday. But when he was twelve he was sent away to school, to the lycée at Rouen. Harriet was heartbroken:

22 oct 1846
    Mon cher, bien cher Enfant,
J'ai été si triste après ton départ pour Rouen que j'eu tombé *très* malade et je suis encore souffrant – Hélas! mon cher fils je suis sur je ne puis pas supporter ma profond chagrin sans l'espèrence de ton avenir – Ton père n'est pas venu me voir depuis ton départ, il ne me écrit pas non plus – Dit moi *tout* ce qui'l ta communiqué à votre départ – *tout*, *tout*, LA VÉRITÉ, aussi tout de tes nouvells et croire moi ta pauvre mère affectionnée.

H. BERLIOZ

Rue Blanche 43

22 Octobre

    Je n'puis pas te renvoyer le papier parcequ'il faut payé seize sous pour l'pacquet au chemin de fer.
    M. et Mad. Vaniée et Joséphine t'aim toujour, on t'dit mille chose affectioné il sont tous tres amiable pour moi – aussi Abel ton camarde t'dit mille amities – Pour moi, Oh! person n'peut t'aimé comme ta pauvre mère.
    Dieu te Benis.
    Ecrit moi apres tu as reçu une lettre de ton père, *il faut écrire à lui tout suit. Il va partir bien tot.*[24]

The last ten years of Harriet's life are unrelievedly desolate. As for Berlioz, he supported Harriet, visited her, looked after her when he could when she was ill; he continued to feel love and affection for her, but he could not live with her. He began to spend long periods abroad, in Austria, Hungary, Russia. In the autumn of 1847, after taking Louis to La Côte for a happy fortnight to stay with the ailing Dr Berlioz, he accompanied his son to Rouen before travelling on to London to take up an appointment at Drury Lane as conductor of a new opera company. Harriet was alone.

The blows fell almost as frequently upon Berlioz, although of a less severe kind. The Drury Lane venture collapsed with the bankruptcy of the promoter. Berlioz returned to a Paris torn by revolution only to learn, as he feared, that his father had died. Harriet survived a strange shooting incident: walking in her garden, she was fired at by a bandit, the ball embedding itself in a tree two inches away from her.[25] In October, death came even closer. She suffered what was to be the first of many severe strokes.[26] She was partly paralysed, with movement on her right side heavily restricted, and her speech was badly affected: in time she became able to speak a little English, but no French. There were four further strokes, and in the April of 1849 Berlioz nursed Harriet through an illness attributed to the cholera epidemic. It hardly seems possible that she could survive so much for so long, or that Berlioz himself was able to sustain his public, let alone his creative, life through this and other crises.

For the last years of her life Harriet existed, nursed night and day, unable to move or barely to speak. Louis wrote to her regularly, and came to see her on leave from his apprentice voyages when he began training as a marine officer. Berlioz spent what time he could spare with her in Montmartre. The only way she could make herself understood was for someone to guess what she wanted and ask, 'Est-ce cela?' so that she could reply 'Oui' or 'Non'.[27] One day Berlioz brought with him a portrait of Harriet, taken twenty-two years before in all the poetic beauty of which not a trace remained. Harriet cried bitterly when she saw the picture; and yet she thanked him warmly 'for the sorrow it had caused her . . . can there be such sweetness in regrets and memories?' She cried, too, when Berlioz was able to make her understand that his sister Nanci had died, without being able to utter a single word.[28] At times even the tears would not flow.

In 1854, when she seemed at last to be dying, Louis was granted a short leave from Cherbourg and was able to spend a few hours beside her bed. On 3 March she died.

In chapter 59 of his memoirs, completed later the same year, and which serves as a kind of epilogue to the work, Berlioz describes his reactions to Harriet's passing in what becomes a memorial tribute to her:

I had been out of the house for two hours when one of the women looking after her came to fetch me and hurried me home. It was all over: she had just breathed her last. A sheet already covered her. I drew it back and kissed her pale forehead for the last time. Her portrait, which I had given her a year before and which, painted in the days of her splendour, showed her as she had been in all her radiant beauty and genius, hung beside the bed on which she lay inert, disfigured by disease.

I will not attempt to describe the grief that took possession of me. It was complicated by a feeling which, though it had never before been so intense, I had always found the hardest of all to bear – a sense of pity. In the midst of all the regrets for our lost love, a

40. *La Mort d'Ophélie*. Title page of first edition of version for soprano or tenor, Paris, 1848.

wave of terrible, overmastering pity swept over me at the thought of everything she had suffered: her bankruptcy, before we were married; her accident; the deep disappointment of her last unsuccessful appearance on the Paris stage; her decision, which she made voluntarily but never ceased to lament, to give up her beloved art; the eclipse of her reputation; the spectacle of second-rate imitators, men as well as women, achieving fame and fortune; our bitter domestic strife; her ungovernable jealousy, which in the end had cause; our separation; the death of all her relatives; the enforced absence of her son; my long and frequent journeys; her distress, half injured pride, half genuine concern, at being to me a constant financial burden which she knew I could barely support; her delusion that she had forfeited the regard of the English public through her attachment to France; her broken heart; her vanished beauty; her ruined health; her growing physical suffering; the loss of speech and movement; the impossibility of making herself understood in any way; the long vista of death and oblivion stretching before her as she lay slowly, inexorably dying. My brain shrivels in my skull at the horror, the pity of it! . . .

I had to attend to the last sad duties on my own. The Protestant pastor who was required for the ceremony, and whose parish covered the suburbs of Paris, lived on the far side of town in the rue de M. Le Prince. At eight in the evening I went to notify him. One of the streets on our route had been taken up, and the cab had to make a detour which took us past the Odéon. The theatre was brightly lit for a play then much in vogue. There, twenty-six years before, I had seen *Hamlet* for the first time. It was there one night that the fame of my poor dead wife blazed up like a meteor; there that I had seen a whole audience break down and weep at the sight of Ophelia in the ecstasy of her grief and heart-rending madness; there that I had seen Miss Smithson, recalled after the final scene, reappear on the stage, dazed, almost appalled by the magnitude of her triumph, and tremblingly acknowledge the applause of the intellectual élite of France. There I saw Juliet for the first and last time. Beneath that arcade I paced on many winter nights in a fever of disquiet. Through that door I saw her enter for a rehearsal of *Othello*. At the time she was unaware of my existence; and had anyone pointed to the pale, dishevelled youth leaning against a pillar of the Odéon, staring after her with haunted eyes, and had prophesied that this unknown young man would one day become her husband, she would have considered him an impertinent fool.

And yet . . . he it is who now prepares your last journey, poor Ophelia, and who will say to the priest in Laertes's words: 'What ceremony else?'; he who was so cruel to you, who was made to suffer so much by you, having suffered so much for you; he who, with all the wrongs he did, can say, like Hamlet:

> . . . Forty thousand brothers
> Could not, with all their quantity of love,
> Make up my sum.'[29]

The next day she was buried in Montmartre. Baron Taylor, Joseph d'Ortigue, Briseux, Léon de Wailly and a 'few other kind spirits' attended the funeral. 'Twenty-five years before,' claimed Berlioz,

all intellectual Paris would have been at her funeral . . . Every poet, painter and sculptor, the entire acting profession, to whom she had given such noble object lessons in the art of movement and gesture and pose, every musician who, listening to her, had sensed the music in her tenderness and the terrible truth in her woe, every lover, every dreamer, aye and more than one philosopher, would have walked in tears behind her coffin.

When Louis's birth was registered, Harriet was described as 'artiste dramatique'; in the entry for her death, there is only the phrase 'sans profession'.

Writing to Adèle at the time, Berlioz seemed more appreciative of the support of his friends. 'A great number of writers and artists' accompanied the coffin to the nearby cemetery; Berlioz remained behind in the garden, overwhelmed by his memories of the past – not simply of the dreadful contrast between Harriet as she had become and Harriet as she once was, but also of the changes in their son Louis:

he is no longer like the dear child I used to watch run up and down these garden paths . . . O cursed ability to recall the past! Perhaps that's the reason I have so painfully succeeded in evoking such impressions in some of my works.[30]

Gautier paid his tribute. Dumas, who almost alone had remained faithful to Marie Dorval in the neglect and destitution of her last years, wrote in *Le Mousquetaire*:

A woman who possessed a great spirit, great beauty and great talent has passed away in the Paris which was her adopted home for more than twenty years: Mme Hector Berlioz is dead. Every artist knows the moving story of the young maestro who, seeing the beautiful English girl playing Shakespeare's heroines at the Odéon fell so deeply in love with her that he managed to unite his poetic, stormy life to Miss Smithson's. Alas, death has come in these days to knock at the door of the gifted couple, and has left a dreadful void: Mme Hector Berlioz is dead.[31]

Jules Janin, in the *Journal des Débats*, recalled Harriet's impact as the interpreter of Shakespeare for a generation:

How sadly, how swiftly they pass, these legendary divinities, frail children of Shakespeare and Corneille. Alas, it was not so long ago – we were young then, filled with the thoughtless pride of youth – that Juliet, one summer evening on her balcony above the Verona road, with Romeo at her side, trembling with rapture, listened – and heard the nightingale, and the lark, the herald of the morn. She listened with a pale, dreamy intensity, bewitching fire in her half-averted eyes. And her voice! a golden voice, pure and vibrant, a voice through which the language and genius of Shakespeare in all their rich, perennial vitality and force found superb utterance. When she moved, when she spoke, her charm mastered us. A whole society stirred to the magic of this woman.

She was barely twenty, she was called Miss Smithson, and she conquered as of right the hearts and minds of that audience on whom the light of the new truth shone. All unconsciously she became a new passion, a poem unheard till then, an embodied revolution. She pointed the way for Madame Dorval, Frédérick Lemaître, Malibran, Victor Hugo, Berlioz. She was called Juliet, she was called Ophelia, and was the inspiration for Delacroix himself when he drew his touching picture. Ophelia is shown in the act of falling, one hand slipping from the branch to which it still clings, while the other clutches to her fair bosom the last sad garland; the hem of her robe is about to meet the rising waters; around her a weeping landscape, and far off, hastening towards her, the wave that will engulf her in her sodden clothes and drag 'the poor wretch from her melodious lay to muddy death'.

She was called, lastly – this admirable and touching Miss Smithson – by another name (Malibran bore it too): Desdemona; and the Moor, as he embraced her, called her his 'fair warrior'. I see her now just as she was then, white-faced as the Venetian woman in *Angelo, Tyrant of Padua*. She is alone, listening to the rain and the moaning of the wind, the beautiful lass, enchanting and doomed, whom Shakespeare out of love and respect lapped round with his noblest poetry. She is alone, and afraid; an unutterable unease troubles the depths of her soul. Her arms are bare, a corner of her white shoulder is visible. The bareness had something pure and sanctified about it, the holiness of the sacrificial victim, the woman about to die. Miss Smithson was marvellous in this scene. She was more like a vision from on high than a creature of our clay. And now she is dead. She died a week ago, still dreaming of the glory that comes so swiftly and so swiftly fades. What images lie there, what worlds of poignant regret! In my youth they used to sing a chorus in homage to Juliet Capulet, a sad funeral march, with the same cry going through it, repeated again and again: 'Throw flowers! throw flowers!' So they passed into the gloomy crypt where Juliet slept, and the dark melody ran its course, telling of the chill and terror of those mortuary vaults. 'Throw flowers! throw flowers! she is dead,' the dirge sang, like an Aeschylean hymn. 'Juliet is dead (throw flowers!). Death lies on her like an untimely frost (throw flowers!). Our instruments to melancholy bells are turned. Our wedding cheer to a sad burial feast. Our bridal flowers serve for a buried corpse!'[32]

By his quotation 'Throw flowers!', Janin enfolds Harriet's obsequies within the funeral procession of the *Roméo et Juliette* Symphony. Liszt's letter of consolation similarly relates Harriet's life to Berlioz's art: 'She inspired you, you loved her and sang of her; her task was done.' The comment might be interpreted as a callous dismissal of Harriet as a mere appendage, an object; in the context, it is more appropriate to think of it as a sensitive compliment, one that Harriet would have appreciated, since it implies an enduring value and significance for her life as an artist.

Berlioz's letter to Louis expresses his sense of loss more simply and personally:

My poor dear Louis,
By this time you will have received my letter of yesterday, and you know everything. I am alone, writing to you in the large room at Montmartre, next to her deserted bedroom. I have just come from the cemetery, after laying two wreaths, one for you and one for me, on her grave. I do not know what I am doing, nor why I have come back here. The servants will remain for a few days. They are putting everything in order, and I shall do my best to make as much as possible for you out of what there is. I have kept

some of her hair. Do not lose the pin I gave her. You will never know what we suffered, your mother and I, but it was those very sufferings that made us attached to one another. It was as impossible for me to live with her as to leave her. At all events, she saw you before she died.[33]

Berlioz could never relinquish anything or anyone that he had loved. On 23 March he wrote to Louis again:

I am going to have a watch chain made for you with your mother's hair, and I hope you will keep it faithfully. I am also having a bracelet made for my sister, and am keeping the rest myself.[34]

Seven months later, Berlioz married Marie Recio, although he knew how much this would upset Louis. He felt he owed it to Marie to make her at last the second Mme Berlioz. She died in 1862, and was buried in a vault in the larger Montmartre cemetery. Berlioz was informed that the smaller cemetery where Harriet was buried was to be demolished, and he made arrangements for the transfer of her remains.

A municipal officer, who had orders to witness the exhumation, was waiting for me. The grave had already been opened. On my arrival, the grave-digger jumped down into it. The coffin, though ten years in the ground, was still intact; only the lid had decayed from damp. Instead of lifting out the whole coffin, the gravedigger wrenched at the rotting planks, which came away with a hideous crack, exposing the coffin's contents. The gravedigger bent down and with his two hands picked up the head, already parted from the body – the ungarlanded, withered, hairless head of 'poor Ophelia' – and placed it in a new coffin ready for it at the edge of the grave. Then, bending down again, with difficulty he gathered in his arms the headless trunk and limbs, a blackish mass which the shroud still clung to, like a damp sack with a lump of pitch in it. It came away with a dull sound, and a smell. The municipal officer stood a few yards off, watching. Seeing me leaning back against a cypress tree, he called out, 'Don't stay there, M. Berlioz, come over here, come over here!' And as if the grotesque must also have its part in this grim scene, he added (mistaking the word), 'Ah, poor inhumanity!' A few moments later we followed the hearse down the hill to the larger cemetery where the new vault stood ready, open. Henriette's remains were laid in it. The two dead women lie there now in peace . . .'[35]

11 Romantic image

ᴈᴧᴇᴈᴧᴇᴈᴧᴇᴈᴧᴇᴈᴧᴇᴈᴧᴇᴈᴧᴇᴈᴧᴇᴈᴧᴇᴈᴧᴇᴈᴧᴇᴈᴧᴇᴈ

Without making such extravagant claims as Berlioz and Janin did under the weight of grief and sympathy, the reflection of Harriet Smithson and her art as an actress can be found in several areas. There was first her impact on the acting profession which, though not exclusively, was most vividly experienced in France. Stendhal, writing in the *New Monthly Magazine* for June 1828, was inclined to temper the enthusiasm of his assessment by belittling the competition:

Our tragic actresses have grown old and ugly and the public is tired of them. You may therefore imagine how this enhances the reputation of Miss Smithson, who seldom appears on the stage without making the female and many of the male members of the audience shed tears.[1]

He then reflects on the limited praise afforded to Kemble, Kean and Macready and concludes:

Finally, however, it is only Miss Smithson whose success has been consistently remarkable. When she played the part of the widowed Queen of King Edward in *Richard III*, the scene in which she parts with her children left not a single eye in the house which was dry. It should be mentioned, however, that displays of maternal tenderness are quite the fashion in France at the moment; and with us fashion in anything, whether good or bad, is all-powerful.

Stendhal was in Italy when the season opened and could not have been present at the earlier performances of the sequence. His comments therefore apply to the more passive aspect of Harriet's acting, her ability to extract pathos from situations of distress, as in the role of Jane Shore. There was palpably an element of fashion in the audience's response: measured in terms of volume of tears shed, Harriet rated very highly. The actors and actresses, however, who attended the English theatre so regularly were drawn by the demonstration of a particular technique rather than an effect. To some extent this interest, too, might be ascribed to fashion; it was in part necessity, for French Classical dramaturgy made few demands on the actor when it came to dying publicly by degrees, and the new drama, including adaptations and translations of Shakespeare, would call for a distinctive range of interpretative skills. To note how Kean or Kemble handled the pillow or the sword of ice-brook's temper was professional common sense. The classical actors sought examples which would help them revive the jaded traditions of the Comédie-Française; the boulevard actors, such as Frédérick Lemaître or Marie Dorval, found a style and spirit of acting which was attuned to the attempts by the Romantic writers to create a different and defiantly contemporary drama.

So far as Harriet's particular contribution was concerned, the quality of truthfulness, generally remarked on in the English performances, was especially distinct in her portrait of madness. A direct comparison was drawn with Mlle Mars, who played a mad role in Soumet's *Emilia*: Mlle Mars possessed 'more grace and intention', but was not 'so truly mad'. According to the *Corsaire*, 'Miss Smithson has shown us true madness in Ophelia; despite the efforts of our own actresses and perhaps through the failings of our authors, we have never seen it before.'[2] The movement from presentation to representation is reflected in a report of an actress being advised to visit an asylum so as to authenticate her portrayal by first-hand observation.[3] Harriet's definition struck an audience as bringing them closer to the thing itself, like Géricault's studies of madmen: it was true to nature, primitive, naive; however graceful the idea or emotion in expression, the actress concealed the art which enabled her to present it, appearing wholly unconscious of the effect she was producing. The connection between Harriet's style of acting and that of Mlle Mars was revived in 1830 when the latter took the part of Doña Sol in *Hernani*, the most analysed production of the century: Mlle Mars created an image of youth and beauty by uniting 'the pathos of Mme Dorval and the primitive ingenuousness of Miss Smithson'.[4]

The identification of Harriet with Ophelia lingered. In 1840 Gautier reviewed the dancer Fanny Elssler's interpretation of Nina:

In her hands the mad girl of the comic opera has become Shakespearean, a worthy sister to Ophelia, a white and slender vision whose eyes alone have life, lit with a feverish ardour in a marble-white face that has the pallor of a Greek statue in moonlight . . . As a mime, Mlle Elssler has no rival, and we can hardly think of anyone but Miss Smithson to compare with her.[5]

The year before, commenting on the same ballerina in *La Gipsy*, a *ballet d'action* in which mime played as important a part as pure dance (and which once appeared in the Opéra repertory in conjunction with act one of *Benvenuto Cellini*), Gautier declared that in the scene where she was falsely accused of theft and where her identity was revealed, Mlle Elssler rose to

the most sublime heights of tragedy . . . Noble pride in innocence, energy, tears, grief, love, intoxicating joy – she runs through the whole gamut of human emotions. Only Miss Smithson or Mlle Dorval could have attained such transports of pathos, such forceful miming.[6]

Marie Dorval had herself earlier been compared to Harriet, for instance when playing Marguerite in a version of *Faust*. Gautier's comments elsewhere about Marie Dorval – that her talent was of a passionate nature, that she did not neglect art but that art came to her from inspiration, that she put herself in the position of the character she was playing and became that character[7] – could be applied to Harriet as suggesting the broad French perception of her Shakespearean acting. The means by which she conveyed that sense of passionate identity were principally her command of movement, gesture and pose: the silent expression of feeling. Any judgment that reaction to Harriet's acting was an ephemeral question of fashion must be modified by the range of reference to it as an absolute standard of excellence years after her career had effectively ended.

Janin placed Harriet's importance in a wider context. Again, he focused upon the moment when she came, 'crowned with flowers and wisps of straw, to scatter upon an invisible tomb imaginary roses', and declared that 'at that very moment we understood the genius and drama which became manifest in that delightful creature, and that the poet Shakespeare was in fact the inspired poet of the great tragic actresses'.[8] Until Miss Smithson, tragedy was a male preserve. Janin argued that Harriet prepared the way for Rachel by accustoming the French public to seeing tragedy as belonging to the women's province as much as to the men's. Janin was, by his critical advocacy, largely responsible for Rachel's initial acceptance. He emphasised the connection by an anecdote in which Rachel, seeing one day a portrait of Harriet in the role of Ophelia, exclaimed with emotion, 'There is the poor woman to whom I owe so much!'[9]

The relationship between Harriet's stage image and graphic art is more complex. It has been argued that 'with the English theatre it was realised that movement and gesture could convey psychological weight', at once providing 'a valid alternative to the static and declamatory style of the French theatre'. After the 1827–28 performances, a 'sense of the poetic possibilities of movement became a feature of Shakespearean interpretation by the most advanced artists'.[10] Until that season, there had been a dearth of French illustrators of Shakespeare, and the series of coloured lithographs by Devéria and Boulanger published as *Souvenirs du théâtre anglais à Paris* in 1827 have a special interest, both as the first substantial interpretation of Shakespeare in France and for their close relationship to the stage performance. Janin's comment about the emphasis on the tragic actress is borne out by the fact that nine of the twelve principal illustrations feature Ophelia, Juliet, Desdemona and Jane Shore, the exceptions being Hamlet and Horatio in the graveyard, Romeo in despair at Friar Laurence's cell, and the attempted murder of Cassio and Roderigo. There is a second, smaller illustration of Ophelia in addition to the main one which shows Harriet's *jeu muet*: in this her hair falls long to her knees, and the image suggests less a posed effect than the arrest of movement by taking the eye to the pronounced curve of her hip and trunk, and by emphasising details such as the gracefully separated fingers.

Delacroix's lithographs and paintings provide a far more profound insight into Shakespeare. As early as 1817 or 1818 he announced his interest by signing a letter 'Yorick'; in 1820 he made a watercolour drawing of the farewell of Romeo and Juliet. There were paintings of scenes from *Othello*, which he saw in the shape of Rossini's *Otello* in Paris as well as interpreted by Kean in London in 1825 and, almost certainly, by Charles Kemble and Harriet in 1827 in Paris. Other plays which he took subjects from were *Macbeth* and *Antony and Cleopatra*. The tragedy which provoked the most extensive response was *Hamlet*.

Two works which have a close relationship, at least in time, to the Paris performances are the lithograph of the Gravedigger scene published in 1828, and a watercolour drawing of Hamlet killing Polonius, which has been described as 'less like a compositional study than a memory sketch'.[11] There follows the series of lithographs, carried out in 1834–35 and 1843, thirteen of which were published that year in a limited edition. Three other plates, discarded from that sequence, were published together with the original thirteen in a second posthumous edition in 1864.

The relationship between the lithographs and stage performance is much looser in literal terms than those of Devéria and Boulanger: whereas theirs were commemorative, these are interpretations.

41. Othello and Desdemona. Painting by E. Delacroix, 1847–9.

Delacroix wrote to Gautier: 'The majority of these plates were done some time ago and having suffered through imperfect reproduction they are in a position of even greater disfavour with the public who prefer the rendered and polished to the search for expression.'[12]

Yet Delacroix was closely interested in the nature of stage performance, as his own accounts of theatre visits demonstrate, quite apart from the inherently dramatic qualities of his compositions and the derivation of many of his subjects (*Pénitence de Jane Shore*, *Mort de Sardanapale*, to cite works of contrasting scale). For the figure of Hamlet, he used a female model. Several of the moments chosen by Delacroix indicate that he must have been relying as much on his own interpretation of the text as on recollections of a particular production. One of the lithographs of 1843 shows Hamlet on the point of drawing his sword to kill the praying Claudius, a scene which was customarily omitted in contemporary English performance and which was certainly not played in Paris in 1827–28. Again, his inclusion of two gravediggers suggests a response to an idealised and imagined realisation, rather than to memories of the 1827 version. The powerful lithograph of the play within the play, with its asymmetrical grouping and focus on Hamlet, is obviously an interpretation, not a record; yet it succeeds in being far more theatrical than the traditional tableau of Devéria, and not just because it depicts a more heightened moment, the pouring of the poison into Gonzago's ear. Delacroix's detail reflects contemporary description: the fan, Hamlet's short jacket and the locket round his neck, for instance.

The one lithograph which disturbs the pattern is the 1843 plate of Ophelia drowning, an interesting choice of subject since it alone depicts what is described rather than enacted in the play. Nineteenth-century stage practice saw a steady growth of interest in the figure of Ophelia, to which Harriet contributed. It became the custom to intensify the force of Gertrude's description by bringing on a bier in the background, and Sarah Bernhardt was the first Ophelia to be carried upon it to provide a physical presence rather than a lay figure. This tradition may itself have been nurtured by Delacroix's work. Janin, perhaps carried away on the tide of his own rhetoric, wrote that Harriet 'was the inspiration for Delacroix himself when he drew his touching image of Ophelia'.[13]

Three paintings also exist, one as early as 1838, of the same subject. There is a strongly sensual quality in the image, created by the loose, partly transparent clothing and the trance-like expression on Ophelia's features, as she lies poised between life and death. The mood is less poignant than quietly triumphant, with the self-absorption that recalls the figure of Aischeh, the Bactrian woman who hangs herself in *La Mort de Sardanapale*. The same sense of barely suppressed eroticism is present in the lithograph of the mad Ophelia, kneeling, with bare arms and prominent breasts; this illustration reproduces the traditional stage properties of the veil mistaken for a shroud, and the hair decorated with straw like a crown of thorns. Delacroix's works at the least testify to the potency of Ophelia as an image for the Romantic period, a symbol both of wounded, self-absorbed sexuality and of the destruction of innocence by an indifferent world. The sculptor Auguste Préault, who is mentioned as having attended the Odéon performances, showed a bas-relief of the same subject in 1849.

There are two further iconographical extensions of Harriet's image, though each is modulated through Berlioz's music. One lies within the oeuvre of Fantin-Latour, some of whose work was rigidly realistic, but who also experimented in the style of the *école de fantaisie*, and created a number of visionary pieces inspired by the music of Wagner, Schumann, Brahms and Berlioz. (There seems a faint biographical echo of Berlioz and Harriet in the circumstances in which Fantin-Latour met his future wife, Mlle Victoria Dubourg – not in his case in the theatre, but in the Louvre, where each was copying Corregio's *Mystic Marriage of St Catherine*.) Fantin-Latour's lithograph of the artist at the Ball in the *Fantastique* is the first attempt to give graphic form to Berlioz's *idée fixe*. Michael Ayrton made a series of four wash-drawings of the same subject in 1967, and commented that he believed Berlioz 'blended his Ariel with his Juliet in the music as I have been forced to blend them in my drawings of the *idée fixe*. In a sense, or at least metaphorically, they become one.'[14] Ayrton also produced drawings which give an impression of Harriet both as Juliet and in her own person.

The image of Ophelia entered French literature through Hugo, in his *Orientales*, published in 1829. Several of the poems in this collection were given epigraphs from Shakespeare. *Fantômes*, composed in April 1828, may be a point of reference for the *Symphonie Fantastique*:

Elle aimait trop le bal, c'est ce qui l'a tuée,
Le bal éblouissant! le bal délicieux!
Sa cendre encor frémit, doucement remuée,
Quand, dans la nuit sereine, une blanche nuée
Danse autour du croissant des cieux.[15]

Berlioz may have known Boulanger's engravings based on *Fantômes*;

42. *Le Bal*. Lithograph by H. Fantin-Latour.

but the most arresting association for him would be the image with which the poem concludes:

> Le pauvre enfant, de fête en fête promenée,
> De ce bouquet charmant arrangeait les couleurs;
> Mais qu'elle a passé vite, hélas! l'infortunée!
> Ainsi qu'Ophélia par le fleuve entraînée,
> Elle est morte en cueillant des fleurs!

Musset, deeply influenced by Shakespeare, referred frequently to Ophelia. Later in the century Rimbaud made the image of Ophelia the centre of an entire poem:

> Sur l'onde calme et noire où dorment les étoiles
> La blanche Ophélia flotte comme un grand lys,
> Flotte très lentement, couchée en ses longs voiles . . .
> On entend dans les bois lointains des hallalis.
>
> Voici plus de mille ans que la triste Ophélie
> Passe, fantôme blanc, sur le long fleuve noir.
> Voici plus de mille ans que sa douce folie
> Murmure sa romance à la brise du soir.

Harriet's performance as Ophelia seems appropriately celebrated by lyric poetry: 'O pâle Ophélia! belle comme la neige!'[16]

The playwrights who saw the 1827 season were stimulated in part by the acting and details of interpretation, but comprehensively by their exposure to Shakespeare's dramatic structure. Their reaction was two-fold: first, to use Shakespeare as an example, a set of criteria, an aesthetic ideal, as Hugo did theoretically in the Preface to *Cromwell*; secondly, they started to provide a more Shakespearean version of a number of Shakespeare tragedies in French. Vigny and Emile Deschamps completed their translation of *Romeo and Juliet* by the end of March 1828 and it was accepted by the *Comité de lecture* of the Théâtre-Français the next month. This, though encouraging, was a far cry from actual performance, which did not occur until 1905: Vigny ascribed the initial delay to the reluctance of the fifty-year old Mlle Mars to risk ridicule in so youthful a role as Juliet (it was even more unthinkable for her to step aside for a younger actress). The production of a version by Soulié at the Odéon was both an indication of the vogue for Shakespeare and a reasonable explanation for an initial postpone-ment. Deschamps, in his *Préface des Etudes Françaises et Etrangères*, called for young actors, willing to play every kind of role, and prepared to study 'the expressive mime and natural style of declamation of the

43. *The Death of Ophelia*. Lithograph by E. Delacroix, 1843.

great English actors'; he also looked forward to a fresh presentation of one of Shakespeare's great tragedies, in French, 'avec toute la pompe d'une mise en scène soignée'.[17]

Vigny responded to the challenge. *Le More de Venise* was accepted by the Théâtre-Français in July 1829 and performed in October when Hugo's *Marion de Lorme* ran into difficulties with the censor. The period of rehearsal was stormy. Ciceri was entrusted with the décor, Albertin was the stage director, but Taylor and Vigny also attended rehearsals and Dumas often joined them at Vigny's request. Michelot began to rehearse the part of Iago but quarrelled with Joanny (the Othello) and was replaced by Périer. Mlle Mars played Desdemona. The excellence of the production, together with Auguste Briseux's organisation of the claque, eventually secured public acceptance, though the overall impact of the play was a little restrained. Vigny seems to have approached the project with the objectivity of a man conducting a literary and dramatic experiment – which he undoubtedly was; but a certain lack of passion and the difficulties of translating Shakespeare into French brought about a transmutation which necessarily softened the bold outlines and colours of the original. At the same time, his work represented an astonishing advance both in its comparative fidelity to the forms of language of the Shakespearean original and in its understanding of Shakespearean structure. Mlle Mars pronounced the notorious word 'mouchoir', and was widely admitted to have been magnificent in the Willow scene. She and Périer showed an ease born from long experience of playing in comedy which made them able to attempt the 'natural' style of acting which was part of the English tradition and which met the intentions of the Romantic dramatists. The production holds great historical interest, for it reflected English theatrical tradition, drawing on memories of the 1827–28 season and incorporating detailed advice from Young, particularly in the acting of Périer as Iago. Vigny, like Dumas and Hugo, involved himself enthusiastically with the visual concepts of his plays and with details of stage presentation and business. 'I was able to pass on to Mlle Mars,' he recalled, 'and to those who created the role of the Moor in French, my ideas, my intentions, and the Shakespearean traditions preserved in England.'[18] An unusual feature of the text is the frequent use of stage directions, which both describe the stage picture on occasion and also in places give precise timings for some of the actions. In act five scene two, where Othello enters Desdemona's bedchamber, the scene heading is pictorial: 'Une chambre à coucher. – Desdemona endormie sur son lit, à moitié déshabillée, en robe blanche, nu-pieds ses cheveux noirs épars.'

Othello enters, holding in his left hand a lamp, in his right a sword. Othello's speech, 'C'est la cause, ô mon âme!', is punctuated by stage directions: 'Il pose son épée et sa lampe sur une table', 'en regardant Desdemona', 'Il l'embrasse', 'Il fond en larmes'.

The description of Desdemona agrees with the engraving made by Devéria and Boulanger of Harriet as Desdemona, although that illustration records the moment of the murder itself; the lamp and the sword accord with Kean's stage practice. Behind the stagecraft of *Le More de Venise* lay Vigny's close observation of the English theatre's performances.

No one apart from Berlioz responded more exuberantly to the Odéon performances than Dumas. For him, that first exposure to *Hamlet* was the discovery of a new world, and he likened himself to Adam waking in Eden on the first day of his creation. In the English acting he found what he was searching for: 'it was men of the theatre forgetting that they were on stage; it was that fabricated life which was transformed into actual life by the power of art; it was that reality of word and gesture which turned actors into living creations of flesh and blood complete with every virtue, passion and weakness, rather than into stilted, impassive, bombastic and sententious heroes. "O Shakespeare, merci! O Kemble et Smithson, merci! Merci à mon Dieu! merci à mes anges de poésies!"' [19]

Dumas watched as the English repertory unfolded, and then set himself to read and dissect the works of Shakespeare, in whom he claimed to find the dramatic qualities of Corneille, the comedy of Molière, the originality of Calderón, the philosophy of Goethe, and the passion of Schiller. The first fruit of this programme was *Christine*, a historical verse drama accepted by the Théâtre-Français in 1828, though not acted until 1830 in a revised version at the Odéon. Thwarted by the opposition of Mlle Mars, Dumas determined to storm the citadel, and for his next attempt offered a historical drama in prose on *Henri III et sa Cour*, a subject which he chanced upon when his eye caught an arresting paragraph in a book lying open in a friend's office.

The work is more melodrama than drama, and owes as much to Pixérécourt's practice as to the theories of Hugo. The characters have no conflicting elements within their composition; the dialogue veers between the simplistic and the strident. Yet the play is highly polished in its construction, and undeniably theatrical. The influence of

Shakespeare, and especially the Shakespeare plays which Dumas had lately seen, is self evident, so far as violence of action and stage imagery are concerned: the recollection of Kemble as Othello stifling Harriet as Desdemona seems to have been Dumas's point of dramatic comparison. Within a historical framework, the emphasis is placed on love outside marriage, and specifically the revenge exacted by the jealous Duc de Guise against the Duchesse and her lover Saint-Mégrin. The incriminating handkerchief makes an early appearance, when the Duc's hand falls idly upon one left in a compromising location by his wife, and it returns later to stifle the death cries of her faithful page. Other more or less direct 'quotations' include an escape from a first floor window by a rope ladder, and the Duchesse's appearance in act five with her hair adorned with flowers. The poisoned chalice, the on-stage wounding of the Duchesse by the cruel grip of the Duc's iron gauntlet, the Duchesse keeping Saint-Mégrin's pursuers at bay by thrusting her arm through the bolts of the door, may all reasonably be attributed to Dumas's response to certain elements of Shakespearean drama as well as to his reading of Scott. Mlle Mars and Joanny performed the two principal roles. The play's first night was a triumph for the almost unknown Dumas, in part because he had persuaded the Duc d'Orléans to attend the opening night with numerous guests, and the play ran for thirty-eight performances.[20] The fact that a work of this nature could be performed at all with such a cast at the Théâtre-Français was indication of a significant change in attitude, though the movement would not be confirmed until *Hernani* the following year.

Besides the general influence of Shakespeare on Dumas, and the excitement which the theatricality of the productions he saw aroused in him, there is one additional link which should be mentioned. The English season furnished Dumas with the subject of what is arguably his most original play, *Kean*. Dumas's Kean is an imaginative creation, and the author never allowed the restrictions of historical accuracy to confine him. All the same, the original Kean is recognisably evoked, an achievement which was helped by the memories of the actor's behaviour in Paris in 1828 and by Frédérick Lemaître's uncanny resemblance to him. In Sartre's version Kean performs, in the play within the play, an extract from *Othello*; in Dumas's script, Kean is acting the balcony scene from *Romeo and Juliet* when he steps out of character to harangue the Prince of Wales and declare, 'I am not Romeo . . . I am Falstaff.'

Dumas responded to some of the more obvious and external features of Shakespeare; one feels he would have been even more enthusiastic about Webster's *Duchess of Malfi* or Middleton and Rowley's *Changeling*. Hugo's study of Shakespeare was more profound. For him, the English performances served to confirm and highlight what he already sensed. As with Dumas, Hugo's plays contain numerous echoes of Shakespearean motifs. In *Marion de Lorme*, the workmen's scene recalls the gravediggers in *Hamlet*, and in *Angelo* Tisbe gives Caterina a potion which results in her being presumed dead and taken to the burial vault. In *Hernani*, the Shakespearean influence seems less simplistic and more pervasive. It would be satisfactory to suggest a link betwen the 'portrait' scene in Gertrude's chamber and 'La galerie des portraits' in act three of *Hernani*, and Hugo's reading of *Hamlet* may indeed have helped suggest the setting. In contemporary performance of *Hamlet*, however, the English practice was to use pictures in little 'not much bigger than two large coins or medallions', carried in the pocket or on a chain round the neck, and it was not until 1840 that Macready transformed Gertrude's closet into a royal picture gallery. But the scene in the tomb – 'Les caveaux qui renferment le tombeau de Charlemagne à Aix-la-Chapelle' – and the swearing on the cross of the reversed sword are familiar Shakespearean effects, while the southern setting, the palace intrigue and the sense of doomed love help to explain why the Romantics found Shakespeare's material so congenial. Indeed, the scenario of act five seems like a distillation of *Romeo and Juliet*, with an echo of *Hamlet* provided by the masked figure who moves like a ghost from hell among the young seigneurs who stand on the terrace like the maskers before the house of Capulet. There is even a resemblance between the stage designs for this act and the settings used for the balcony scene in the English theatre. Hernani's drinking of the poison and Doña Sol's decision to follow him to death recall the double suicides of Romeo and Juliet and Antony and Cleopatra – as does the language:

> Mort! non pas! nous dormons.
> Il dort. C'est mon époux, vois-tu. Nous nous aimons.
> Nous sommes couchés là. C'est notre nuit de noce.[21]

It is, in fact, in his use of language that Hugo seems most to reflect Shakespeare, first in his ability to create a texture of imagery and secondly in his understanding of character as essentially poetic. In the moments before they hear the distant sounding of the horn which brings their doom as surely as the lark heralds the separation of Romeo and Juliet, Hernani and Doña Sol explore their brief happiness in a purely lyrical mode:

HERNANI: Ah! qui n'oublierait tout à cette voix céleste!
   Ta parole est un chant où rien d'humain ne reste.
   Et, comme un voyageur, sur un fleuve emporté,
   Qui glisse sur les eaux par un beau soir d'été
   Et voit fuir sous ses yeux mille plaines fleuries,
   Ma pensée entraînée erre en tes rêveries!
DOÑA SOL: Ce silence est trop noir, ce calme est trop profond.
   Dis, ne voudrais-tu pas voir une étoile au fond?
   Ou qu'une voix des nuits tendre et délicieuse,
   S'élevant tout à coup, chantât? . . .
HERNANI: (*souriant*)   Capricieuse!
   Tout à l'heure on fuyait la lumière et les chants!
DOÑA SOL: Le bal! – Mais un oiseau qui chanterait aux champs!
   Un rossignol perdu dans l'ombre et dans la mousse,
   Ou quelque flûte au loin! . . . Car la musique est douce,
   Fait l'âme harmonieuse, et, comme un divin choeur,
   Éveille mille voix qui chantent dans le coeur!
   Ah! ce serait charmant![22]

Hugo's poetic response to Shakespeare was, for all its sensuous music, in some respects an unnatural achievement. The language of Shakespeare cannot be transposed into French with any consistency or ease. Berlioz's admiration and understanding of Shakespeare was as great or greater than that of any of his contemporaries; like Delacroix, he was fortunate to be able to create works to express that deep perception either in forms freed from the restrictions of words, or in forms to which words could be the adjunct and accompaniment.

Berlioz drew directly on six Shakespeare plays. First in time was *The Tempest*, in the form of the *Fantaisie* which was first performed as an independent piece in 1830 and was later rearranged to become the final section of *Lélio*. The overture on *King Lear* was written in 1831, while Berlioz was recovering at Nice from the treachery of his Ariel. *Roméo et Juliette*, the centrepiece, was performed in 1839. There are two compositions which relate to *Hamlet*, *La Mort d'Ophélie* and the *Marche Funèbre* for the last scene. Finally, there are two operatic works; first, the setting of 'How sweet the moonlight sleeps upon this bank' from *The Merchant of Venice* in act four of *Les Troyens*, and the delicately exuberant variation on *Much Ado About Nothing* – 'a caprice written with the point of a needle'[23] – of his last great work, *Béatrice et Bénédict*.

Inevitably, there are many associations with Harriet adhering to these works; they may not always be relevant in terms of pure music, but they frequently form an inescapable part of the circumstances of composition, performance or publication. The *Marche Funèbre* was written in the aftermath of the exhausting struggles with a Harriet who was ceasing to reflect Ophelia and who had become bitter, a pitiful alcoholic in the process of physical deterioration. It may, too, reflect Berlioz's grief at the death of his father in 1848, as well as a performance he saw that year in London. *La Mort d'Ophélie*, with words by Legouvé, is even more poignant. When it was published in 1848, Berlioz was in London, and Harriet alone in Paris. The vignette of Ophelia which decorated the first edition anchors the ballade to Harriet's performances at the Odéon; the coronet of flowers and the downcast, pained eyes form a pathetic image of abandoned love. Legouvé's rendering of Gertrude's description emphasises the idea of Ophelia singing her own obsequy:

> Elle flottait toujours chantant,
> Chantant quelque vieille ballade,
> Chantant ainsi qu'une naïde
> Née au milieu de ce torrent.

It was not only the dark notes to which Berlioz responded. The *Fantaisie* on *The Tempest* forms the musical and dramatic climax to *Lélio, ou le Retour à la Vie*, and Berlioz seems to have sensed instinctively one of the play's major structural ideas by emphasising the opposition between Caliban and Miranda. The artist as composer stands in the same relation to the *Fantaisie* as Prospero to his magic island world, and in its context within *Lélio* the piece evokes a comparable tension between the self-delighting sufficiency of art and the wider demands of society. At the close, the *idée fixe* is heard once more; the dreamed image remains in the artist's quickened mind. *Béatrice et Bénédict*, the other major work based on a comedy, is a wonderfully vital, if slightly elusive, opera; Berlioz described it as one of the liveliest and most original things he had done. Ronald Eyre's recent retranslation of the libretto into English, using Shakespeare's text wherever possible, reasserts the relationship between the two works while never obscuring the essential differences. Berlioz had first considered basing 'un opéra italien fort gai' on *Much Ado About Nothing* as early as 1833, perhaps under the influence of his first reciprocated love for Harriet.[24] It is significant, though, that when he took up the subject again nearly thirty years later he chose to concentrate not on the romantic absorption between Hero and Claudio but on the more mature, wittier, sharp-tongued and sharp-eyed relationship between Beatrice and Benedick: Shakespeare's criticism of the contrasted conventional romance is maintained by musical expression rather than by plot. The absence of Don John, or an equivalent, in Berlioz's version leaves an uncomfortable hiatus at the opera's centre; he did not invent a wholly satisfactory context in which Beatrice and Benedick must inevitably reveal their love for each other. Yet in Ronald Eyre's adaptation, as triumphantly performed at the 1980 Buxton Festival, the problem was alleviated by allowing Beatrice to overhear Benedick searching for a rhyme. Berlioz's variation coruscates over the patterns of the original, exploring in musical terms the varied tones and emotions of both the structure and language of *Much Ado About Nothing*; it possesses a vivacity and lightness of wit that is wholly Shakespearean. The suggestion of melancholy tenderness in Berlioz's Hero seems to echo the wistful Harriet of 1833.

Roméo et Juliette is Berlioz's most extensive Shakespearean work, though defying every attempt to categorise it. It is a symphony, and yet at times moves close to opera or oratorio. It is musically self-sufficient, but in many places almost compels the imagination towards pictorial representation. The Prologue and the Finale stress the narrative element and the dramatic setting, following Shakespeare's use of the Chorus and the slow, formal stepping back from the instantaneous love and passionate deaths of Romeo and Juliet. But when Berlioz creates his musical evocations of the love scene, the Adagio, and of the agony and death in the Capulets' tomb, he avoids the tyranny of words. As he explained in his preface,

> just because to depict so sublime a love is so dangerous for a composer, he has perforce given his imagination a freer rein than sung speech, with its precisely defined meanings, would have allowed him, and has turned instead to the language of instruments, a language richer, more varied and highly developed, and by its very indefiniteness far more effective in such an instance.

Berlioz left a glowing description of a performance of *Roméo et Juliette*, at the Grand Theatre in St Petersburg in 1847. For once, he was satisfied with the performers, and with the 'prolonged and systematic rehearsal'.

> I remember it as one of the great pleasures of my life. And I was in such good form that I had the luck to conduct without a mistake, which at that time did not often happen to me. The Grand Theatre was full. On all sides uniforms, epaulettes, tiaras, diamonds, flashed and rippled. I was recalled I do not know how many times. But I confess I paid little heed to the public that day. I sang the divine Shakespearean poem to myself, for

myself; and it had so great an effect on me that after the finale I fled trembling to a room at the back of the theatre.[25]

Rather than recall Harriet by the haunting melody of the *idée fixe*, it may be a more appropriate memorial to keep in mind that it was her art in interpreting Ophelia and Juliet which brought Shakespeare to Berlioz like a flash of lightning; it was Harriet who revealed to him the essence of dramatic art, and allowed him to perceive 'the divine Shakespearean poem'. Berlioz's capacity to fuse intense personal experience with masterful understanding of dramatic art was never more fully expressed than in *Roméo et Juliette*:

> Premier amour, n'êtes-vous pas plus haut
> Que toute poésie,
> Ou ne sériez-vous point dans notre exil mortel,
> Cette poésie elle-même
> Dont Shakespeare lui seul eut le secret suprême
> Et qu'il remporta dans le ciel?

Sainte-Beuve, writing to Alfred de Vigny and hailing him as 'Shakespearien de ce côté', associates him with a depicted landscape in which 'for ever glides some long and slender form, weeping, divine like Smithson';[26] Antoni Deschamps addressing Berlioz in verse, predicts:

> Vous braverez la mer et les vents en furie;
> Car vos étoiles sont les beaux yeux d'Ophélie.[27]

Berlioz sought in his life a love that could not exist 'dans notre exil mortel'. His idealisation of that love in Harriet brought to them both intense joy and years of unhappiness. That he and others were enabled to express the image of that poetic ideal was in part because of the originality as an actress of Harriet Smithson.

Notes

1. Childhood in Ireland

1. William Oxberry, *Dramatic Biography*, vol. 2, pp. 195–208. Oxberry (1784–1824) was a member of the Drury Lane company. The *Biography* was edited by his widow with the help of Leman Rede, her second husband, from materials collected by Oxberry. His son, also William, acted for Harriet in Paris in the 1832–33 season.
2. *Ennis Chronicle*, 7 March 1800.
3. Oxberry, *Dramatic Biography*.
4. William S. Clark, *The Irish Stage in the Country Towns, 1720–1800*. See generally for details of W. J. Smithson's career up to 1800.
5. See John Clancy, 'Around the town of Ennis with Father Clancy', *Molua* (Dublin, 1945).
6. *Ennis Chronicle*, 7 January 1790.
7. *Ennis Chronicle*, 29 May 1791.
8. *Ennis Chronicle*, 15 October 1801.
9. Oxberry, *Dramatic Biography*.
10. *Ennis Chronicle*, 13 February 1808.
11. *Ennis Chronicle*, 17 February 1808.
12. *Ennis Chronicle*, 20 February 1808.
13. Oxberry, *Dramatic Biography*.
14. 'The Smithsoniad', National Library of Ireland, Ms 8115.
15. *Freeman's Journal*, 27 May 1814.
16. See La Tourette Stockwell, *Dublin Theatres and Theatre Customs, 1637–1820*.
17. Frederick G. Tomlins, *A Brief View of the English Drama*, p. 113.
18. Walter A. Donaldson, *Fifty Years of Green-room Gossip*, pp. 246–7.
19. *Freeman's Journal*, 28 May 1814.
20. W. J. Lawrence, 'The history of the old Belfast stage'. Typescript, 1897, National Library of Ireland, Ms 4291.
21. J. W. Croker, *Familiar Epistles*, p. 47.
22. Quoted in Lawrence, 'The history of the old Belfast stage'.
23. See Christopher Murray, *Robert William Elliston, Manager*.
24. Leigh Hunt, *Critical Essays on the Performers of the London Theatres* (London, 1807), p. 200.
25. Charles Lamb, 'Ellistoniana', *Englishman's Magazine*, August 1831.
26. For this and other details of Harriet Smithson's performances in Birmingham, see *Aris' Gazette*, and Playbill Collection, Birmingham Central Library.
27. *Aris' Gazette*, 25 August 1817.

2. Years of apprenticeship

1. The principal sources used to chart Harriet Smithson's acting career in London are: Oxberry, *Dramatic Biography*; John Genest, *Some Account of the English Stage, from the Restoration in 1660 to 1830*; *Theatrical Observer*; *Theatrical Inquisitor*; Playbill Collection, British Library.
2. *The Times*, 21 January 1818.
3. *European Magazine*, January 1818.
4. *Bell's Weekly Messenger*, 1 February 1818.
5. *Theatrical Inquisitor*, 12 February 1818.
6. George Soane, *The Innkeeper's Daughter* (London, 1817).
7. See Geoffrey Ashton and Iain Mackintosh, *The Georgian Playhouse*.
8. Leigh Hunt, *Examiner*, 7 September 1817.
9. *Examiner*, 13 June 1819.
10. Pichot, *Historical and Literary Tour of a Foreigner in England and Scotland*, vol. 1, p. 220.
11. For details of salary, see *Receipts of Performances, Drury Lane*, vol. 8. British Library, Add. Mss. 29, 711.
12. Genest, *Some Account of the English Stage*.
13. Playbill, 31 July 1819, Margate Public Library.
14. Harriet Smithson, letter to Elliston, 14 August 1819. Private collection, Richard Macnutt, Tunbridge Wells.
15. Playbill, 6 September 1819, British Library.
16. James R. Planché, *Recollections and Reflections*, vol. 1, pp. 127–8.
17. William Hazlitt, 'The drama', no. 3, *London Magazine*, March 1820.
18. Playbill, 29 November 1819, British Library.
19. Manuscript list of plays, Theatres Royal, Dublin. Royal Irish Academy.
20. Joseph Cowell, *Thirty Years Passed Among the Players in England and America*, p. 47.
21. Articles of Agreement in *Collection of Memoranda* etc. arranged by James Winston, vol. 21 (1820–22), vol. 22 (1823–25), vol. 23 (1826–30). British Library, ref. C. 120. h. l.
22. James Winston, *Drury Lane Journal: Selections from James Winston's Diaries, 1819–1827*, ed. A. Nelson and G. Cross.
23. *New Monthly Magazine*, October 1821.
24. *New Monthly Magazine*, October 1821.
25. *Examiner*, 7 October 1821.
26. *Theatrical Observer*, 6 October 1831.
27. *Theatrical Observer*, 25 September 1821.
28. *Theatrical Observer*, 20 November 1821.
29. Frances A. Kemble, *Record of a Girlhood*, vol. 1, p. 188.
30. *Theatrical Observer*, 9 February 1822.
31. *Bell's Weekly Messenger*, 18 November 1821.
32. *Receipts of Performances*, vol. 8.
33. Sir Walter Scott, letter to Robert Southey, 4 April 1814, in *The Letters of Sir Walter Scott*, ed. Sir Herbert Grierson (12 vols; London 1932–7).
34. *British Stage*, September 1818.
35. R. J. Broadbent, *Annals of the Liverpool Stage*, p. 141.

3. The walking lady

1. See Christopher Murray, *Elliston*.
2. *Receipts of Performances*, vol. 8.

3. Henry Crabb Robinson, *The London Theatre 1811–1866: Selections from the diary of Henry Crabb Robinson*, ed. E. Brown, p. 101.
4. This correspondence is reproduced by M. J. Baldensperger in *Revue Germanique*, May–June 1908.
5. *Theatrical Observer*, 23 September 1824, and Oxberry, *Dramatic Biography*.
6. *The Times*, 28 January 1825.
7. *The Times*, 1 February 1825.
8. Pichot, *Historical and Literary Tour*, Vol. 1, p. 262.
9. *The Times*, 27 October 1817.
10. *Examiner*, 4 October 1818.
11. Eugène Delacroix, letter to Pierret, 27 June 1825, in *Correspondance Générale d'Eugène Delacroix*, vol. 1., ed. A. Joubin.
12. *Ibid.*, 18 June 1825.
13. *Ibid.*
14. Carl Maria von Weber, letter to his wife, 28 March 1826. Translated by N. Currer-Briggs, in *Weber in London, 1826*, ed. D. Reynolds.
15. F. W. Hawkins, *The Life of Edmund Kean*, vol. 2, p. 292.
16. *Pandore*, 14 May 1828.

4. Shakespeare in France

1. See Helen P. Bailey, *Hamlet in France, from Voltaire to Laforgue*.
2. Denis Diderot, *Oeuvres Complètes* (20 vols., Paris, 1875–7), vol. 8, p. 476.
3. François-Marie A. de Voltaire, *Oeuvres Complètes* (52 vols., Paris, 1877–85), 'Lettre à l'Académie', vol. 30, pp. 355–6.
4. *Ibid.*
5. Voltaire, letter to the Comte d'Argental, 30 July 1776, *Oeuvres Complètes*, vol. 46, p. 473.
6. *Examiner*, 26 November 1821.
7. See Joseph-Léopold Borgerhoff, *Le Théâtre Anglais à Paris*, ch. 1, and Victor Leathers, *British Entertainers in France*, ch. 7.
8. François Guizot, *Shakespeare et son temps*, p. 152.
9. *Ibid.*, pp. 177–8.
10. Stendhal, *Racine et Shakespeare*, ed. H. Martineau, p. 43.
11. Etienne-Jean Delécluze, *Journal de Delécluze*, ed. R. Baschet, p. 353.
12. Delécluze, *Journal*, pp. 97–8.
13. See Borgerhoff, *Le Théâtre Anglais à Paris*, and Leathers, *British Entertainers in France*, for further details.
14. N. P. Chaulin, *Biographie dramatique des principaux artistes anglais venus à Paris*.
15. Donaldson, *Fifty Years of Green-room Gossip*, p. 174.
16. *Theatrical Observer*, 31 August 1827.
17. Countess Granville, letter to Lady Carlisle, 6 September 1827, in *Letters of Harriet, Countess Granville, 1810–1845*, ed. Hon. F. Leveson Gower.
18. Borgerhoff, *Le Théâtre Anglais à Paris*, pp. 72–3.
19. *Morning Chronicle*, 11 September 1827.
20. *Journal des Débats*, 8 September 1827.
21. *Journal des Débats*, 10 September 1827.
22. Kemble, *Record of a Girlhood*, vol. 1, p. 185.
23. *Theatrical Observer*, 4 January 1822.
24. *Gazette Musicale*, 7 December 1834.

5. 'Fair Ophelia'

1. *Globe*, 30 August 1827.
2. Armand A. J. M. Ferrard de Pontmartin, 'Les Acteurs Anglais à l'Odéon' in *Souvenirs d'un vieux critique*, vol. 1.
3. Alexandre Dumas, *Mes Mémoires*, ed. P. Jossérand, vol. 2, p. 419.
4. *Journal des Débats*, 13 September 1827.
5. E. Suddaby and P. J. Yarrow (eds.), *Lady Morgan in France*, pp. 89–90.
6. *Théâtre Anglais; ou collection des pièces Anglaises jouées à Paris.*
7. Alexandre Dumas, *Impressions de voyage en Suisse*, vol. 2, p. 75.
8. *Courier*, 22 September 1827.
9. Delécluze, *Journal*, pp. 455, 456.
10. Arthur C. Sprague, *The Stage Business in Shakespeare's Plays: A Postscript*, p. 17.
11. Sprague, *The Stage Business in Shakespeare's Plays: A Postscript*, p. 18.
12. François R. de Chateaubriand, *Sketches of English Literature*, vol. 1, p. 278.
13. Charles Jarrin, *Mémoires*, ch. 45, quoted in Julien Tiersot, *Berlioz et la société de son temps*, p. 53.
14. *Gazette Musicale*, 7 December 1834.
15. See M. Moreau, *Souvenirs du théâtre anglais à Paris.*
16. *Globe*, 18 September 1827.
17. Dumas, *Mémoires*, vol. 3, p. 18.
18. Countess Granville, letter to Lady Carlisle, 1 October 1827.
19. *Figaro*, 14 September 1827.
20. Delacroix, letter to Soulier, 28 September 1827.
21. Charles-Augustin Sainte-Beuve, *Portraits contemporains*, vol. 3, p. 394.
22. *Athenaeum*, 23 April 1828.
23. Armand Ferrard de Pontmartin, 'Hector Berlioz' in *Nouveaux samedis*, vol. 18, p. 101.
24 Oxberry, *Dramatic Biography.*
25. *Figaro*, 15 September 1827.
26. *Corsaire*, 11 October 1827.
27. Quoted by Dutton Cook, 'Harriet Smithson', *Gentleman's Magazine*, June 1879.
28. George Osborne, *Proceedings of the Musical Association*, February 1879.
29. Hector Berlioz, *The Memoirs of Hector Berlioz*, translated and edited by David Cairns, ch. 18.
30. *Ibid.*, p. 111.
31. *Ibid.*, pp. 111–12.
32. Ferrard de Pontmartin, *Nouveaux samedis*, vol. 18, pp. 101–2.

6. 'La Belle Irlandaise'

1. *Globe*, 22 September 1827.
2. *Courrier Français*, 20 September 1827.
3. *Pandore*, 21 September 1827.
4. *Journal des Débats*, 27 September 1827.
5. Countess Granville, letter to Duke of Devonshire, 5 October 1827.
6. *Literary Chronicle and Weekly Review*, 20 October 1827.
7. *Quotidienne*, 10 October 1827.
8. *Corsaire*, 10 October 1827.
9. *Journal des Débats*, 18 October 1827.
10. *Mercure de France au dix-neuvième Siècle*, vol. 19, p. 595.
11. Countess Granville, letter to Duke of Devonshire, 8 November 1827.

12. *Mercure de France*, vol. 19, p. 235.
13. William Macready, *Macready's Reminiscences*, ed. Sir F. Pollock, vol. 2, p. 443.
14. *Journal des Débats*, 17 October 1827.
15. See Margery E. Elkington, *Les Relations de société entre l'Angleterre et la France sous la Restauration*.
16. Moreau, *Souvenirs du théâtre anglais à Paris*.
17. Donaldson, *Fifty Years of Green-room Gossip*, p. 175.
18. *Theatrical Observer*, 7 November 1827.
19. Antoni Deschamps, *Dernières paroles* (Paris, 1835), p. 325.
20. *Quotidienne*, 5 March 1828.
21. See *Journal des Débats*, 5 March 1828, and *Literary Chronicle*, 15 March 1828.
22. *Pandore*, 5 March 1828.
23. *Journal des Débats*, An 13, 1 nivôse.
24. *Globe*, 12 April 1828.
25. *New Monthly Magazine*, June 1828.
26. Edward Fitzgerald, letter to Fanny Kemble, 17 November 1874 in *Letters of Edward Fitzgerald to Fanny Kemble* (London, 1895).
27. Eleanor Ransome, ed., *The Terrific Kemble*, p. 211.
28. *Ibid.*, pp. 209–10.
29. *Réunion*, 18 April 1828.
30. Alfred de Vigny, letter to Pauthier, 17 May 1828, in *Alfred de Vigny, la vie littéraire, politique et religieuse* (2 vols., Paris, 1913), ed. L. Séché, vol. 1, p. 376.
31. *Globe*, 29 May 1828.
32. *Ibid.*, 23 July 1828.
33. *Ibid.*
34. Delacroix, letter to Hugo, 'ce mercredi 1827'.
35. *Mercure de France*, vol. 19, p. 30.
36. Dumas, *Mémoires*, vol. 3, p. 18.
37. *Courrier Français*, 13 September 1827.
38. Delécluze, *Journal*, p. 462.
39. Friedrich M. Baron von Grimm, *Correspondance littéraire, philosophique et critique par Grimm, Diderot etc.* (16 vols., Paris, 1877), vol. 6, pp. 318–19.
40. *Pandore*, 19 September 1827.
41. *Mentor*, 12 November 1828.
42. Joseph d'Ortigue, 'Hector Berlioz', *Revue de Paris*, December 1832; reprinted in *Le Balcon de l'Opéra*.
43. Berlioz, *Memoirs*, p. 110.
44. Berlioz, *Memoirs*, p. 113
45. Harriet Smithson, letter to a female friend, 6 October 1828, reproduced in part in *The Times*, 11 October 1828.
46. *Galignani's Messenger*, 3 October 1828.
47. Hector Berlioz, *Correspondance Générale*, ed. P. Citron. (Hereafter referred to as *Corr.* with volume, number of letter, correspondent and date, i.e. 1, 113, to Ferrand, 2 February 1829.)
48. Berlioz, *Memoirs*, p. 141.
49. *Corr.* 1, 117, to Albert du Boys, 2 March 1829.
50. Berlioz, *Memoirs*, p. 142.
51. Harriet Smithson, letter to Charles Kemble, 23 January 1829, Folger Shakespeare Library.

7. The 'idée fixe'

1. *The Times*, 11 October 1828.
2. *Dramatic Magazine*, 11 May 1829.
3. *Theatrical Observer*, 11 May 1829.
4. *Covent Garden Theatre, General Ledger 1822–29*. British Library, Add. Mss. 23, 167.
5. *Examiner*, 24 May 1829.
6. *New Monthly Magazine*, 1 June 1829.
7. *Theatrical Observer*, 18 May 1829.
8. *Theatrical Observer*, 2 June 1829.
9. W. Clark Russell, *Representative Actors*, pp. 379–80.
10. *Corr.* I, 129, to Rocher, 25 June 1829.
11. Christopher North (John Wilson), *Noctes Ambrosianae*, May 1830 (4 vols., Edinburgh, 1854).
12. *Corr.* I, 152, to Ferrand, 6 February 1830.
13. Charles Baudelaire, *La Fanfarlo*, ed. C. Pichois (Monaco, 1957), pp. 87–8.
14. *Corr.* I, 156, to Hiller, 3 March 1830.
15. *Corr.* I, 152, to Ferrand, 6 February 1830.
16. *Corr.* I, 167, to Nanci Berlioz, 30 June 1830.
17. D'Ortigue, *Revue de Paris*, December 1832.
18. *Corr.* I, 165 to Rocher, 5 June 1830.
19. *Corr.* I, 162, to Ferrand, 13 May 1830.
20. *Journal des Débats*, 12 May 1830.
21. *Athenaeum*, 29 May 1830.
22. *Courrier des Théâtres*, 12 May 1830.
23. *Constitutionnel*, 12 May 1830.
24. Juste Olivier, *Paris en 1830*, ed. A. Delattre and M. Denkinger, pp. 40–1.
25. Berlioz, *Memoirs*, p. 156.
26. Berlioz, *Memoirs*, p. 149.
27. Berlioz, *Memoirs*, p. 165.
28. *Corr.* I, 158, to Ferrand, 16 April 1830.
29. *Corr.* I, 193, to Ferrand, 12 December 1830.
30. Harriet Smithson, letter to Louis-Philippe, 15 August 1830. British Library, Add. Mss. 33, 965, f. 89.
31. *Journal des Débats*, 6 December 1830.
32. *Courrier des Théâtres*, 4 December 1830.
33. See Berlioz, *Memoirs*, ch. 34, and *Corr.* I, 216, to Ferrand, 12 December 1830.
34. *Corr.* I, 217, to Vernet, 18 April 1831.
35. Harriet Smithson, letter to Kenneth, 15 February 1831. (Garrick Club Collection, London.)
36. *Nottingham Review*, 10 June 1831.
37. Manuscript journal of 6th Duke of Devonshire. Chatsworth.
38. *Age*, 16 June 1832.
39. Harriet Smithson, letter to Thiers, 31 October 1832. Manskopf collection, Frankfurt. Quoted *Corr.* II, p. 34.
40. Berlioz, *Memoirs*, pp. 257–8.

8. Episodes in the life of an artist

1. *Galignani's Messenger*, 24 November 1832.
2. *Courrier des Théâtres*, 22 November 1832.

3. *Artiste*, December 1832.
4. *Journal des Débats*, 25 November 1832.
5. *Artiste*, January 1833.
6. *Courrier des Théâtres*, 6 December 1832.
7. Berlioz, *Memoirs*, p. 258.
8. *Corr.* I, 293, to Nanci Pal (née Berlioz), 26 November 1832.
9. Berlioz, *Memoirs*, pp. 258–61.
10. *Ibid.*, p. 260.
11. Heinrich Heine, 'Berlioz, Liszt, Chopin' in *Heine in Art and Letters*, ed. Mrs W. Sharp, pp. 20–1.
12. Berlioz, *Memoirs*, p. 260.
13. *Ibid.*, pp. 260–1.
14. *Corr.* II, 296, to Harriet Smithson, between 10 and 18 December 1832.
15. *Corr.* II, 300, to Seghers, 16 December 1832.
16. Jacques Barzun, *Berlioz and the Romantic Century*, vol. 1, p. 234.
17. Stendhal, *De l'Amour*, ed. H. Martineau (Paris, 1938), p. 43 and p. 47.
18. *Corr.* II, 304, to Adèle Berlioz, 20 December 1832.
19. *Corr.* II, 303, to Liszt, 19 December 1832.
20. *Corr.* II, 307, to Albert du Boys, 5 January 1833.
21. *Corr.* II, 308, to Nanci Pal, 7 January 1833.
22. D'Ortigue, *Revue de Paris*, December 1832.
23. *Artiste*, January 1833.
24. *Ibid.*
25. See Berlioz, *Memoirs*, ch. 10.
26. *Corr.* I, 314, to Dr Berlioz, 3 February 1833.
27. Félix Marmion, letter to Nanci Pal, 10 February 1833, quoted *Corr.* II, pp. 74–5.
28. *Corr.* II, 322, to Dr Berlioz, between 22 and 28 February 1833.
29. *Corr.* II, 323, to Dr Berlioz, 23 February 1833.
30. *Corr.* II, 327, to Rocher, 12 March 1833.
31. *Corr.* II, 330, Rocher to Berlioz, between 24 March and 10 April 1833.
32. See Berlioz, *Memoirs*, p. 265; and *Corr.* II, 332, to Adèle Berlioz, 3 April 1833.
33. *Corr.* II, 337, to Adèle Berlioz, 30 May 1833.
34. *Corr.* II, 336, to Adèle Berlioz, 27 April 1833.
35. *Corr.* II, 337, to Adèle Berlioz, 30 May 1833.
36. *Corr.* II, 338, to Ferrand, 12 June 1833.
37. *Corr.* II, 339, to Hiller, 11 July 1833.
38. *Corr.* II, 341, to Ferrand, 1 August 1833.
39. *Corr.* II, 342, to Ferrand, 30 August 1833.
40. Ferdinand Hiller, *Künstlerleben*, pp. 63–143.

9. Berlioz's muse

1. *Corr.* II, 347, to Adèle Berlioz, 6 October 1833.
2. *Corr.* II, 348, to Liszt, 7 October 1833.
3. *Corr.* II, 347, to Adèle Berlioz, 6 October 1833.
4. *Corr.* II, 357, to Ferrand, 25 October 1833.
5. *Corr.* II, 364, to Spontini, 7 December 1833.
6. George Sand, *Histoire de ma vie* (10 vols., Paris, 1856), vol. 9, p. 121.
7. *Quotidienne*, 4 December 1833.
8. See Berlioz, *Memoirs*, pp. 266–9; and *Corr.* II, 363, to Adèle Berlioz, 28 November 1833.
9. *Corr.* II, 370, to Adèle Berlioz, 26 December 1833.

10. Berlioz, *Memoirs*, p. 270.
11. *Corr.* II, 360, to Adèle Berlioz, 3 November 1833.
12. *Corr.* II, 445, to Mme Berlioz, 11 October 1835.
13. *Corr.* II, 395, to Liszt, May 1834. The French translation of Moore's 'This world is all a fleeting show', set by Berlioz as *Méditation religieuse*, is more resonant than the original.
14. *Corr.* II, 397, to Adèle Berlioz, 12 May 1834.
15. *Corr.* II, 399, to d'Ortigue, 31 May 1834.
16. *Corr.* II, 401, to Rocher, 31 July 1834.
17. *Corr.* II, 408, to Ferrand, 31 August 1834.
18. *Corr.* II, 409, to Adèle Berlioz, 23 September 1834.
19. *Galignani's Messenger*, 29 November 1834.
20. *Corr.* II, 427, to Vigny, 10 February 1835.
21. Théophile Gautier, *Histoire du Romantisme*, p. 161.
22. *Corr.* II, 458, to Rocher, 23 January 1836.
23. *Corr.* II, 439, to Adèle Berlioz, 2 August 1835.
24. *Corr.* II, 430, to Adèle Berlioz, 17 April 1835.
25. *Quotidienne*, 24 March 1836.
26. *Corr.* II, 474, to Adèle Berlioz, 1 July 1836.
27. Harriet Smithson, letter to Butler, 14 September 1836 (Garrick Club Collection). Quoted *Corr.* II, p. 302.
28. *Journal des Débats*, 19 December 1836.
29. George Sand, letter to la Marquise de la Carte, 18 December 1836 in Sand, *Correspondance Générale*, ed. G. Lubin, vol. 3.
30. Marie d'Agoult, letter to Sand, 26 March 1837, quoted in Jacques Vier, *La Comtesse d'Agoult et son temps*.
31. Harriet Smithson, letter to Edward Sainte-Barbe, March 1836. New York Public Library. Reproduced by Ralph P. Locke, *Nineteenth Century Music*, vol. 1, no. 1 (July 1977).
32. *Journal des Débats*, 8 May 1837.
33. *Corr.* II, 506, to Dr Berlioz, 29 July 1837.
34. *Corr.* II, 501, to Sand, 20 June 1837.
35. *Corr.* II, 509, to Sand, 17 September 1837.
36. Joseph d'Ortigue, *De l'Ecole musicale italienne et de l'Académie royale de musique à l'occasion de l'opéra de M. H. Berlioz* (Paris, 1839).
37. Berlioz, *Memoirs*, p. 300.
38. Berlioz, *Memoirs*, p. 301.
39. Berlioz, *Memoirs*, p. 301.
40. Berlioz, *Memoirs*, p. 303.
41. Berlioz, *Memoirs*, p. 303.
42. Harriet Smithson, letter to Adèle Berlioz, 28 July 1839. *Corr.* II, p. 564. (Adelina Ganz Collection, London.)
43. *Corr.* II, 655, Emile Deschamps to Berlioz, 21 June 1839.

10. The tragic dénouement

1. *Journal des Débats*, 24 November 1839.
2. *Corr.* II, 683, to Dr Berlioz, 26 November 1839.
3. *Corr.* II, 635, to Adèle Berlioz, 1 March 1839.
4. Berlioz, *Memoirs*, p. 310.
5. *Corr.* II, 731, to Dr Berlioz, 22 September 1840.
6. *Corr.* II, 511, to Mme Berlioz, 12 October 1837.

7. *Corr.* II, 667, to Nanci Pal, 28 September 1839.
8. Ernest Legouvé, *Soixante ans de souvenirs*, vol. 1, ch. 16.
9. *Corr.* II, 755, to Ferrand, 3 October 1841.
10. *Corr.* II, 765, to Nanci Pal, 5 February 1842.
11. Félix Marmion, letter to Nanci Pal, quoted *Corr.* II, p. 726.
12. See Berlioz, *Memoirs*, pp. 310–11; *Corr.* III, 784, to Nanci Pal, 23 October 1842; *Corr.* III, 772 *bis*, to Snel, 28 August 1842.
13. *Corr.* III, 791, to Nanci Pal, 9 December 1842.
14. *Corr.* III, 800, to Morel, 16/17 January 1843.
15. *Corr.* III, 815, to Morel, 18 February 1843.
16. *Corr.* III, 832, to the treasurer of the Opéra, May 1843.
17. Louis Berlioz, letter to Nanci Pal, 21 February 1843, quoted *Corr.* III, p. 81.
18. *Corr.* III, 839, to Adèle Suat, 8 June 1843.
19. George Osborne, *Proceedings of the Musical Association*, April 1883.
20. Legouvé, *Soixante ans de souvenirs*, vol. 2, pp. 318–19.
21. *Corr.* III, 910, to Nanci Pal, 23 June 1844.
22. *Corr.* III, 923, to Adèle Suat, 18 October 1844.
23. *Corr.* III, 926, to Nanci Pal, 30 November 1844.
24. Harriet Smithson, letter to Louis Berlioz, quoted *Corr.* III, pp. 368–9.
25. *Corr.* III, 1210, to Nanci Pal, 11 July 1848.
26. *Corr.* III, 1236, to Adèle Suat, 1 November 1848; also *Corr.* III, 1237, to Nanci Pal, 10 November 1848; and *Corr.* III, 1247, to Nanci Pal, 24 February 1849.
27. *Corr.* III, 1297, to Adèle Suat, 12 January 1850.
28. *Corr.* III, 1331, to Adèle Suat, 15 May 1850.
29. Berlioz, *Memoirs*, pp. 567–70.
30. Hector Berlioz, letter to Adèle Suat, 7 March 1854, in *Au milieu du chemin*, ed. J. Tiersot.
31. *Mousquetaire*, 11 March 1854.
32. *Journal des Débats*, 20 March 1854, translated by David Cairns in Berlioz, *Memoirs*, pp. 570–1.
33. Hector Berlioz, letter to Louis Berlioz, 6 March 1854, in *Correspondance inédite*, ed. D. Bernard.
34. Hector Berlioz, letter to Louis Berlioz, 23 March 1854, in *Correspondance inédite*.
35. Berlioz, *Memoirs*, p. 611.

11. Romantic image

1. *New Monthly Magazine*, June 1828.
2. *Corsaire*, 12 September 1827.
3. *Ibid.*, 23 January 1828.
4. Victor Pavie, letter to his father, 26 February 1828, in André Pavie, *Médaillons romantiques*, p. 117.
5. *La Presse*, 3 February 1840.
6. *Ibid.*, 4 February 1839.
7. Théophile Gautier, *Histoire du Romantisme*, p. 274.
8. Jules Janin, *Rachel et la Tragédie*, p. 67.
9. Janin, *Rachel et la Tragédie*, p. 69.
10. Paul E. A. Joannides, 'English literary subject matter in French painting, 1800–1863' (Cambridge Ph.D. dissertation, 1974), vol. 1, pp. 91–2.
11. *Ibid*, p. 195.
12. Delacroix, letter to Gautier, *Correspondance*, 6 August 1843.
13. *Journal des Débats*, 20 March 1854.

14. Michael Ayrton, *Berlioz, A Singular Obsession*, p. 22.
15. Victor Hugo, *Orientales*, in *Oeuvres Complètes*, ed. J. Massin, vol. 3.
16. Arthur Rimbaud, *Oeuvres*, ed. S. Bernard (Paris, 1960), pp. 46–7.
17. See Emile Deschamps, *Préface des études françaises et étrangères*, ed. H. Giraud, pp. 45–55.
18. Vigny, letter to Charles de la Rounat, 3 May 1862, *Correspondance*, ed. E. Sakellaridès (Paris, 1905).
19. Dumas, *Théâtre Complet*, vol. 1.
20. Dumas, *Mémoires*, vol. 3, ch. 119.
21. Hugo, *Hernani*, act 5 scene 6.
22. Hugo, *Hernani*, act 5 scene 3.
23. Hector Berlioz, *Briefe von Hector Berlioz an die Fürstin Carolyne Sayn-Wittgenstein*, ed. La Mara.
24. *Corr.* II, 311, to d'Ortigue, 19 January 1833.
25. Berlioz, *Memoirs*, p. 534.
26. Sainte-Beuve, letter to Alfred de Vigny, 14 August 1828, in Sainte-Beuve, *Correspondance Générale* (Paris, 1935–).
27. Antoni Deschamps, *Dernières Paroles* (Paris, 1835), p. 75.

Bibliography

Harriet Smithson's few surviving letters are widely scattered and largely concerned with professional engagements. Of especial interest are her early letter to Elliston (Macnutt collection); her appeal to Louis-Philippe of 1830 (British Museum); and the long letter to her agent Kenneth of 1831 (Garrick Club collection). From the time of her arrival in Paris in autumn 1832, most of her correspondence is referred to or quoted in full in *Berlioz: Correspondance Générale*. One important exception is the letter to Sainte-Barbe published by Ralph P. Locke in *Nineteenth Century Music*, vol. 1, no 1 (July 1977). Other unpublished letters include one to Peter Moore, 7 July 1819, and another to Elliston, 8 March 1820 (Yale University Library); one to the Manager of the Theatre Royal, Newcastle, of 1829 (Macnutt collection), and an undated note of apology to the Misses Henry (Diederichs collection, University Library, Amsterdam; copy in National Library of Ireland).

'The Smithsoniad' (National Library of Ireland) is a sustained attack on Harriet's father, and provides detailed insights into the sordid business of theatrical touring in Ireland.

Some details about performances, salary, box-office receipts and so forth can be gleaned from the Drury Lane account books and Covent Garden ledgers, as well as from James Winston's collection of memoranda, all in the British Library. There are useful manuscript lists of plays and performers for the Theatres Royal, Dublin in the Royal Irish Academy.

The following bibliography represents only those works I have found most useful, or which throw particular light on Harriet Smithson or on the theatrical and aesthetic context of her career. More extensive bibliographies are those of Jacques Barzun in *Berlioz and the Romantic Century* (New York, 1969) and of Hugh Macdonald in *The New Grove Dictionary of Music and Musicians* (Macmillan, 1980); for the English theatrical background, that of J. F. Arnott and J. W. Robinson, entitled *English Theatrical Literature 1559–1900* (Society for Theatre Research, 1970), remains indispensable.

Allevy, Marie-Antoinette, *La Mise en scène en France dans la première moitié du dix-neuvième siècle*. Paris, 1938.

Ashton, Geoffrey and Mackintosh, Iain, *The Georgian Playhouse*. (Hayward Gallery exhibition catalogue.) London, 1975.

Ayrton, Michael, *Berlioz, A Singular Obsession*. London, 1969.

Bailey, Helen P., *Hamlet in France, from Voltaire to Laforgue*. Geneva, 1964.

Baldick, Robert, *The Life and Times of Frédérick Lemaître*. London, 1959.

Ballif, Claude, *Berlioz*. Paris, 1968.

Barbier, Auguste, *Souvenirs personnels et silhouettes contemporaines*. Paris, 1883.

Bibliography

Barraud, Henry, *Hector Berlioz*. Paris, 1955.

Barzun, Jacques, *Berlioz and the Romantic Century*. 2 vols. 3rd edition. New York, 1969.

Berlioz, Hector, *Memoirs*. Trans. and ed. David Cairns. Revised edition. London, 1970.

Correspondance Générale. ed. P. Citron: vol. I, 1803–32; vol. II, 1832–42; vol. III, 1842–50. Paris, 1972– .

Le Musicien Errant (1842–52), ed. Julien Tiersot. Paris, 1919.

Au milieu du chemin (1852–55), ed. Julien Tiersot. Paris, 1930.

Lettres de musiciens écrites en français du 15ème au 20ème siècle. 2 vols. Turin, 1924–36.

Correspondance inédite (1819–68) ed. Daniel Bernard, Paris, 1879.

Briefe von Hector Berlioz an die Fürstin Carolyne Sayn-Wittgenstein. ed. La Mara. Leipzig, 1903.

Borgerhoff, Joseph-Léopold, *Le Théâtre Anglais à Paris*. Paris, 1913.

Boschot, Adolphe, *Une vie romantique: Hector Berlioz*. Paris, 1919.

Broadbent, R. J., *Annals of the Liverpool Stage*. Liverpool, 1908.

Cairns, David, *Berlioz and the Romantic Imagination*. (Exhibition catalogue). London, 1969.

Carlson, Marvin, *The French Stage in the Nineteenth Century*. Metuchen, 1972.

Chateaubriand, François René de, *Sketches of English Literature*. 2 vols. London, 1836.

Chaulin, N. P., *Biographie dramatique des principaux artistes anglais venus à Paris*. Paris, 1828.

Clark, William S., *The Irish Stage in the Country Towns, 1720–1800*. Oxford, 1965.

Comboroure, Cosette, 'Harriet Smithson 1828–1837'. *Berlioz Society Bulletin*, 86 (January, 1975).

'Harriet Smithson and the Parisian public in 1832–33'. *Berlioz Society Bulletin*, 96/97 (Summer/Autumn 1977).

Cook, Edward Dutton, 'Harriet Smithson'. *Gentleman's Magazine*, 244 (June, 1879).

Cowell, Joseph, *Thirty Years Passed Among the Players in England and America*. New York, 1845.

Croker, J. W., *Familiar Epistles* 2nd edition. Dublin, 1804.

Daniels, B.-V., 'Shakespeare à la romantique: *Le More de Venise* d'Alfred de Vigny'. *Revue d'Histoire du Théâtre*, 27 (1975).

Delacroix, Eugène, *Correspondance Générale*. ed. A. Joubin, 5 vols. Paris, 1935–7.

Journal. ed. A. Joubin, 5 vols. Paris, 1932.

Delécluze, Etienne-Jean, *Journal*. ed. Robert Baschet. Paris, 1948.

Souvenirs de soixante années. Paris, 1862.

Deschamps, Emile, *Préface des études françaises et étrangères*. ed. H. Giraud. Paris, 1828.

Descotes, Maurice, *La Drame Romantique et ses grands créateurs (1827–1839)*. Paris, 1955.

Donaldson, Walter A., *Fifty Years of Green-room Gossip*. London, 1881.

Donohue, Joseph, *Dramatic Character in the English Romantic Age*. Princeton, N. J., 1970.

Theatre in the Age of Kean. Oxford, 1976.

Doran, John, *Annals of the English Stage*. 3 vols. London, 1888.

Downer, Alan S., *The Eminent Tragedian William Charles Macready*. Cambridge, Mass., 1966.

Draper, E. W. M., *The Rise and Fall of the French Romantic Drama*. London, 1923.

Dumas, Alexandre, *père*, *Impressions de Voyage en Suisse*. 2 vols. Paris, 1852.

Théâtre Complet. 15 vols. Paris, 1863–74.

Mes Mémoires. ed. P. Jossérand, 6 vols. Paris, 1954.

Eddison, Robert, 'Souvenirs du théâtre anglais à Paris, 1827',
   Theatre Notebook. vol. 9 (1954–5).
Elkington, Margery E., *Les Relations de société entre l'Angleterre et la France sous la
   Restauration.* Paris, 1929.
Evans, David-Owen, 'L'Odéon et le drame romantique'. *Revue d'Histoire Littéraire de
   la France,* 34 (1927).
   Le Théâtre pendant la période romantique (1827–48). Paris, 1925.
Eymard Julien, *Ophélie ou le narcissisme au féminin.* Paris, 1977.
Fèrrard de Pontmartin, Armand A. J. M., *Nouveaux samedis.* 20 vols. Paris 1865–
   81.
   Souvenirs d'un vieux critique. 10 vols. Paris. 1881–89.
Gautier, Théophile, *Histoire de l'art dramatique en France depuis vingt-cinq ans.* Paris,
   1858–9.
   Histoire du Romantisme. Paris, 1874.
Genest, John, *Some Account of the English Stage, from the Restoration in 1660 to 1830.*
   10 vols. Bath, 1832.
Gilman, Margaret, *Othello in French.* Paris, 1925.
Granville, Harriet, Countess, *Letters 1810–1845.* ed. Hon. F. Leveson Gower, 2 vols.
   London, 1894.
Guest, Ivor, *Romantic Ballet in Paris.* London, 1966.
Guizot, François, *Shakespeare et son temps.* Paris, 1852.
Hawkins, F. W., *The Life of Edmund Kean.* 2 vols. London, 1869.
Heine, Heinrich, *Heine in Art and Letters.* ed. Mrs W. Sharp. London, 1892.
Hiller, Ferdinand, *Künstlerleben.* Cologne, 1880.
Honour, Hugh, *Romanticism.* London, 1979.
Hopkinson, Cecil, *A Bibliography of the Musical and Literary Works of Hector Berlioz.*
   ed. Richard Macnutt. 2nd edition. Tunbridge Wells, 1980.
Houssaye, Arsène, *Souvenirs de jeunesse: 1830–1850.* Paris, 1896.
Howarth, W. D., *Sublime and Grotesque: A Study of French Romantic Drama.* London,
   1975.
Hugo, Victor, *Oeuvres Complètes.* ed. J. Massin, 18 vols. Paris, 1967–70.
Janin, Jules, *Histoire de la littérature dramatique.* 6 vols. Paris, 1853–8.
   Rachel et la Tragédie. Paris, 1869.
Joannides, Paul, 'English literary subject matter in French painting 1800–1863'.
   Ph.D. dissertation, 2 vols. Cambridge, 1974.
Johnson, Lee, *Delacroix.* London, 1963.
Jullien, Adolphe, *Hector Berlioz: sa vie et ses oeuvres.* Paris, 1888.
Jusserand, Jules J., *Shakespeare en France sous l'ancien régime.* Paris, 1898.
Kemble, Frances A., *Record of a Girlhood.* 3 vols. London, 1878.
Lawrence, W. J., 'The history of the old Belfast stage'. Typescript, 1897. National
   Library of Ireland, Ms 4291.
Leathers, Victor, *British Entertainers in France.* Toronto, 1959.
Legouvé, Ernest, *Soixante ans de souvenirs.* 2 vols. Paris, 1886–7.
Lennox, Lord William Pitt, *Plays, Players and Playhouses.* 2 vols. London, 1881.
Locke, Ralph P., 'New Letters of Berlioz'. *Nineteenth Century Music,* vol. 1, no. 1 (July,
   1977).
Lubin, Georges, *Drame perdu pour une étoile sans emploi* – in *Hommage à G. Sand,* ed.
   Léon Cellier. Paris, 1969.
Macready, William Charles, *Reminiscences,* ed. Sir F. Pollock, 2 vols. London, 1875.
Magnin, Charles, *Causeries et méditations.* 2 vols. Paris, 1843.
Maurice, Charles, *Histoire anecdotique du théâtre.* Paris, 1856.
Millner, Simon L., *Les Illustrateurs Français de Shakespeare.* Paris, 1939.

Bibliography

Moreau, M., *Souvenirs du théâtre anglais à Paris*. Paris, 1827.

Moreau, P., *Le Théâtre romantique*. Paris, 1949.

Murray, Christopher, *Robert William Elliston, Manager*. London, 1975.

Odell, George C., *Shakespeare from Betterton to Irving*. 2 vols. New York, 1920.

Olivier, Juste, *Paris en 1830*, ed. A. Delattre & M. Denkinger. University of North Carolina Studies in the Romance languages and literatures, 19. Chapel Hill, 1951.

Ortigue, Joseph d', *Le Balcon de l'Opéra*. Paris, 1833.

Osborne, George A., 'Musical Coincidences and Reminiscences'. *Proceedings of the Musical Association*, 3 February 1879 and 2 April 1883.

Oxberry, William, *Dramatic Biography and Histrionic Anecdotes*. 5 vols. London, 1825–6.

Pavie, André, *Médaillons romantiques*. Paris, 1909.

Partridge, Eric, *The French Romantics' Knowledge of English Literature (1820–1848)*. Paris, 1924.

Pichot, Amédée, *Historical and Literary Tour of a Foreigner in England and Scotland*. 2 vols. London, 1825.

Planché, James Robinson, *Recollections and Reflections*. 2 vols. London, 1872.

Planta, Edward, *New Picture of Paris, or the Stranger's Guide to the French metropolis*. 15th edition. London, 1827.

Porel, Paul and Monval, Georges, *L'Odéon: Histoire administrative, anecdotique et littéraire du second Théâtre Français*. 2 vols. Paris, 1876–82.

Ransome, Eleanor (ed.), *The Terrific Kemble*. London, 1978.

Reynolds, D. (ed.), *Weber in London, 1826*. London, 1976.

Robinson, Henry Crabb, *The London Theatre 1811–1866: Selections from the Diary of Henry Crabb Robinson*, ed. Eluned Brown. London, 1966.

Russell, W. Clark, *Representative Actors*. London, 1869.

Sainte-Beuve, Charles-Augustin, *Portraits contemporains*. 3 vols. Paris, 1847.

Sand, George, *Correspondance Générale*, ed. G. Lubin, 9 vols to date. Paris, 1964–

Schrickx, Willem, 'A Shakespeare Season on the Continent: Brussels 1814 and its prelude in Amsterdam'. *Neophilologus*, 61 (1977).

Sessely, Annie, *L'Influence de Shakespeare sur Alfred de Vigny*. Berne, 1928.

Sprague, Arthur Colby, *Shakespeare and the actors, the stage business in his plays, 1660–1905*. Cambridge, Mass., 1945.

The Stage Business in Shakespeare's Plays: A Postscript. Society for Theatre Research, no. 3, 1953.

Stendhal [Beyle, Henri], *Racine et Shakespeare*, ed. H. Martineau. Paris, 1928.

Stockwell, La Tourette, *Dublin Theatres and Theatre Customs, 1637–1820*. Kingsport, Tenn., 1938.

Stratman, Carl, *Britain's Theatrical Periodicals, 1720–1967. A bibliography*. New York, 1972.

Suddaby, E. and Yarrow P. J. (eds.), *Lady Morgan in France*. Newcastle, 1971.

Théâtre Anglais; ou collection des pièces anglaises jouées à Paris. Paris, 1827–8.

Tiersot, Julien, *Berlioz et la société de son temps*. Paris, 1904.

Tomlins, Frederick G., *A Brief View of the English Drama*. London, 1840.

Trapp, Frank A. *The Attainment of Delacroix*. Baltimore, 1971.

Vier, Jacques, *La Comtesse d'Agoult et son temps*. Paris, 1955.

Vigny, Alfred de, *Oeuvres complètes*. Pléiade edition. 2 vols. Paris, 1955 and 1960.

Voltaire, François-Marie Arouet de, *Oeuvres complètes*. Moland edition, 52 vols: vol. 30, 'Lettre à l'Académie'; vol. 46, 'Lettre à d'Argental'. Paris, 1877–85.

Wicks, C. Beaumont (ed.), *The Parisian Stage*, part II *(1816–1830)*. Alabama, 1953.

Wicks, C. Beaumont and Schweitzer J. W. (eds.), *The Parisian Stage*, part III *(1831–1850)*. Alabama, 1960.

Williamson, J. *Charles Kemble, man of the theatre*. Lincoln, Nebraska, 1970.
Winston, James, *Drury Lane Journal: Selections from the Diaries of James Winston, 1819–1827*, ed. Alfred Nelson & Gilbert Cross. London, 1974.

Newspapers and periodicals

Age
Aris' Gazette
Artiste
Athenaeum
Bell's Weekly Messenger
Berlioz Society Bulletin
British Stage and Literary Cabinet
Constitutionnel
Corsaire
Courier
Courrier Français
Courrier des théâtres
Dramatic Magazine
Ennis Chronicle
European Magazine
Examiner
Figaro
Galignani's Messenger
Gazette Musicale
Gentleman's Magazine
Globe
Journal des Débats
Literary Chronicle and Weekly Review

London Magazine
Mentor
Mercure de France au dix-neuvième siècle
Monde Dramatique
Mousquetaire
Musical Quarterly
New Monthly Magazine
Nineteenth Century Music
Nottingham Review
Pandore
Presse
Proceedings of the Musical Association
Quotidienne
Rénovateur
Réunion
Revue Germanique
Revue du dix-neuvième siècle
Revue de Paris
Romantisme
Theatrical Inquisitor
Theatrical Observer
Theatrical Observer (Dublin)
The Times

Index

Index

Index

Index

Oxberry, William, 4, 5, 28, 29, 41

Paganini, Nicolò, 130, 150, 160, 162
Paris, theatres and companies:
  Comédie-Française, 58, 84, 85, 177;
  Odéon, 51, 52, 56, 58, 59, 69, 71, 72, 75,
  77, 86, 89, 94, 97, 98, 99, 133, 172, 173,
  184, 187, 191; Opéra, 116, 119, 120, 149,
  155, 159, 160, 167; Opéra-Comique, 102,
  110, 115, 119; Porte-Saint-Martin, 33, 46,
  48, 49, 95, 97, 154; Salle Chantereine, 47,
  139, 165; Salle Favart, 50, 82, 89, 90, 98
  127, 133; Salle Ventadour, 154, 157;
  Théâtre-Français, 43, 47, 48, 51, 59, 68,
  72, 79, 86, 89, 96, 155; Théâtre-Italien,
  50, 54, 71, 82, 89, 100, 126, 142, 149,
  150; Théâtre-Nautique, 152, 154; Théâtre
  des Nouveautés, 116; Théâtre du Palais
  Royal, 133, 142; Théâtre des Variétés,
  157; Vaudeville, 137, 142
Parsons, Foster, 4
Pasta, Giuditta, 71, 84
Payne, John Howard, 26; *Adeline*, 31; *Junius
  Brutus*, 94; *Thérèse*, 25, 26, 31
Penley, Samson, 33, 46, 51
Perier, C.-P., 186
Picard, L. B., 99
Pichat, M., *Léonidas*, 48
Pichot, Amédée, 19, 37, 39
Pixérécourt, René-Charles G. de, 26, 187
Phillips, Miss Louise, 110, 124
Planché, James Robinson, 23, 36, 41
Pleyel, M. Camille, 121
Pocock, Isaac, *Rob Roy Macgregor*, 110
Porto, Luigi da, 82
Préault, Auguste, 58, 182
Price, Stephen, 101, 110

Rachel, Mlle (Elisa Félix), 178
Racine, Jean, 44, 47, 49; *Britannicus*, 59
Recio, Marie-Geneviève, 165, 166, 167, 168,
  175
Reynolds, Frederick: *The Dramatist*, 26;
  Laugh When You Can, 10; *The Will*, 7
Rimbaud, Arthur, 184
Ristori, Adelaide, 164
Robert, Alphonse, 147, 153
Roberts, David, 32, 34, 41
Robinson, Henry Crabb, 33
Rochefoucauld, Sosthène de, Vicomte de la,
  50, 51
Rocher, Edouard, 114, 142, 153; 156
Rossini, Gioacchino A., 79, 137; *Il Barbiere
  di Siviglia*, 89; *Otello*, 79, 179
Rowe, Nicholas, 86, 126; *Jane Shore*, 29, 84,
  86, 106, 108, 109, 125, 126, 127
Rubini, Giovanni B., 142

Sainte-Beuve, Charles-Augustin, 58, 72, 115,
  193
Samson, Joseph-Isidore, 128, 133
Sand, George (Aurore Dupin, baronne
  Dudevant), 130, 138, 149, 157, 158, 159
Saqui, Mme, 22
Sartre, Jean-Paul, *Kean* (Dumas), 188
Schiller, J. C. F., 187
Schlesinger, Maurice, 130, 156
Schumann, Robert, 182
Schutter (journalist), 130
Scott, Sir Walter, 28, 37, 50, 89
Scribe, Eugène, 166
Serres, J. T., 24
Seymour, Frank, 109
Shakespeare, William, 24, 34, 36, 39, 43,
  44, 45, 46, 47, 48, 49, 55, 57, 58, 60, 61,
  63, 67, 68, 69, 72, 75, 76, 77, 82, 84, 94,
  95, 99, 100, 111, 112, 116, 120, 125, 139,
  140, 151, 157, 161, 162, 173, 174, 179,
  182, 184, 186, 187, 188, 189, 190, 191,
  192, 193; *Antony and Cleopatra*, 36, 179;
  As You Like It, 12, 37; *Coriolanus*, 12, 36,
  92; *Hamlet*, 10, 33, 36, 44, 45, 46, 47, 55,
  56, 57, 59, 60, 63, 66, 67, 69, 71, 75, 77,
  79, 86, 87, 94, 95, 99, 101, 106, 124, 126,
  130, 137, 139, 148, 149, 154, 169, 172,
  179, 187, 189, 190; *Henry IV part I*, 36,
  139; *Henry V*, 36; *Henry VIII*, 34, 36;
  Julius Caesar, 36, 37; *King John*, 12, 36,
  37; *King Lear*, 36, 44, 89, 94, 121, 190;
  Macbeth, 29, 36, 44, 90, 91, 92, 95, 110,
  179; *Measure for Measure*, 36; *The
  Merchant of Venice*, 89, 94, 96, 190; *Much
  Ado About Nothing*, 190, 191, 192; *Othello*,
  33, 36, 37, 44, 46, 47, 79, 80, 86, 88, 94,
  96, 139, 172, 179, 188; *Richard II*, 36;
  Richard III, 12, 36, 39, 47, 52, 94, 124,
  176; *Romeo and Juliet*, 2, 36, 44, 47, 52,
  69, 71, 72, 77, 86, 87, 89, 95, 96, 97, 137,
  138, 139, 161, 184, 188, 189; *The Tempest*,
  117, 190; *Titus Andronicus*, 92; *The
  Winter's Tale*, 3, 36
Sheridan, Richard Brinsley: *The Rivals*, 52,
  124; *The School for Scandal*, 46, 82
Siddons, Sarah, 8, 10, 45, 108
Smith, Horace, 108
Smithson, Harriet Constance: birth, 2;
  childhood, in Ennis, 4; school in
  Waterford, 5; début in Dublin, 7–8;
  Belfast, 9–10; Birmingham, 11–12; début
  at Drury Lane, 13–15; in melodrama,
  15–18; Margate, 20–1; letter to Elliston,
  22; Bristol, 22; at Royal Coburg, 22–4;
  Dublin, 24–5; Drury Lane salary, 25;
  Desdemona to Kean's Othello, 26;
  pronunciation, 27; benefits, 28;

214

Index

P1